The End of the

Road

Part 1 of the Motorcycle Chronicles

Roan Poulter

The Motorcycle Chronicles

The End of the Road

All Roads South

The Long Road Home

By Roan Poulter

Other titles under pseudonym

Chapter 2 Selfhelpless

By Dr. Richard Cranium

Chapter 3 Eros' Game Series

Vol. 1 – The Station Agent

Vol. 2 – The Bandit of Tombstone

Vol. 3 – The Soul Surfer

Vol. 4 – The Aristocrat

By Anne Carter

ISBN: 0615613187
ISBN-13: 978-0615613185

DEDICATION

This book is dedicated to my wife Karrie, and of course my kids Aleksa and Kaden. Without their limitless patience and ability to put up with my frenetic mind, I could have never finished this beast.

You're the best.

Lyman (Liquid Studios) Winn, Molly Bailey and Tatiana Stahmann, without you three, I would have been coverless.

Ginger Bess, you lent Anne a beautiful voice.

I am eternally grateful to all of you.

THE END OF THE ROAD

Prologue

On a warm Friday dusk, just as the sun dips below the horizon, a motorcycle that looks like it was stolen from a museum pulls into the parking lot at the Annabelle Hotel in Jefferson City Missouri. The bike sounds deep and throaty, with an occasional misfire like good punctuation. The rider and bike are each covered in a fine coat of dust and grit, probably the byproduct of passing by some late season planting operation. The rider sets the drab olive colored motorcycle on its kickstand and swings their leg off. It isn't until the rider steps off the motorcycle that it becomes a she. The long legs and leather jacket hide most of her feminine features while riding, although it is the improbability of a woman on that sort of bike that would throw most people. When the helmet comes off, her short dark brown hair makes her look like a flapper from the 1920's, maybe some female aviator or circus daredevil. The first lines have begun to accumulate at the corners of her eyes, other than that she looks like she's in her twenties. Heads turn to watch her, she's an interesting animal to even the most jaded observer.

Most people wouldn't recognize the old Indian motorcycle for the piece of history it was. The 1944 Indian was one of only 1000 motorcycles created to convince the United States government to flood the Nazi's with Allied soldiers riding to battle on two wheels. She strokes the headlight like one might caress an obedient dog. She puts both hands on her back and arches it, trying to relieve the knots that are the constant companion of a long ride.

Her tall, lean physique suggests she was a runner earlier in life. From the parking lot she looks out across the road to the bars competing for her attention. She gives them each a smirky knowing smile, noting the lighting levels and possible rapist hiding outposts, all data to be computed in decisions later tonight.

Walking into the hotel, the sway of her hips removes any lingering doubts about her gender. Her boots cause the same pronounced sway to her posterior that high heels do, but with the tight leather pants and now unzipped jacket, it is nearly pornographic. The front desk is staffed by a twenty something young man, standing just in front of the worst family picture the woman had ever seen. The boy in the picture looks like he just got pinched or needed to take a shit. The rider hopes that a family of proprietors excited enough to have their picture hanging in the lobby, will care enough to run a clean joint. It looks clean; and something about it just felt right.

When the rider provides her identification it shows her name is Anne Carter, from Salt Lake City, Utah. The man behind the counter doesn't know who she is, the name sounds familiar, but he sees a lot of names in the course of his day. Annie, for her part is happy to be unrecognized. Ever since Oprah picked her book to highlight and Lifetime optioned it for a movie, she was entirely too recognizable for her own good.

"How are the bars across the street," Anne asks.

"Uhmm, I don't really go to bars." The boy looks at her blankly. He has an infinitely forgettable face.

"What have you heard," Anne asks again. She has a desire to grab the boy by his hair and bash his face into the counter repeatedly, but resists.

"That the fishbowl and Teasers are good. Whatever you do though, don't go to the Basement. It's filled with those Goth type people." Anne studies the young man's face, but finds it almost devoid of emotion. He looks like a grown up version of one of the Vienna choir boys. Anne considers asking more questions but decides that she will undoubtedly be met with additional blank stares and generic answers. She picks up her bag, takes the key and heads up to her room.

Inside the room is clean. That is better than some of the places she has stayed on this trip. She tears off the top blanket and deposits it on the floor. After watching a Dateline NBC expose on hotel rooms, she now assumes every top blanket is thoroughly covered in semen. She pulls out a Ziploc baggie and puts the remote in it. Basically it seems everything in a Hotel is covered in semen.

Anne avoids looking at her phone, sure that it has multiple messages just waiting to deliver some variation of unfortunate news. *No one ever leaves a message with good news.*

She checks the shower, it too is clean and she chuckles to herself. Inside her bag are two pair of jeans and an assortment of t-shirts socks and underwear. The bag smells a little like a homeless person. She takes the bag into the bathroom and dumps its contents into the tub along with a few tablespoons of dust and sand. She strips what she's wearing off and grabs the bottle of body wash out of her bag. The hot water starts to flow and she feels almost instantly better. The steam feels like it's helping to dislodge the dirt from her pores. One by one she takes her clothes and washes them with the soap, rinsing them in the shower head that is about the height of her throat. *Who decided to put the shower heads so low that I have to wash my hair on my knees?* As she finishes each item she rings it out and hangs it on the shower rod. Leaning her head down and bending her knees she is almost able to get the spray of water on her head. When she turns the water off the bathroom is so thick with moisture that it's raining.

She steps out of the tub and opens the bathroom door to help spread the humidity out. She glances back at the tub and chuckles again. *Sorry bout that.* The clean tub has been unceremoniously replaced with one displaying a prominent dirt/scum ring around its base.

She takes some of the clothes off the shower rod and opens up the ironing board. The iron hisses and spits as it hits the soaking wet fabric. She considers wearing the vintage Nirvana t-shirt that reminds her she was young once, but instead goes for something a little dressier, more befitting someone her age.

Looking in the mirror at her naked body, she stops to appraise. *Not bad for an almost 40 year old.* She thinks of a time that she stood in front of a mirror and hated what she saw. Years of mirrors that tore at her, held her captive within her domestic cage. She hated mirrors as only a woman could hate mirrors. The sound of her mother's voice telling her that she was 'too fat for that dress', or of Bill's voice joking that she had not worked off the baby weight yet rang loud in her memory. Before the tears could well up and ruin her makeup she turns away from the mirror and finishes getting ready.

Passing the boy on her way out, she is tempted to ask him about dinner options, but he just looks too dim. He looks milk fed, like some over aged veal.

Outside the heat of the day is passed and the night is electric. Anne was trapped in St. Louis for two weeks waiting on 'The General'. The General sits in its parking spot, like an obedient Labrador retriever or codependent girlfriend. Anne tips her imaginary hat as she walks by, avoiding the recommended bars and heading immediately toward her destiny at the Basement.

Chapter 1 - Missouri, we have a problem

Well, I'll never be head of the PTA now. The thought brings Anne back from the edge of the dark oblivion. Not quite asleep, but not totally awake, it had felt intensely real. For a moment she had been the housewife and mother again, folding clothes, wiping noses and waiting for her life to begin. Only when she snapped out of it, her life looked like an old VHS movie on fast forward, zooming right past where she had wanted to be and ending up in this damn mess. Just a month ago her own mother had informed her that she was a whore, and at this moment Anne was having a hard time making a meaningful argument against the declaration.

Anne begins to wonder how it all turned out like this. She knows she should leave, but resents being forced to flee her own Hotel room. By rights the man child lying next to her should leave, but Anne knows there's no way he's leaving, hell, he probably couldn't stand up right now. He looked so delicious, all young and beautiful, with his little stomach muscles. She had been so hot when they hit the door that her clothes almost took themselves off. He had smelled so good; some cologne that in the moment of passion had made him seem like an exotic Parisian or Arab Prince, but now seemed more likely to be Axe Body Spray.

An hour ago she felt like her blood was on fire, telling herself a thousand lies to get in that position; under him with her legs spread wide. *Wouldn't mom be proud?* Only now were all the lies laid bare, like a naked prisoner on a concrete floor under fluorescent lights, curled into a fetal ball. She wanted to hit him in the face, tear out his eyes. He had lied to her, she was sure of that. She also knew she wasn't special, just a great story to tell his friends. She had been a mark; something easily attained and easily discarded. She might as well have been a Kleenex. Just like always, the moment they separated she hated him; almost as much as she hated herself.

Anne rolls over on her side and looks at the small leather pouch on the bedside table. The zipper is open with an assortment of necklaces and earrings spilled out from it. Inside the bag she sees something silver shining and reaches over to see what it is. A small silver ring sits in the middle of her hand, its weight somehow greater than the sum of its mass. It's a simple thing, white gold, scratched and pocked, with just one small diamond, hardly big enough to see. She tries to slip the ring on her finger, but can't get it past the second knuckle. Licking her finger and with a small grunt the ring slips into place. She stares at the ring for a long moment and starts to feel tears welling in the corners of her eyes. Suddenly the world becomes a little clearer, showing a few more lines and liver spots than she remembered.

"I'm gonna go get some ice," she says quietly, as much to the air as to the passed out and snoring form on the bed beside her. It sounds honest anyway. Anne doesn't see any movement from the lump, besides the gentle rhythm of his breathing. *He's still breathing, that's a good sign considering how drunk he is.* Anne grabs her bag and satchel and looks around the room to make sure she hasn't forgotten anything. *There's my favorite hair scrunchy.* The black fabric and elastic hair loop lies under his outstretched arm on the bed. *Sometimes it's just not worth it.* The idea of somehow waking up this young drunken idiot, beautiful body or not, now made her want to retch. She was too busy judging herself to stand the idea of seeing any sneering judgment in his eyes.

The door clicks shut softly behind her. *I am free.* How a tasteful evening of consensual sex with a total stranger she picked up in a bar had degenerated to him being unable to sustain an erection, puking on the carpet, and forcing her to flee her own room seems mystifying. *Well, maybe it's really not that mystifying.*

Mental note: Never pickup a heavily tattooed, bleary eyed, hot young boy in a dark club in Missouri

Correction: Never pick up a boy in a dark club in Missouri

Correction #2: Never pick up a boy in Missouri

Correction #3: Never go to Missouri

As she power walks down the hallway as fast as her feet will carry her while pulling her boots on, she finally makes her way to the front desk. Anne needs desperately to escape the Hotel and the train wreck in her room, but it is extremely important not to seem too rushed here. *Be cool.* Eventually a twenty something blonde tank of a girl with too much hairspray and a bad complexion finally responds to her repeated finger strumming on the countertop.

"Can I help you Ma'am," she says in a sleepy mid-western drawl. She looks like the kind of girl you would expect to meet in a bowling alley.

I think she was asleep back there. On her breath lingers the pungent aroma of stale coffee, but Anne resists the urge to step away from her. She must have been in the back sleeping; her hair is all matted on one side and her forehead has the red imprint of her fist on it. *It's so hard to find good help these days.*

Anne has a chance to look into the office behind her and is horrified by what she sees. Papers and old coffee mugs litter a desk in layers that might stretch back to the Carter administration. Anne remembered the cookies from this afternoon and just hoped they had not been set down anywhere in that office. Most likely the whole office was covered in semen as well.

The girl seems somehow totally oblivious to Anne's sense of haste until she says loudly, "Checking out."

"But it's three A.M.," the girl says. *As if I don't own a fucking watch.*

"I know."

"Okay then," she shuffles through the card index and pulls out the details of the stay. She looks at the card and with a double check, and then looks at Anne with wide appraising eyes. *Shit.*

"Are you really Anne Carter, like from Pandora's Lust on TV?" she sounds so excited, her voice is doing that squeaky thing that some might find irresistible, but at this instant it just makes Anne want to jam a gas soaked rag into her mouth.

"Who?" Anne tries to stay positive sounding. "I actually need to get going, gotta flight to catch at 5:30".

Anne lies to her because she can. Lies are cheap and it's not the first she's used tonight. *I will not allow Pretty Polly here to judge me.* She was familiar with the name but it was doubtful she could pick out her picture. *Just check me out you stupid bitch.* Anne glances at her watch and realizes that the liability in room 214 will either be dead or come looking for her pretty quick. The girl tosses the card in the trash and gives Anne a huge smile. Anne tries to smile back as hard, although it makes her a little sick on the inside.

As Anne turns to go, she hears over her shoulder, "Her legs fluid and strong, like drawn gold, beckon me toward the hidden gem. Mine own flame rises." *I am not getting away that easy. I knew it.* Anne considers just bolting. If she didn't have a significant fear that the guy in her room might drown in his own vomit tonight, she would just bolt, but unfortunately her taste in men is yet again coming around to bite her. The check in card had all the information someone would need to track her down. She needs some loyalty from this girl should the worst come to fruition. *I fear Midwest Pollyanna here was looking when I took the tattooed boy to my room.*

"How much did you like it," Anne asks trying to sound seductive and not irritated.

"Long I delved between the milky white luxury of my Goddess," she repeats a line from Anne's own book to her. *Somehow she makes it sound dirty; no, that's not the right word, more like unclean. Oh God, my kingdom for a normal person in this town.* Anne knows how to reply, she literally wrote the book on how to reply. But Anne won't play that game. *She can't make me.* Anne pushes up the little counter extender and makes her way to the girl. They are inches away. *Wow, her breath is even worse on this side of the counter.*

"I need you to forget that I was ever here," Anne tries to make clear to her blank Midwestern face.

She smells of lightly sour milk as Anne gets closer she grits her teeth against the inevitable. Suddenly her mouth is on Anne and her hands are wrapped around her skull. Her tongue probes her like this is an alien abduction. Anne is not even sure what to do with her tongue; this girl seems to be using up all the space in both their mouths. As

Anne ponders the atrocities that are happening, she freezes as she hears something, trying to wave her arm to alert the girl to a new presence.

Just then who should walk down, but the liability from tonight in his boxer shorts. *Oh God, I had thought to be ten miles away from here before he opened the door.*

"I thought you went to get ice," he says and looks at Anne hurtfully. *I hoped you were asleep, or dead.*

Abruptly the tongue machine lets go of Anne's head and retreats to the safe confines of her filthy office, presumably embarrassed. *I was the one that got violated.*

The boy really does have a rocking body and for a second Anne reconsiders, she can't see any judgment in his eyes, but she knows it will come. She has to be twice his age, the math is emotionally devastating. *I really have to start giving my bedmates better inspections.*

"Why don't I come join you back there?" Anne nods and smiles, because her head is about to burst. She's not sure if he wants to come back and ravage her for the world to see, or just bend her over the front desk like a twenty dollar whore. Either way, she's past being excited about anything he has to offer tonight.

Suddenly the office door opens and Beth the front desk girl reemerges. Anne had not noticed her name badge before, but since they had now swapped saliva it seems lady like to call her by name.

"I'm in." Anne tries to comprehend her meaning. She looks up the stairs and sees a sly smile on the boys face. *How in the hell did I end up the bologna in this Dysfunction sandwich? I would rather have dental work done without Novocain, than spend another second with either of them.*

"Why don't the two of you head up and get started." Anne has sentenced this night to the death penalty. Without another word or a glance she turns on her boot and heads toward the front door. Just as she pushes the door open she can hear hurried footsteps and the sound of her own words spouting in unnatural combinations from the girl's lips. She resists the urge to look back, to see the train wreck unfold in all its horror. Sitting on the General, she would like to have a good cry, but he simply won't allow it. With a thunderous roar they exit the parking lot and head West.

Chapter 2 - The escape

The Missouri night air is cold but refreshing. The bounce and jostle of the bike thumping across the flat Missouri highway has a soothing effect, like a baby being bounced in its mothers arms. The old Indian rumbles along with an occasional backfire to announce its presence and scare off any would be attackers. The six grand she paid to have the guy in St. Louis overhaul the bike may have been a waste. *What the hell do I know about motorcycles, wasn't this Bill's pet project?* The wobble is gone from the front end, but the engine doesn't sound right. It seemed like a long shot when the mechanic proposed it. A quick glance at the little bubble compass bobbing away on the speedometer indicates that in some general sense they were heading west. Toward home, whatever that means. More like toward a house she owns, a storage shed she rents to hold all her belongings, and a bunch of people who used to mean something to her. Anne scans the horizon, hoping for a gas station where she can fill up and get something to wash the bad tastes from her mouth.

Mental note: Get a pack of gum in case you need to make another quick exit from a Hotel.

Anne tries desperately to see the humor in the situation as she pulls into a Chevron gas station, seemingly the only sign of life on this desolate stretch of road. The lights under it are bright and hurt her eyes after an hour on the pitch black road. The bike takes two and a half gallons of fuel and according to the sign, they have a special on Gatorade. *Who drinks that crap? I know that shit's not fruit. Don't lie to me; I know what fruit tastes like.* Inside the store she sets a bottle of tea and a package of Mentos on the counter before hitting the bathroom. Rinsing her face with the industrial smelling hand soap in the dispenser is not an option. *Oh yeah, you're all about standards; now.* She rinses her face as well as well as she's able in the scalding hot water. For a split second she makes eye contact with the reflection. What she sees on the surface is a woman who looks younger than the thirty seven year old who is referenced on her driver's license. She is attractive with just the beginnings of some wrinkles around her eyes. She wears very little makeup. Her hair is a mess, but that's really the helmet's fault. Her breasts are still full and relatively ample, thanks to a generous payment plan to her plastic surgeon almost ten years ago. She wonders if she ought to have them redone. *Cause that's what's wrong with us, the great Slut Poet?* For a moment she can almost see the bored housewife from a previous life staring back at her; the woman who raised her children and kept an immaculate house while the world passed her by. No, that woman's not here anymore, it was just a figment of her imagination. *The Slut Poet is still here.* That unfortunate title had been gifted to her by Rush Limbaugh and it had stuck even in her own mind.

Is this really where you've brought us? She averts her gaze and washes her hands once more for good measure before walking to the counter. The guy behind the counter looks like he's been here for days, some kind of permanent fixture in his bar stool slump. *I probably don't need to pay; I think you could rob the place without him ever noticing a thing.* His shoulder length hair and dangling ear lobes make Anne think he's probably been in an unlistenable band more times than he can count. His fingernails show black paint at the edges and his skin is nearly transparent he's so white. No telling what his real hair color is, it looks like he may be drinking the dye to get it that black. For a minute Anne has the desire to try and talk some sense into him, tell him about a future that could be his. When they lock eyes he has a white contact lens in one eye. *Fuck me, what a douche bag.* He is obviously some parent's shining failure; someone right now is sitting in a singlewide trailer, wondering where he or she went wrong. *Is there any helping this boy, really? I guess my mothering instinct is as dead as I feared.* Just as Anne breathes a sigh of relief, sure he will ring her up without a word he looks up at her and with a condescending laugh says, "Rough night?"

With that small phrase and the little chuckle, it is as if all Anne's worst fears of judgment and persecution have come true. She could not have been hurt worse if a line of protesters outside were screaming 'Whore' at her. She feels hot tears welling up, her humiliation now seemingly complete. She works hard to suck her tears back in. Then it turns, turns to hate. *How dare this sack of shit judge me?* She wants to go over the counter and fuck him up. Make use of those self defense classes she took. She is screaming and crying and fuming at the cashier, but all on the inside. From the vantage point across from her, it appears nothing is wrong; she is an adult and has learned to bury all those horrible feelings behind the gentle façade of ambiguity.

"Nice bike," he says. Anne tries to bring herself back. She appeases his interest with a curt nod, but turns to leave as quickly as she has her card back in her hand.

He isn't interested in having a discussion about Bill's exhaustive search for a classic bike. He probably doesn't know the difference between a Harley-Davidson and an Indian. He doesn't care about how Bill found it on a website dedicated to old Indians. He doesn't want to hear about the process of finding replacement parts for a Prototype bike that's older than his dad. He wouldn't care about the Indian company making only a thousand of these bikes to try and sell to the United States Army at the tail end of World War II. He wouldn't care that this bike is one of only twenty known models left running.

Anne realizes by walking away that any chance for a meaningful human interaction is gone. He had probably not meant anything offensive in his first statement, but it was done. Her right leg swings over the bike and the engine roars to life. It's possible she might have missed an opportunity to meet a friend for life. They might have spent his shift talking about hopes and dreams and their own individual observations on what it means to really make it in life. She might make things all right for him, he might make them all right for her, but instead Anne moves on with the callous negligence that has overtaken the discourse of her life. Anne doesn't want to care about him; she can't afford to care about him. She needs him to fade into the distant shadows of memory, consigned to the same data repository as bad movies burned TV dinners. If years later Anne stumbles upon the same gas station and by chance he still works here, she hopes to have forgotten he even existed.

Miles roll by, the air's getting cooler and the hotel options aren't exactly opening up. It seemed like a bad idea to bed down within a mile or two of the last hotel, which put her out of the town and into this no man's land. The General is pretty recognizable, and the last thing Anne wants is some Tribal Tattooed vomit boy tracking her down with some crazy drama. She can feel the weariness seeping from her shoulders down toward her hands. Her eyelids are getting heavy and she knows she made a mistake. *It wasn't really safe to drive, but what other choice did I have?*

The purple morning dawns while the road just keeps on rolling out ahead of her. No signs of life, no place to rest. *Time to get creative; we're not going to find a Holiday Inn anytime soon.* Then she spots a dirt road taking off across the tree-covered farmland. She slows down and weighs her options. *Die looking for a hotel, or sleep on the ground?* Up ahead there looks like an old farm road taking off into the forest, there might be somewhere to catch a nap. *There might be somewhere you can get gang raped by a group of genetically deficient hillbillies too.* Too tired to play the 'what if' game with herself she takes the road. Anne slows way down on the dirt, to keep from laying the bike down on the soft corners. The street tires on the General aren't the best on the rocky dirt road and the headlight doesn't exactly illuminate the world. The dirt road is well groomed and even, but better safe than road rashed. A mile or two in, the road forks, bringing to mind the poem of Robert Frost, and with his poignant words, Anne and the General take the road less traveled, or at least less graded anyway.

There are no houses or signs of life along the road except the weathered fence running around an overgrown orchard. There's a break in the old split rail fence and the motorcycle is just able to squeeze through. Anne finds a rock to put under the kickstand to keep the General from sinking into the soft soil. Only when she stands on her own feet does she realize just how tired she really was. *Stupid bitch, what do you think your reaction time is right now, three seconds; if you're lucky?* With a long stretch, the muscles in her back and legs scream in protest. *You're getting old Rock Star.* Anne opens her bags, spilling the contents on the ground, refilling it with anything soft enough to be considered a pillow. She lays out her cold weather jacket and pants off the rack like a mat. Anne looks at her makeshift bed and wonders just how it came to this The sun is just making it's debut; Anne hopes she picked a spot that will be shaded for at least a couple of hours. It feels good to be able to close her eyes. *I'm safe here, at least for now. Hopefully I don't dream of vomiting boys with tattoos and Herpes.* She starts the counting, 1, 2, 3,4,5,6,7,8,9, 10…. Before long she is snoring softly, the hard mask of protection shed in that brief moment between sleep and wake. Here she looks peaceful, happy and content.

Chapter 3 - Breakfast in Hell

Buzzing flies and the occasional piercing ray of sunlight through the leaves end Anne's siesta most unpleasantly. Stretching out her tired muscles and walking around, Anne feels better, but her stomach is rumbling so loudly she's almost embarrassed. The crash site was actually an orchard, which would have worked out better if it had been a little later in the season. The small green nubbins on the trees look inedible, although it doesn't stop her from trying one. *Whoo, that's some bitter shit.*

Anne shakes out the jacket and pants and tries to will the moisture out of her gear before rolling it up, hopefully limiting the moldy smell in coming days. There is a swallow of iced tea from the night before, which actually seems to make her hungrier than if she had just stuck with nothing. Hitting the aftermarket start button, the General roars to life. *That's better than kicking this old bastard for twenty minutes.* Anne wishes for a second that she had not thrown the GPS away, it would have been handy to locate a diner this morning. *That was a poor choice.* In fairness, the GPS had led her on one too many wild goose chases. It had made a satisfying crunch sound as it hit the ground at sixty miles an hour.

Anne knew she ought to have a GPS on her adventure, but there was something genuine in asking directions. Maybe it was just a good excuse to have to socialize with people. Anne pulls the phone out of her jacket and notices she has several hundred new emails and two voicemails. *Ignore the emails and call the voicemail.* The signal in the orchard is not great, but it sounds like her Editor Elizabeth. Something about Lifetime and revisions, it is difficult to hear the message. Everything always sounded like a panic from Elizabeth; as if Anne was not a big girl capable of making her own decisions. *I know when I need to be in LA.* Everything is potential downside and the end of the world with her. Anne kicks a stone across the ground, as if that would serve a lesson to Elizabeth. *I told her I would be incommunicado mas grande until this fall. Probably should have explained what incommunicado meant.*

You're just pissy because you're hungry. Elizabeth meant well. She had been the first real agent to give Anne's book a shot, so in truth Anne wouldn't have ever said any of those things to her. After hundreds and hundreds of rejection letters, she knew very well that sting. Before the Pandora's Lust collection, Anne had spent so many days writing, each time sure that this would be her great first work. She had written almost a half dozen books. A half dozen well crafted, heart on her sleeve, tear her guts out books. Books she had begged her husband to pay to have printed by some vanity publisher, just to own boxes and boxes of unsold books. *I still wouldn't put the Pandora's Lust collection above even one of those books.* But it was the one that hit. It was the one that put her in Costco, Barnes and Noble, and Wal-Mart; selling out book signings all around the country. It got her on Oprah. This from the book she wrote as a joke.

One day after receiving what seemed like the millionth rejection letter, she sat down and started writing the sappy erotica poetry that would eventually become Pandora's Lust. Who would want to read a book of poetry with a thousand variants on the word vagina? *Everyone apparently.* Enough people so that they read and read, discussed and begged for new poems, demanded a movie and made her a household name. Only it couldn't be done in a movie, so Lifetime agreed to make a series of it. Now it was their most popular and highest rated series. Who would have guessed that the little Mormon housewife would hit big on a book of sex poems? All because of a joke, a test to see if she gave the mindless masses what they wanted, would they take the hook? Well now the hook was set and Anne had all new and exciting problems. Many Church groups had tried to have her book banned; the explicit sex was just too much for them. Then of course there was the issue of a woman having written a pornographic book of poetry, everyone assumed you wanted to fuck them. As if writing a book about whores made her a whore. She had intentionally pushed the limits of decency trying to get someone's attention, a publisher, her husband, God. So she had written a book about bondage and orgies and sex slaves, she had only tried to give them what she thought they wanted. Some of the dirtiest scenes made her laugh out loud, they seemed so forced and contrived, like a preschool acting out a scene from Schindler's list. Of course, there were only two people who knew it was written as a joke, Anne and the one she shared those kinds of secrets with. *So when everyone else isn't laughing, maybe the joke is on us?*

Tracing her way back along the dirt road to where the asphalt starts, Anne is glad to be back on solid pavement. She ponders the whole North, East, South, West thing for the umpteenth time that month, and decides to keep heading west. She wonders about seeing Minnesota and the Boundary waters, but it seems unlikely she could make it to LA in time for the new season.

What mattered was moving forward. Away from the shit storms her lack of good judgment tended to leave in wake. *I still wish I hadn't left that schrunchy.*

Not too many miles ahead there appears an old rail car style diner alongside the road. The lack of cars out front suggests just how great the food is, or is not, but Anne parks the General anyway and decides to take her chances. *That's how hungry I am.* The door opens roughly after putting her shoulder into it. Bill could have fixed that door, Bill and his shed full of tools. *Just shave a sixteenth off that corner and you'll be golden. Stop thinking about Bill.*

Anne stands at the "wait to be seated" sign for as long as she can. There are only a couple of occupied booths so finding an open seat is easy, finding one that doesn't look like it requires a current tetanus shot to sit in is not as easy. It is a long search, but finally there is one that only requires a light brushing to clear away old toast crumbs. The utensils, wrapped in a wrinkled napkin, have remnants of someone else's food on them and Anne seriously considers just getting up and moving on. *There must be something else not too far away.*

Only just that minute an older lady marches up on the table. "Can't you read? Please wait to be seated." Her two fifty frame is squeezed in all the wrong places by an ill-fitting house dress. She looks like a bad caricature of a waitress from some 70's diner sitcom. Anne laughs to herself half expecting her to tell her to 'eat my grits'. She is leering at Anne, giving her that look of 'admit you're wrong'. Only now Anne has decided that this is a point of order. *I wasn't wrong, so I'm not going to apologize. If she is going to sit and read her Harpers Magazine where she can't keep her eyes on the front door, to hell with her.* She hands her the menu in a huff, scoops up the extra utensils and pulls out her little pad. Anne puts off all thought of eating elsewhere, so she can be a thorn to this old haggard bitch, anything to add to her misery.

"Whadle'yahave," she asks in a most grating manner. *Your face smashed with a hammer.* "Clean Utensils to start, if it's not too much trouble," Anne states plainly. Anne continues without allowing a retort.

"Bacon, not quite crispy, two eggs over medium and wheat toast. Oh, hot water for tea; and if you could find me some real sugar." When Anne looks up from the menu, the old woman is scowling intensely, having not written a thing. *What is it with this bitch? Goddamn it I hate this fucking state.*

"You mean the Slim Pickins breakfast?" Anne feels her unpleasantness rising like a geyser of acid ready to spew. Anne can hear the echo of her mother, telling her that only petty people say petty things.

"Actually, I mean exactly what I ordered, in exactly the way I ordered it. Bill me what you must." Apparently Anne had reached the maximum bitch customer factor, because the old waitress spins on her granny heels and stomps off in what any reasonable God fearing woman would describe as a 'huff'.

Anne leans back as much as she can in the rigidly upright, damn near puritanical booth. *Why can't they just make these seats at a slight angle?* Now that the irritation took over Anne bunch's up her jacket and helmet into the corner to make her own recliner. Closing her eyes is a poor choice, because a minute later she is snoring softly, deep asleep. The sound of a teapot being slammed on the table wakes her faster than an ice water enema. "Bitch," Anne says under her breath and theoretically out of the Sea Hag's earshot as she had begun the march back to whatever hole she crawled out of. Only the hesitation in her step at that instant makes Anne realize that the declaration had not been out of her range of hearing. *Who knew old women could hear that far?* To her credit she continues walking. Anne doesn't see her again. Tucked in her messenger bag is a canister and stainless clamp. She's running short on Jun Chiyabari Himalayan Autumn Black Tea. *I need to email Elizabeth to send me another round.* The tea fills the metal orb and the clamp closes securely without any leaves sticking out, so as not to threaten to make a reappearance between her teeth later. Searching each coffee cup for hidden bodaggets is a fruitful exploration, but finally yields a cup that doesn't need to be thrown away or autoclaved. *Are they washing these dishes with a dead rat, or what?* Wiping a smear of some old lady's lipstick off, Anne pours the steaming water over the clamp. Brown rivulets start to trail the ball and the delicious aroma fills the booth. A search through the sugar depository for the brown packets of raw sugar yields nothing. Only after a search of three other tables does even white sugar make an appearance. *Why are we so afraid of a little sugar, but never think twice about ordering a plateful of carbohydrates that could serve an entire Ethiopian village?*

The irony of that last thought makes her laugh a little, the yard pig in the booth across the room is devouring a stack of pancakes like she has been trapped on a desert island, yet three empty packets of saccharine lay discarded next to her cup. *Never mind those kinds of details.* Just as she lifts the hot brew to her lips a young man sets a plate of food in front of her. Anne doesn't know how she was so lucky to have skipped another altercation with the Sea Hag, this young man seems very pleasant and the food looked just as she had ordered it. The arrangement on the plate is odd, as is his continually standing over her watching. Anne pulls her shirt up to make sure she wasn't flashing a nipple or something. She looks at the plate, looks at him, looks at the plate, and looks at him.

"Looks good," she says.

"Does it look Porotic my Lady?" *Never mind, I'm not hungry anymore.* That was why the placement looks so strange; it is eggs bacon and toast in the shape of a giant Phallus and associated testes. Anne feigns a smile and even giving him thumbs up and a wink. *But that's all I'll do.* Suddenly his arm is in front of her face and Anne panics, drawing back hard; wasn't this how that movie Misery started? But as he pulled up his sleeve she could see her own words forever emblazoned on his forearm. 'Dip the wick, oh my beast of burden. Hard hands on the virtue of my loins is most desired', his tattoo reads. *How the hell did he recognize me?*

Now Anne tries the knowing glance and gaze hold, trying to convey that their secret pact must be kept from the conservative pundits that would surely seek to destroy them; but still he will not leave. Anne starts to shovel the food into her mouth. She needs sustenance. She needs to get away from this scary boy before he tries to take a lock of her hair or throw her in a pit, cut her skin off and wear it around with his penis tucked between his ass cheeks. *Maybe that's a little dramatic.* The tea should have been cooled a little bit as it burns the shit out of her tongue trying to guzzle it. She closes her eyes in pain for only a second. Suddenly the boy is sitting across from her with his hands out to presumably hold hers.

All is lost. Save yourselves!

His staring into her eyes is getting uncomfortable. *I might make out with a dairy princess that smells like a toilet, but I will not spoon a rabid fan; even if he puts me into a pit in his basement.*

Mental note: Maybe you could swallow your tongue to commit suicide like they used to do in the movies.

The food is almost gone and the tea is at least not quite scorching anymore; or her nerves have been seared closed, hard to tell really. She is seconds from making an escape when he says it.

"Don't you think I would make an awesome Darian?" *What did this deranged short order cook just say? He was obviously totally insane; the part has already been cast and the first season is over. Look at his haircut, he thinks he is Darian. Why does everybody want to be Darian? There are more characters than just him. I guess because he's the underdog hero.*

"You would," Anne says, because it doesn't cost her anything. Luckily he just smiles, lost now in the glowing warmth of the confirmation of his awesomeness. Anne is throwing her tea making supplies into her bag as fast as she can, while sliding out of the booth. She reaches into her pocket and pulls out a fifty. *This is no time to ask for change.* She throws it on the table and stands up, throwing the bag with her tea supplies over her shoulder. Suddenly he shakes off his haze and stands up. He grabs the fifty and holds it out to her with a kind of pouty and feigned hurt face.

"I could never take your money, not after all this." His smile is sickeningly sweet and his hand lingers in front of her.

"Really I insist…" she starts. But right at that moment he removes his hand from in front of her and extends it to shake. Anne reaches her hand out and clasps his overly warm, slightly wet palm. Then he goes in for the 'bro hug'. *Please don't go for the kiss. Please don't go for the kiss.* A second later he releases her and they stand staring at one another awkwardly.

Anne tries to smile, but doubts that it looks like anything other than that a child that just shit their pants or screwed the cat. This boy has serious problems. *I need to leave.* He scribbles a note on the bill and places it lovingly in her jacket pocket along with the money; it instantly makes her itch and want to take a shower. *Where's a good sexual harassment lawyer when you need one?* Anne braces, as she thinks for sure he is going to try and kiss her this time; and closes her eyes. Then he is gone, almost running into the kitchen with awkward jerky motions. *Fly, while you still can you fool!* She pulls the fifty and the bill from her pocket and throws them on the table before collecting her helmet. The note had his email and phone number on there. It says his name is Evan. That makes sense; Anne never met an Evan that wasn't a freak. *Must be a cursed name.*

Outside, the bike roars to life just as he comes out the back to harass her further. *I have not completed my escape.* He waves his arms and surprisingly even to her, she lifts the front visor of her helmet to hear what he has to say.

"Friend Me on Facebook, my handle is Evan Darian Slutpoet Johnson, EVAN DARIAN SL………………"

Mental note: Never join Facebook.

THE END OF THE ROAD

Anne nods her head as she pulls away and hits the gas. Looking in the side mirror his ever shrinking form was still waving as she crested the hill and sped toward anywhere else but there.

Chapter 4 MarJean's Bar and grill; and felony criminal assault

At the next fork in the road, it is either on to Kansas City or a little detour around the capital of Missouri that takes her through Lee's Junction. Anne weighs in her head the plusses and minuses of a major metropolis like Kansas City. She is fully aware of the barbeque phenomenon, the use of lots of sauces in conjunction with that delicious smoke. But somehow it just doesn't seem like a good idea. She needs to avoid major cities to avoid major pitfalls like the one she had been nearly trapped in the night before.

As the main freeways pressed on toward Kansas City with its choking exhaust fumes, The General takes the exit for the spur route and heads south toward the small town. As the speed limit reduces and reduces it starts to feel like the bike is moving backwards. Time, it seems, is moving backwards as well. There are none of the strip malls and franchise rows that plague so many cities; this is a real small town. The main street is picturesque like something out of a Rockwell painting. This could be a town you could get a real feel of nostalgic Americana. *It might also be the meth capital of Missouri for all I know.* Anne pulls the bike up along the deserted main street. This is the downside of a small town on a Sunday. The Bible belt was notorious for shutting down while the good, God fearing white folks of the city were busy bible thumping and Jesus worshiping.

The biggest problem with that whole situation is the difficulty in finding a good meal on the Sabbath. Walking up and down the street she peeks into storefronts and restaurants only to find them all dark or uninhabited. After two blocks of nothing, Anne rounds a corner to find an open sign blaring its neon sex glow into the noon sun. Opening the door her nostrils are filled with old cigarette smoke, sour beer and redneck sweat. *Not two bad meals in a row? Shit!* Once again, Anne is face to face with a sign declaring that she should wait for some hostess that was obviously too busy working on her doctoral dissertation to pay attention to any lowly customers who might saunter in. A quick glance around doesn't reveal a soul. She steps hesitantly further and further into the bar, realizing that she may bring the ire of the hostess down upon her. "Hello," Anne half yells, half questions. "Hello back," a far off voice yells back and a portly but kind looking woman emerges from the back room. She is built like a brick shit house, but with a bigger ass. She introduces herself as MarJean, with a capital J, which she says is nonnegotiable, even though Anne can't imagine a scenario where she would ever write her name down.

"I'm sorry honey; I didn't know there was anybody out here. I was in the back warshin some dishes." Anne finds herself desperately dreaming that she really was washing the dishes, after the experience this morning, she would relish the opportunity to eat off a clean plate with a clean fork.

"You should'a just found a seat, you ain't gotta wait fer me." She waves dismissively at the sign. Anne gives the sign a dirty look of her own as they make their way toward her table.

"What'll ya have," she asks.

"What'll you suggest," Anne shoots back.

"For the lady, probably a salad, er something you can push around your plate, not eating, but also not messing up my clean table." Anne laughs out loud, wondering exactly where this plain speaking woman came from.

"I was hoping for a steak actually," Anne states pleasantly, "And not just to push around my plate, but to eat."

"The rib eyes are beautiful today."

"You sure you know what a good cut of meat looks like?" Now it is MarJean's turn for a laugh.

"Don't I look like I know what I'm talking about?" Here MarJean shows off her physique that does seem to indicate an intimate knowledge of all things food.

"You sold me." Anne folds up the menu and hands it back, having never even looked at it.

"And just how do you want that cooked?" This feels like a test to Anne, some kind of right of passage into the cool kid club. If she orders it anything above medium, she will have lost.

"Rare as you dare", she says with a smile, "but warm please".

MarJean smiles and walks back into the kitchen. This leaves Anne alone with only her thoughts, which is quite often a dangerous endeavor. She feels like she has met MarJean somewhere before, but can't place it. Most likely she reminds her of someone from her life before. For a split second she wonders what her old self would tell her new self. *I would have never ordered a steak. Not because I didn't want one, but because I would have been afraid to look like the kind of girl that would order a steak.*

Looking around the bar, there are what seems like hundreds of cardboard cutouts of beautiful women pushing all sorts of alcohol and beer. There would have been a time that they would have offended her; especially after the birth of her son, when she had put on those thirty extra pounds, sitting at home, being milked hourly like a Herford.

Suddenly MarJean is back with her plate. It was miraculously fast, in fact Anne is wondering how she could have done it, til she looks around again and notices that it is really only the two of them. Without a word she slips the plate down in front of Anne and sits in the seat across from her. She looks eagerly at Anne, as if anticipating for her that first bite.

"Sooooo?" MarJean questions just as the first small bite passes Anne's lips.

"Wow, it's really good", Anne says with her mouth still partially full of deliciously seared beef. Actually Anne really thinks she probably undersold just how good this steak really was. It was still red in the center, but warm all the way through, still sizzling a little on the end.

The spice rub has salt and pepper, but there is also a hint of brown sugar and possibly fresh basil. It is quite possibly one of the best steaks she has ever eaten.

Anne gives MarJean a little more appraising look while she cuts and chews her meal. The woman was certainly not beautiful; probably in her mid fifties, with salt and pepper grey hair. She is wearing jeans and a purple blouse that did little to hide her copious cleavage, or help it for that matter. She is wearing a wedding ring, just a simple band of gold.

"Owner, or do you just work here?"

"I own the place, lock stock and barrel."

"With your husband?" Anne asks without knowing. Suddenly the simple happy demeanor of the host drains away, making her seem somehow older and infinitely sadder.

"My husband and I bought this bar and the restaurant next door about ten years ago. He was the chef and I took care of everything else. We did pretty well for a local place, got wrote up in the paper and everything. He died about six years ago and I just didn't have the energy to keep the restaurant and the bar open. The bar sells booze and booze means money, so I kept the bar open." A long moment of awkward silence follows. Anne knows she shouldn't have asked about being married, it doesn't seem like it can ever be a good subject to bring up.

"My husband died two years ago", Anne is shocked to hear the words coming out of her mouth. This was something she did not readily share with people close to her, much less total strangers. But somehow the shared tragedy of the loss and a sense of anonymity made her feel safe. It felt to her like she was in an Alcoholics Anonymous meeting, at least some kind of Anonymous meeting.

"Is that your bike outside?" MarJean asks.

"It was actually my late husband's" Anne confesses. "I remember nights he was working on it that he didn't come to bed until two or three in the morning. When he bought it, it was just a box of random parts and a frame. I told him he had lost his mind. I used to bring his dinners down to him in the garage; he had parts and pieces everywhere. He would get all excited and show me how some little rod was just the right fit and how it wasn't a part that existed anymore. Truth is he loved that bike a whole lot more than he loved me at the end."

MarJean said nothing while she spoke, just nodding and being an attentive listener. Now she stood up suddenly, "Want to come see the kitchen?" A second later, Anne shook off her haze and followed silently.

As Anne walked into the kitchen she noticed MarJean preparing two coffee cups.

"What're you making?" Anne asks.

"Tea" she replies simply.

"Oh, it's your lucky day. I have something very special."

MarJean smiles at this but somehow she doesn't look as excited or affable anymore. Anne quickly retrieves the stash from inside her jacket and pours the tea clamp half full. Plopping it in her cup she fills it with hot water. As MarJean stirs slowly and starts to smell; she can't help herself but smile. This is tea the way God intended it. She puts a little sugar in from one of the large glass cylinders with the chrome tops. Anne smiles with great satisfaction after noticing that it's raw sugar.

Looking around the kitchen it has quite an array of equipment. Shiny stainless steel counters, with grills, mixers and any number of kitchen gadgetry that Anne could even hardly guess toward its purpose filled the room to capacity. To the other side of the kitchen was a door into a dark space. As Anne looked at it, MarJean nodded toward it, as if granting her access.

The door swings easily and Anne is greeted with a copious amount of spider webs and dust. But beneath all that is a beautiful little restaurant with exquisite woodwork on the walls and sparkling chandeliers hanging from the ceiling. It has the feel of an old mansion that was left with the dust covers on for a dozen or so years.

"That was Harold's dream. I can't count how many nights he spent cutting and piecing together what he thought would be THE place to

be on a Saturday night. I can't hardly stand to go in there."
MarJean's eyes start to shine here and Anne feels she should say
something, offer some consolation.

Anne runs her hand over a wall panel and smiles before making her
way back into the kitchen.

"Bill was just about done with the bike when I got my book deal. I
flew out to New York, then book tours around the country, then off
to Hollywood to shoot the series. When everything fell apart and I
came home to an empty house, just the General sitting in the Garage,
polished up and ready. So I boxed everything and set off."

Certainly she was skipping some details in her account, some would
say she was deliberately hiding the truth from herself. MarJean didn't
seem to mind at all. There seemed to be some kind of an unspoken
bond between the two women, something that only tragedy and
suffering could create.

"So where to now?" MarJean asks.

Anne shrugs her shoulders to indicate that she doesn't know. She
knows she's heading west, but people want to know a destination,
not a direction. There must be an end to all this, a goal, something
worth making the journey. Only Anne didn't have an end game for
this, she just knew it felt good to keep moving.

*Exactly where am I heading? That is a hell of a good question, which I wish I
could contemplate while sitting in a soft lazy boy, but I have a feeling I have
overstayed my welcome and should get moving.* Just then the door opens and
three men in their twenties come in laughing and carrying on.

She is instantly a little jealous. Anne had friends like that. Their loud
laughter seems to draw a stark contrast to her quite often silent and
solitary life on the road. They're busting each other's balls about
something when their eyes finally adjust and focus on the two of
them.

"Holy shit Maggie, who knew the gate swung that way?" This from
the corn fed blonde, who follows his comments up with a lick
between his fingers. He's probably two fifty and based on the

Orange T-shirt it appears he works road construction. Actually, they all look like they work road construction, or should. Anne feels intimidated, so she says nothing.

Anne looks at MarJean, trying to gauge if these are friends of hers or not. She looks weary; the final sparkle gone from her eyes. Anne considers saying something back to the boys, but now she knows MarJean, and she's afraid it would hurt her. Maggie, she actually looks like a Maggie, has reverted to her fake cheery face that she put on when Anne came in. *She puts on her mask like a Knight straps on his armor.* Anne is embarrassed, she should say something, defend her. *Slut Poet to the rescue? I doubt it.*

In the end Anne says nothing. She walks up to the bar and slips Maggie a hundred dollar bill from her pocket. MarJean tries to give her change, but instead of accepting Anne tries to look sincere when she thanks her for a wonderful meal. Her mask drops for just a second, long enough for the guys in the back to make another comment. Anne tries real hard not to listen, made easier by the blood pounding in her ears. This is not fair; if she were a man those boys wouldn't be saying this. If Bill had been here; she stops there. For a moment he was at home, waiting for her; and the agony of the realization of truth is almost more than she can bear. Her own wound torn open again, she raises to leave.

MarJean's mask is back up as she yells back at the boys, "don't be pissed at her for trying to get some action; the sheep don't blame you."

They howl with delight, but to Anne it feels like somebody just stabbed her. They ruined a moment of actual connection and gratitude. MarJean's voice and smile belie the inner sorrow and depth that she showed just moments prior. They both needed something here today, a real genuine connection with another human being, but instead they were both retreating to their safe places, MarJean's mask and Anne's road. Anne tries thanking her again, but the mask stays firmly in place now. Anne walks out into the blinding sunlight as Maggie and the boys are yelling something back and forth. She can't hear them because she's outside the door. She can't hear them because the blood's pounding in her ears, telling her that impotent rage causes ovarian cancer.

But as she didn't hear them, they didn't see her. They didn't see the sugar canister in her hands. They didn't realize the streets are completely deserted. They didn't consider the fact that while Anne might be too puny to fight them, she was very capable of stealing a spoon. And Anne is especially doubtful that they thought she had it in her to pour the contents of that sugar canister into their gas tank, using the spoon to hold the spring seal open.

Guess that makes it a sure thing, I will not be staying in this town tonight.

Mental note: Hell hath no fury….like a woman….with a sugar canister and a solid head start?

Chapter 5 Stranded with herself

The miles roll on and Anne is split between stroking her bravado and looking in the rearview mirror with a growing sense of panic and impending doom. It was an impetuous move and in retrospect seemingly overdone. She should have let a severe look of disgust suffice for her retaliatory actions, but this is what she does. She sensed the offense and overreacted stupidly. So here she is again, fleeing the scene of a cowardly crime. *What crime? My continuing crimes against humanity, my daily shot of mayhem that I feel compelled to inject into the lifeblood of our once fair community.* Truthfully, Anne feels more ashamed now than she probably would have been if she had just left it alone. There was a good chance MarJean was outside with those boys trying to figure out what happened. She might very well be leading the vigilante posse to rid their fair town of outlaw rebel scum; sounds about right. *String up the Slut Poet.*

What probably angers Anne the most is that she didn't get rewarded for her act of civil cowardice. Deep down she pictured MarJean giving her a wink as the three good ole boys ran around pumping their fists in the air grabbing their heads. The tickertape parade rains down on her as Anne rides triumphantly through town, having shown that every action has a reaction. That's how it should have gone anyway. Anne tries not to think as the General pounds out the miles below her.

Mental note: Thinking is dangerous business.

The light is failing and Anne is treated to a spectacular sunset. The only problem with it is the angle, right now it is directly in her sight line, if only it was Ninety degrees to the right or left of where it is, so she could turn her head to see it, instead of having it emblazoned on her retinas. Even with the tinted lens down Anne is forced to pull over to put sunglasses on. The vibration strip on the side of the highway tries to loosen Anne's fillings until she finally brings the General to a full and complete stop. While she reaches for her glasses in her bag, the bike starts to shudder; she pulls in the clutch and feathers the throttle, but too late. The engine dies and she is left with only the radiance of hot motorcycle and a whiff of rich smelling exhaust. This is a bad sign. She hits the starter and the bike still has good starting sounds, but the occasional sputter won't grow into the throaty sound it needs to keep going. Now the gasoline smell is strong, so it's flooded. After a moment Anne turns off the key and gets off. The world begins to darken as she stares at the bike, somehow trying to will it back into normal operation. She sets her helmet carefully on the asphalt, doing her best to remain calm. Staring at the bike and the various parts contained therein doesn't help much; because although she can clearly see the bike and the aforementioned parts, she is reminded immediately that she doesn't actually know anything about engines, carburetors or really anything but where to put gas in and check the oil. Anne had read Zen and the art of motorcycle maintenance in High School, or at least read it until the main character got to the school where he had the nervous breakdown and it started waxing philosophical. But that wasn't much help anyway; he was riding a Honda. This is the General. It has, stuff, like, uhm positrack and Johnson confabulators that no Honda could even dream of.

Mental note: Wishing the bike better will not fix anything.

Eventually the reality of her complete ignorance of all things mechanical helps to calm her mind. She has no way to knowledge or tools to fix this bike, to pretend like she does is stupid. With that thought she pulls her phone out. Six more emails and a voicemail from Elizabeth and Jordan. *Stabbing pain, panic and frustration.* Anne knows this is a bad time to call Jordan, but she needs Elizabeth's help right now. The phone rings and the sickeningly sweet voice of her literary agent picks up.

"Anne, how are you?"

"I'm broke down just across the border from Kansas."

"Are you alright, are you hurt? Do I need to send help? What are your coordinates?" The mothering reaction is to be expected; it's her thing.

"Elizabeth," Anne is finally able to break in, "I'm fine. I just need you to send a tow truck to me, I'm on Intersta—." This time it's Elizabeth's turn to cut Anne off.

"Never mind, I know where you are, GPS locator on the phone, remember? I have a ticket in with AAA, they're on their way." *Occasionally this whole mothering thing is pretty awesome.*

"Wow, thanks Liz."

"Well, one good turn deserves another right?" *I should have called someone myself.* She takes the awkward silence for capitulation.

"There's a Convention in Kansas City this weekend, I have you a prime speaking spot."

This is Anne's personal hell. If they allow a Q & A, there will be three hours of varying fan worship and protesting Religious crazies. Anne desperately wants to say no, this was supposed to be her time, but she is feeling quite humble at this very moment. Somehow maybe this will make up for the sugar stunt. *Don't ask how it all works out, it's a cosmic thing.* Anne agrees to the pirate demands and Elizabeth texts Anne the information. Then she is gone and all that can be heard is the wind softly skipping down the highway, bringing a soft scent of dust with it. Anne is left alone with the General. The bad General, the General who strands his troops in the middle of some inbred Limbo, not quite Kansas, but somehow still Missouri.

Actually the General here has done pretty well. This was not Anne's first bike. She grew up riding motorcycles, either that or be left behind by all her boy cousins tear assing around her grandparents' farm. When she got older there was a really nice BMW, in fact, the BMW she had owned would not have left her in this predicament. Or at least that is what Anne's harsh looks at the General are meant to convey. Because the bike before her was not rebuilt to be a method of transportation, it was a status symbol, a golden idol. It was meant to impress, meant to elicit ooh's and ahh's.

Thinking of the BMW brings up happy and sad memories, moments of bliss and horrible moments that left her wishing she could forget.

I used to ride that bike with Bill on his just ahead. My heart was pounding; never sure whether it was more out of love or fear. The General only has the one seat, because Bill didn't want anyone that comfortable behind him ever again.

Anne wondered if there wasn't some wisdom in that, now she felt no draw to have someone weighing her down.

The phone is still on the seat, as if asking to be used. *I need to call Jordan.* It shouldn't be this hard.

I remember the last phone call to Bill, the awful silence, the sniffling and the questions you couldn't answer. The silence, the awful, thundering silence that echoes in your head, that's why you can't call Jordan.

Jordan and Anne had spoken every day of his natural life until the world went to shit. It's surely not his fault; he shouldn't be punished, but it all just felt so hard, so painful. *I keep telling myself it's not my fault. I need to call.*

Just pick up the phone and call him you miserable bitch.

The numbers on the phone are by last name, but Anne can't remember what she put for his last name. Then there it is, under Jordan, no last name. *I'll bet he wishes that were true sometimes. Who wouldn't want to be the son of the Slut Poet?*

Now you're just being self depreciating, hoping you can send yourself into a shame spiral so you won't have to make the call. But you have to make the call.

The number is dialing before Anne has a chance to outthink herself. The ringing is so loud in her ear she has to hold the phone away. When the voice says hello, Anne hopes upon hope it's Jordan, just to painfully recognize the voice of Debbie.

Why can't Jordan ever answer the phone?

Anne considers hanging up, but surely Debbie's got her glasses on by now and seen that it's me.

"What do you want Annie?" Her tone shifts to flat contempt the second she realizes it's Anne. She sounds as lovely and caring as ever.

"I need to speak with Jordan." There's a silence, Anne imagines it allows the old woman time to ponder whether or not she should be allowed to speak to Jordan. Then she screams "Jordan", the echo forcing Anne to hold the phone away from her ear; then there is only silence on the other end of the phone. It seems to stretch on toward eternity, the only audible sound the pounding in her chest. She is looking for something to say, anything at all to break this horrible silence. "Did the check come alright this month?" Anne asks. Nothing but silence on the other end. Then like a poisoned dart she whispers in the phone as I hear Jordan coming for the phone, "we get your money just fine."

Anne tries to quickly retort with "Thanks Mom", but the line is silent. *Boy I thought the Slut Poet thing bothered me.* Then Jordan is on the phone.

"It took you long enough to call me," he starts.

"Hey, how's school," Anne asks with as happy a voice as she can muster, avoiding any direct response to his first statement.

"Where are you," he asks back, ignoring her question in turn.

"I'm on the book tour; I have a stop in Kansas City to speak at some convention tomorrow."

"Why haven't you called?" This is a harder question than just the mechanics of why she hasn't called. Anne isn't sure what to say here and her silence probably serves to fill in some gaps, true or not.

"I have a new girlfriend," his voice tears into the fabric of Anne's brain. Immediately she wants to slip into full mothering mode, but she realizes that that time has passed, that she gave up that right.

"That sounds great; who's the lucky gal?" *Act cool.*

THE END OF THE ROAD

This time it's his turn for the silence. Anne stands on the side of the road, kicking small rocks into the dwindling twilight, trying to decide how to move her pieces across the board when Jordan says, "I wish you could meet her." This is a stab at Anne's heart. He's saying more than what he's saying. *We should both be saying things. I can't do this anymore.*

"Hey honey I have to go. The General's broke down and I see the tow truck coming." Anne knows this is a lie, but it shouldn't be much longer, so maybe it's not. More silence as she waits for him to say something.

Say something, say anything. Tell him what to do.

"I got to go," Anne finally manages. She cannot handle the silence, it is ripping her guts out and stomping them into the asphalt. For a moment she feels like she might be sick.

She is getting ready to click the red button that will end this suffering when a faint voice says, "I miss you mom." Then the line is dead and the only thing left to prove that they ever even spoke is the phone signaling her that their call lasted two and a half minutes.

Why is it I only seem to have bad memories?

Chapter 6 The worst Klingons you've ever seen

The old tow truck rattles along the highway toward Kansas City. They seem to be heading east, which is frustrating for Anne. This is technically backwards, which means she is getting further away from escaping Missouri. The tow truck driver's name is Tim and so far he's a pleasant surprise in an otherwise bad situation. He spent almost ten minutes walking around the bike. It's nice for Anne to have someone who appreciates the General, most people look but don't know enough to understand why it's cool. A 1944 Indian Chief 442 is an exceedingly rare bike; old Harley's litter the ground everywhere, Hell you can't throw a dead cat without hitting a Harley. Of course that's because Harley Davidson stayed in business, while the Indian corporation has folded multiple times.

The flat army green sets a field that blends into the horizon while the Generals' star shines like the sun. The brown leather seat was hand worked and looks like an old catcher's mitt; only for a butt. His only disappointment is that Anne didn't do the restoration herself; he wants stories about how she found it in a junkyard and piece by piece restored it to glory. Anne does her best to relay the stories as Bill told her, but pretty soon she finds herself contradicting her own words. She tells him what the guy Bill bought it from told him, which was a lot. It had been his father's; he bought it with his first saving account after coming back from World War II. Indian had produced 1000 of these bikes trying to sell the Army a contract to put them in place of the Harley Davidson. Turned out they were just too late, and anyway the Army had decided to go with the Jeep anyway. Tim ends up telling Anne more about Indians than she ever knew. When they pull into Kansas City an hour or so later he points her toward the convention center, where her name is on the billboard. *Oh God, no; have mercy.* Tim sees her name and thinks that's about the most awesome thing ever, but all Anne can see is the Star Trek logo. This isn't a Fantasy convention, this is a Trekkie convention. These might seem synonymous to the average Joe, but for those unlucky enough to have been caught in one of these, there is a huge difference. Already, the night before it starts, Klingons and Romulans roam the sidewalks and malls like street gangs. Anne tries to laugh because she can't cry. *What does Erotic poetry have to do with Star Trek?*

"Does this city have a decent bar," she asks.

"Gotta pretty damn good one actually, Howl at the Moon." Anne isn't sure if that's the name or the activities proposed within, but at this point she's ready for anything. They pull into the Hilton and Tim takes her around the front. Elizabeth picked this hotel obviously, it's right next to the convention center. That sounds like a poor choice to Anne. She pictures a Federation officer storming her room, determined to bring her to the convention center dressed in Ohura's uniform, funny ear piece and all. No, this isn't going to work.

"Is there a more accessible place to this 'Howl at the Moon'?" He just chuckles to himself and pulls back out into the road. The hotel they stop at is not as nice as the Hilton, but the chances of being raped by a group of evil Ferengue traders are lessened, and that seems like a net gain to her. Tim tells her he'll take the bike to his shop and call her in the morning. Anne smiles and says thanks for the tenth time before heading into the front desk of the hotel.

She finds it strangely comforting that it is a man checking her in. He asks her how many nights she will be staying, to which she replies, "as few as possible." That doesn't seem to make her any friends, by the sour look on his face.

"Will you need the shuttle to the convention center in the morning?" Anne doesn't seem to have a pithy response to that question. She knows that she probably will need the shuttle, but she had not figured to be staying in a hotel with enough geeky patrons to warrant a shuttle. He gives her the rate and she exclaims, without thinking really, "I'm with General Electric." This gives her the deepest possible corporate discount.

He looks her up and down and says, "YOU'RE with GE?" *This is where you really have to sell it.*

"I'm with a subsidiary of General Electric." *Bang zoom, three points, field goal and check mate. Still with the cheapness?* He sneers and adjusts the rate to save her almost eighty bucks. The huge influx of people for a convention causes hotels to raise their rates, sometimes by a factor of three. Anne doesn't need the money, but it makes her feel better knowing that he won't get it.

Pushing the door to her room open it is obvious that it has been smoked in at some point. It has that hotel room disinfectant smell to it. She showers the road grime off her and my clothes as best as she can, rubbing the soap into the clothes, then removing them and squishing them clean with her feet while she washes her dirty parts. As she opens her bags she can immediately smell that she doesn't have anything clean. With disgust she takes all the clothes with the exception of the cleanest outfit and dumps them unceremoniously into the trash can. There was a mall just down the road. She throws on the outfit and walks out into the daylight.

A mall always seems a little surreal to Anne, today it is an absolute geek festival. Not only are there the obligatory teenie boppers, but there are also members of every galactic federation or whatever they are. As she walks along pondering how to outfit herself for this leg of the journey, more designer options are available than she would have thought. She could go high end, maybe some Louis Viutton, or chic hot with Abercrombie and Fitch. There is a Hot Topic, which really draws at her in this moment, but she knows that Elizabeth would not approve. In the end she finds a store with thirty something slender and attractive clothes. It's the kind of store most frequented by divorcees and single moms looking for number two. After an hour of trying on clothes she leaves with two full bags of pants, shirts, panties and socks. There was something truly liberating about throwing away all your clothes. Going out shopping for a new wardrobe allowed her to reinvent who Anne Carter was.

She is dressed and primped and ready for a night out. Anne's hair is appropriately messy, not too, but just the right amount. Again she is shocked at how good she looks for her age. *This would have made Bill forget about that stupid motorcycle. Stop that.*

She takes a couple of deep breaths. *Now I'm ready.* She walks out of the room and the air is electric. *That's what you said in Jefferson City. Quiet, we agreed never to mention that again.* Anne hits the lobby and sees the 'Howl at the moon' sign across the street. She tries not to even look at the douche bag working the desk as she walks by.

Just as she touches the door the clerks words hit, "Good to have you staying with us Ms. Carter." So he figured out who she is, who cares? It did seem like he tried to make an extra emphasis on the Z sound in Ms., but maybe that was just her sensitivity. *Remember Jefferson City, just think about how that worked out for us last time.*

At the entrance to the bar there is a strikingly handsome young man waiting. Anne does her best to walk slowly, allowing him to fully appreciate her entrance. They lock eyes and he smiles charmingly, right until the moment that his girlfriend or wife notices him and punches him in the arm before storming off. Without a word and with only a parting glance he was off after her. *Strike one.* The guy at the entrance let's Anne walk in with only showing her Drivers License.

"Wow", he exclaims.

"Wow what?" Anne asks with more of a sultry tone than she intended.

"You look great for thirty eight." Anne tries hard not to blink, not to punch him in the mouth. She contains her rage for this most improper of utterances, reminding herself that men just don't get it.

"Thanks", she says in a tone that doesn't indicate that she would like to crush his trachea. His blank stare indicates that he has no idea he just crushed her by stating a number that was unwelcome.

"It's five bucks", he says with the same tone. Now her anger is closer to the surface. *What is the cutoff age to get into a bar for free? Am I a decade past, or just three years?* Taking a deep breath she takes out a twenty and flips it to him, continuing on without further conversation. She can hear his voice saying something about change, but she's past that now. Time for the future, something good to happen.

As she walks in there is a moment of realization, a moment where she hears a piano, no, two pianos. Her jaw hangs open as she realizes that she just paid to get into a dueling piano bar. *What the FUCK Tim? How am I supposed to have a good time at a piano bar? No one has a good time at a piano bar, although you are legally required to do so.*

Mental Note: Never get bar recommendations from a tow truck driver.

Anne's anger is palpable; sure that she has been played for a fool. *I planned my whole night around this place.* She starts to think the best solution is just to bail on the whole evening when a very well built waiter comes over and asks her what she wants. She is tempted to be honest with him, *give me some attention,* but now her game feels off balance. She tells him nothing, moving to the bar instead of to one of the tables surrounding the pianos. The small dose of male attention, no matter how purely inspired, helps her to try to make the best of it. *But how can I be the center of attention if there is actually a dais of piano playing monkeys in the middle of this place? And I don't play piano.* She gets a drink and sits on a stool nursing her bloated but wounded self worth and a double Cranberry Vodka. She finishes her drink and orders another. She finishes that and orders another. Things start to get soft, warm and tingly. She knows that if she has a couple more drinks, she'll be ready for something. Not sure what that thing is; probably fight, fuck or puke, maybe all simultaneously. The booze starts to slow everything down, but on the plus side the music begins to sound better to her. Anne sings along with the pianos and enjoying herself immensely from her barstool when someone comes up next to her.

"Has anyone ever told you, you look like Anne Carter?" Annes smiles and shakes her head yes, forgetting that it's bad to be recognized. *Tonight I want to be worshiped.*

"That would be, that she is I, my good man. The Slut Poet at your service." She is too drunk and should go home, but her Jiminy Cricket stayed at the hotel room and the little devil has even passed out in a pool of his own vomit. At this point Anne is Id, all Id. *Fuck Sigmund Freud!* The young man excitedly pulls Anne to the table and introduces her to his group of friends. She is taking pictures and having pictures taken of her. She is yelling and being loud. Suddenly a strong hand presses down on her shoulder and she is sitting. This quiets her down for a minute. Around the group there is a lot of nerdiness there, although there is an attractive boy with brown hair wearing a hoodie. Anne orders a water, she starts to sense that she's getting too drunk. The water comes and she drinks it quickly, too quickly. *Oh God, I'm gonna puke.* Anne tries to loop prim and proper as she sprints toward the bathroom. She makes it there, but just in time to throw up into the sink. *You should have eaten, I told you so. No you didn't. Yes, I did. Well, that's a fine suggestion now.* She stands up and tries to wash the mostly liquid vomit down the sink, but it clogs and starts to look like quite a mess for someone. *Best at this point to just step to another sink I think.*

She stands at the clean sink and rinses her mouth out. She looks like a drunken slob, even by fairly low standards of drunken slobberness. *Who is this asshole?* The stranger that stares her in the eye seems distantly familiar, but not very familiar. She looks like someone who used to be in old photographs of a family she knew. She was a better woman than this; she was a mother that took care of her children when they were sick, not regressing on the evolutionary scale to the slime that first crawled from the sea and puked into a sink. Anne wants to cry and break the mirror, but that would ruin her makeup and mess up her hair. *That's better.* Someone else comes in and she begs a stick of gum off her. She's looking at her like she recognizes Anne, but doesn't ask. *His gum is much better tasting than the vomit.* As Anne walks back up to the table they greet her like an old friend. They have ordered her another glass of water; she is cautiously optimistic that she won't puke this one up. For the first time that night she really looks at the people around the table; they are wearing Star Trek T-shirts. *We have spotted the enemy, and they are us.* Anne would bail, but now she feels committed to the group. She tries to take it easy drinking two more waters while listening to the government sanctioned three Billy Joel song minimum. *Fuck that piano man, I should have been an actor so I could get out of this place.*

She begins to name the nerds, the first based on his brown skin and epicanthic fold is a Samurai warrior, next to him is Nose Zit, and next to him is the dark haired boy in the hoodie she had noticed earlier, apparently his name is Carter. He has beautiful brown eyes and long lashes. He keeps flashing glances at her and Anne needs that right now. The big fat girl next to him is Kate, which sounds better that Tits McGhee like Anne had been calling her in her head until someone used a name. She looks Latina, not aboriginal Indian stock like most of them, but with almond eyes, long brown hair and copious cleavage. Anne is shocked at how drunk she still is, she almost wonders if someone slipped something in one of her drinks.

The Samurai warrior suddenly orders a round of Tequila for the table. *This is an odd group.* Surprisingly, out of the eight people at the table, only Anne, Kate, Samurai and Nose Zit are doing shots. That should mean they all get two. But somehow, Anne gets three, and shuffles one to the boy in the hoodie. *I shouldn't be doing any shots.* Time shifts again and the fuzziness returns. A girl at the table next to the group glances over and gives Anne a scornful look. Anne can feel her hands balling into fists. She can see in her mind what it would look like to bash the girls head into the table. But Anne is so drunk that all her anger looks more like a child trying to play at being a grown up. They flash the lights. People are leaving but Anne is not sure she can stand. Suddenly she is helped up, vigorously. People are yelling and she notices there is vomit on the table in front of her. *I am never coming here again, that's just unacceptable and disgusting.* The vigorous helpers magically transport her to the door and dump her unceremoniously on the asphalt outside. Her face cushions the landing, but now for some reason it hurts and her hands are bleeding, or her face, probably both.

"Good thing my face broke the fall," she yells at the black T-shirted hooligans. Less vigorous hands are helping her up and asking arbitrary questions. *Something about a Hotel, what hotel?*

Anne tries to think, but at this moment she's not even sure she was at a hotel. The faces don't look quite as excited as they were when they met her. *Somebody worship me.* Then she is put in the back of a car, her face glued to the leather by drying vomit. She wakes up when they pull her limp body out and notice she has thrown up all over her shirt and face. Anne can hear them talking about her, asking if they s should take her to the hospital. Anne starts to cry, not out of shame, she's still too drunk to feel the shame that will come later. She cries for the loss of another night, another window of opportunity that slipped through her fingers. She cries for the blouse that will have to go in the garbage. No one wants to help her, but they are doing it anyway. She tries to tell them that she loves them, that she appreciates what they're doing. Everything comes out mumbles and whispers, which no one is close enough to hear. Nose Zit has her feet; she assumes the Samurai warrior has her head. Someone in front of her is carrying her shoes. *When did I lose my shoes?* They get her into the hotel elevator with only a small exchange with the Hotel staff. The world goes black somewhere near the elevator.

The impulse to throw up is strong and Anne flails wildly in the dark. There is a toilet and she barely makes it. She goes three times and then lies back down on the cool tile floor. *It feels so good against my face.* When she wakes up again, there is lighter. Anne realizes she is on the floor of a bathroom, but not her bathroom. She tries to stand up, but has to immediately vomit again. When she's done she stands at the vanity, holding herself up. She runs the sink and drinks several gulps before needing to vomit. Again she stands at the vanity. She runs the sink and takes a couple of smaller drinks. She sees a tube of toothpaste and takes a little bit on her finger. Wiping it back and forth on her fuzzy teeth she looks at her reflection. The mascara she put on so carefully had been smeared across her face. It had been waterproof, but apparently not drunk proof. Even the most enchanted observer would say she aged ten years in the course of the night. Now the shame comes to wash over her, as if the nausea needed a replacement. Her head hurts and so she tries not to think. *Please don't think. Please don't think what Bill would say. He would probably say that my face looking like this is the only thing that kept me from being raped.* Anne feels into the secret pocket in her pants and feels the small vial. Shaking her head she opens the vial and puts a small amount of whit powder on the space between her thumb and forefinger. Closing her eyes she takes a quick snort. The kick is harder than she thought it would be, hopefully it is enough to get her back to her hotel. A famous Rock and Roll star once told her that Cocaine was like having Four Wheel drive on a vehicle, it was for getting out of trouble, not into it. She looks around for her purse, but it isn't in the bathroom. Anne makes her way to the door and opens it a crack.

In the room are two beds with three people asleep in them or at least it looks like human forms under the blankets. The room is totally dark, who knows what time it is. The door creaks softly as Anne tries to push through into the room. She waits a second, looking for any motion from the lumps, then pushes again. Less squeak the second time and she is able to get out of the door. Anne looks around the room frantically for her bag and shoes. Big hot tears are welling up in her eyes, the reason for which seems unknown to her. She could be crying of embarrassment, shame some residual sadness from her outburst tonight. She steels her jaw and sniffs her tear away. *I guess having to walk back to my Hotel barefoot will teach me a lesson.*

The door is locked when Anne gets to it. She twists, then tries another lock, but nothing seems to open the stupid door. There isn't enough light to see what the problem is.

Suddenly she hears a voice. "Feeling better?" it's a woman. Anne just wishes she could figure out the Goddamn door. Humilated and now cornered, she turns to face her questioner. Turns to face the look of condemnation, the superiority that watching Anne make a fool of herself must bring someone.

"How do you open this stupid door", Anne asks the girl, who she can now see is Kate.

"I don't know. Come lay down, it's too early. We'll give you a ride in the morning." Now Anne is trapped. She knows this is what to do. Otherwise she needs to get a new drivers license and credit cards. Like a petulant child she walks toward the bed and sits on the edge. She's still a little dizzy, and so tired. She slips her pants onto the floor, obviously no one here was going to take advantage of her. She lies back and is out almost before her head hits the pillow. Kate says sleepily, "I think you should change the Slut Poet thing, maybe Harlequin poet." Anne smiles.

Her dreams are vivid. Faceless men are tearing at her clothing, ravaging her body. She can feel herself yearning for them. Then Anne is awake and hot. Kate must have put the blanket over top of them and someone did not turn the A/C low enough. Slowly as the dream fades into waking she notices that Kate is close behind her. The soft warm pillows of her breasts are pressed into Anne's back.

THE END OF THE ROAD

Kate's arm is draped over Anne's waist; it is only shocking for a moment that her pants are undone. Kate must have stopped when she sensed Anne wake up. Anne wonders what to do, should she protest, should she go with it? Instead Anne pretends to go back to sleep. She closes her eyes and gives a fake yawn.

Slowly the hand on her waist starts to rub her side. The fingers slip under her blouse and trace along her belly. The finger traces the outline of the top of her panties, tantalizing in its exquisite trepidation. Suddenly her hand slips under Anne's shirt, cupping her breast. Anne is not sure when to stop playing possum, but when her bra pops free she turns over and almost instantly Kate's mouth is on her. Her lips are so soft it's like kissing a cloud. She is almost ravenous in her style, and any restraint she may have held before is abandoned as the hands roam her chest, stopping to squeeze her breast or pinch her nipple. Her legs are straddling Anne's, hot and pulsing.

Kate is a voluptuous girl with large heavy breasts. Anne's hands squeeze and knead them, Kate moaning softly into her mouth. Suddenly Kate starts kissing her neck, then down her throat and to her breast. Anne's blouse is totally open, leaving her naked to the world. Kate kisses her stomach and Anne feels a tingling below as she knows what comes next.

Softly and quietly her panties are slipped from her and now she is without covering. The blanket has been pushed almost off the bed as Kate moved down. Anne scoots up to allow Kate room to work without falling off the bed. Her tongue is magical, darting when it should dart, slow long licks when she should do that. Anne feels her moment getting close, her hands clenched into fists to keep from grabbing Kate's hair and pushing her deeper inside.

Suddenly Anne notices movement from the other bed. It is the boy in the hoodie. His eyes are as wide as an owl's. Under his sheet, his own hand is moving with a furious pace. Anne smiles seductively, arching her back more for a titillating effect than for herself. Her nipples are rock hard, all the elements are right for her to finish. Her mouth opens slightly just before she closes her eyes and the world shifts. There are fireworks and marching bands and a great sense of release. The ringing in her ears subsides a moment later. She pushes gently on Kate's shoulders to stop her.

Anne looks over at the bed, but the boy is playing possum, as if he wasn't awake during the show. Kate rolls onto her back, stroking Anne's arm as if to remind her that it was someone else's turn. Anne gives one more furtive glance at the boy, but his eyes are shut so tight one might think they were glued. She would have preferred to involve him, to have that particular itch scratched, but she sure as hell wasn't going to force him.

"Too bad", she says with more than a little regret. With that she slides over on top of Kate, working her own way down. *No, Slut Poet might still be more correct.*

Chapter 7 What have I done?

The pain is excruciating. A dull throb behind her eyes is keeping time with a lightning pain that passes from the top of her head and explodes out her ears. Anne would race to the toilet to vomit, but her stomach feels like a yawning black hole, she's beyond hunger, straight to nausea. *Where am I? This is not my hotel room.* It takes her a minute to allow the flood of memories to come racing back. Looking out the window it looks like Seven AM. Lying next to Anne is Kate, the girl she had the tryst with. Only she doesn't look quite as good as she did last night. No one else seems to be awake but her and her headache. *What happened to Cocaine being there to help you get OUT of trouble, not into it?* She slips her pants on and locates her shoes on a chair. Her purse takes a bit more detective work, hiding under a pile of clothing and shopping bags on the desk. With her items in hand she is free to finally escape the dreaded door. Looking back toward the bed is a large pile of sheet. Anne tries to retrace her steps, but she quite clearly remembers being with Kate, the hot Brazilian girl. The thing that is on the bed is every bit of 200 maybe 225 pounds. *You have a problem.* Anne is trying to rewrite history just as she rolls over. It's Kate. Big old, huge ass Kate. She looks pretty even now, if you could just cut her off below her breasts. Maybe she could be tied to a treadmill and fed grass clippings and water for a couple of months. *That could work.* They're staring at each other; Anne smiling to keep from running screaming. Suddenly Anne looks at her watch and sees that she really does have to go. Without a word she turns, opens the locks and slips through the door. In the long dark anonymous hallway she feels instantly relieved. No longer face to face with her reality, she can start to rewrite how things went last night. Each step toward the elevators gets her farther and farther from the truth and much closer to a sense of self respect. In a moment of panic she wonders where her phone is, only breathing a deep sigh of relief when she finds it in her purse. That would have been an even more awkward situation to have to knock on that door.

She punches the number into the phone and Tim picks up.

"Hello".

"Hey, Tim, it's Anne".

"I'm not done with the bike yet if that's what you're gonna ask. I told you…"

"I need a ride; actually I'm not even sure where I am. The Hilton I think."

"Where did you need to go? Aren't you speaking at the convention center?"

"I think I was supposed to be speaking twenty minutes ago."

"Well walk outside and look across the street."

"Oh, okay. Thanks Tim."

Now that's a funny coincidence.

Anne passes Nose Zit on her way down the hall and he is smiling like the village idiot this morning. Anne does her best to interpret patterns in the carpet as they pass. The elevator will not come no matter how many times she hits the button, so she heads for the stairs. She makes it all the way to the next floor before walking out half dead and hitting the elevator button. *That's enough stairs for the rest of this hangover.*

Outside the convention center it is pandemonium as characters from across the galaxy gather for a meeting of epic nerdiness. Never have so many assembled virgins and social outcasts looked so comfortable. Here they are accepted; here they don't have to hide from the cynical world. They aren't pushed aside by the jocks; here they are the Masters of the Universe. *Some may quite literally be the Master of the Universe.* Only Anne can't find where to get into this Geek Palace, not without waiting in line with the costumed freaks. *I will speak to them and take their money, but by God I won't wait in line with them. Wait, now we have standards?*

Mental note: Standards are always easier to follow in the daylight with a hatful of sobriety.

She calls Elizabeth, who picks up on the first ring and asks, "Where have you been?"

"Just tell me how to get into this thing. I am not waiting in line."

"They sent a Limousine over two hours ago."

"Well, I was busy then, at uhmmmm. Well, where do I get in now? I'm standing out front and I'm not going in those doors."

"Go around the north side. There will be a VIP entrance somewhere on that side." Anne walks around the North side, only it's the south side, *oh shit look at the sun dumb ass*, now she walks around the REAL North side, head pounding every step and sees it. In comparison this entrance has no one at it. She tries to walk in until almost getting body checked by a rather large girl in a security t-shirt.

"This entrance is for Green badge presenters only" she tells her. Anne wishes that getting dismissed here and now would end this suffering. She has a desperate desire not to have this conversation, *but I guess I must.*

"My name is Anne Carter, I'm speaking somewhere here."

The security Hag's face turns white and she starts apologizing, "Oh my God, I am SO sorry. I didn't recognize you, are you alright?" Anne is in no mood for explanations, especially to this behemoth. Anne wants to say something shitty to her, but she needs as many people on her team as she can get right now. *The other team is doing fine, ranks swelling by the moment.*

"Stomach flu", Anne finally mutters. Security hag steps back a little. Then she rushes Anne inside and she is shown to the green room. Inside is a veritable Cornucopia of has beens. There were at least two Federation security officers, three freaky aliens and one Captain. Of course there were various Klingons and Kardashians or whatever; they were all slinging some hash. Every one of them had some sort of product line or major sponsor that they pushed. A woman Anne thought she should recognize came up to her. Anne remembered her from some Star Trek show, her inner eight year old wanted to ask for an autograph, but as it was, she hit her up for a job. Anne tries to explain that she doesn't have any say over casting, Hell; she doesn't really have any say over dialogue. Lifetime brought her along because she told them they had to. She is as wanted on that set as a chancre on a man's nut sack. You might get used to it, but you're never gonna love it.

She is nice enough to loan Anne her makeup and hair product. Reemerging from the bathroom there are more interested stares than there were before. Anne gives the bag back to the woman, who tries to again remind her to speak to casting. Anne nods with as much smile as she can muster at the moment. Finally she is alone with her Chai and a donut that she can't even get a full bite of down. She is in the green room forever, which is good because she needs the rest. When she awakes with a start, she realizes just how comfortable the couch really is. At some point the guy who played the Ferengi bartender gives her a glass with two plop, plop, fizz, fizz's in it. She hopes it doesn't have any strings attached, the idea of making out with an alien is not appealing this morning. When it is finally her time she feels almost like a human, the memories of past transgressions washing away. *I need to remember that fizzy shit.* She takes the podium and there are only like a hundred people there. This isn't a big crowd, but she's up against George Takai, seriously, it's Sulu. She has a go to speech prepared for this kind of thing. Inspirational stuff mixed with some metaphors from the book, but she doesn't feel like doing that today. Instead she throws the ball out to them, for what they want to hear. The crowd is kind of shocked, but get over it fast as someone asks what she has been doing lately.

"Well, I've been on the road. I'm driving across the country on a 1944 Indian. I'm on my way back to Los Angeles after doing some signings and stuff along the way."

"What about books," someone yells out.

"The new Pandora's Lust book is about halfway done." *Bullshit, you finished it months ago.*

"I will have several other books coming out in limited release next summer." No reaction to that. People didn't want her other stuff, 'Death comes for us all' proved that. They haven't sold enough copies of that book to pay for the printing, even at the reduced rate. There were probably hundreds of mental institutions and nursing homes with copies of that book, minus the cover, indicating that no royalties had been paid.

"I'm really out here looking for material for a new book." There is some murmuring approval at this and I think, *Maybe I ought to do a book about the trip. Of course none of you will buy it because it's the wrong genre and you're too busy buying a costume for your next Star Wars Bingo and Orgy night.*

The presentation continues on for an hour or so and at the end Anne actually starts to feel less wrung out. Actually, she feels better than she has all day. *I need to remember that Alka Seltzer thing.* People have copies of Pandora's Lust they want signed. She doesn't charge, maybe she should, it would shorten the line for sure. After thirty or so it's done. A couple of people have stayed to talk, these are known as lingerers. One young boy is obviously obsessed with Darian. Anne gets it, she wrote it like that. She wrote him to be the boy she would have been madly in love with when she was this kid's age. He's reacting how a 17-year-old boy in his socioeconomic demographic should react, not nearly as uniquely as he would like to believe. She was surprised he could still grip a pen with all the masturbating he must do each day. The other man that stayed hadn't said a word. He has a book and she tries to ignore the boy who will not shut up. At first she thought the older man was the boy's father, but it doesn't seem like that now. The man is tall, with short hair and a few days beard growth. He has chiseled features, not the kind of person usually at one of these, he is absolutely striking. He is tall and well muscled under his shirt, but in an athletic way, not like he can't tie his own shoes muscles. He laughs at something Anne says and as she turns her head to notice he has a tattoo on the underside of his arm, not big but quite intriguing. She is ignoring the boy, painfully, but thoroughly. *He wants to be alone with me.* Anne decides to give the boy the attention he doesn't want and after a couple of snuffs he is gone. She is now alone with him.

"I was hoping you would sign this," he says. It's a copy of 'Death comes for us all'; this is the first copy she had seen out in the wild.

She's not even sure where he could have got it. She looks confused and babbles something incoherent.

"It's changed the way I see the world," he says.

I love you. Let's make babies.

She is positively captivated by him, now he's closer and the smell of his masculinity sets her nerves on edge. She is fumbling with her words and he loves it, or so his wide smile would indicate. Anne takes the book from his hand and they touch, just barely, just perfectly. She wants to touch his hand again; she wants to touch his face. She wants to see his tattoo; she wants to know all about him. She is trying not to blow this; she is good at blowing things. *Oh you're the fucking master of that, Slut Poet. No, tonight I am a Harlequin Poet.*

"We should have dinner while I'm in town." *Too much, way too much.*

"I would like that very much."

The hangover is gone. She feels like a million bucks, until the door opens and a form slides into the room. And there she is; Kate. Fat slovenly Kate, who had so captivated her so many hours before. Now she looked disgusting, especially next to this beautiful man, whatever his name is. Kate is close enough to see the body language Anne is using with this man. Right behind her is the whole group, Samurai warrior, Nose Zit, and the Brunette who had bore witness to the deeds. *How could you do that?* But what Anne finds with a sudden moment of clarity is that she is not most disgusted with Kate. Anne can see tears in Kate's eyes, she gets it. Anne should have a sign that says, "This is the kind of men I can get," or "You're too gross for me fatty." She turns abruptly and Anne makes no move to stop her. She pushes the crowd out the door and they are gone with the thundering silence. For a minute Anne fears she will run in and start screaming obscenities or details of what had happened, but Anne knows better. She's going to go and fill that void with a pint of ice cream and a box of Kleenex. She will seal off that little part of her heart that has been damaged, until a thick layer of scar tissue forms there. Get enough scar tissue and nothing can hurt you, unfortunately very little can really touch you either. Nothing gets past the scar, that's what she needs to learn. Anne turns back to the man, but now the glow is gone. She is ashamed and embarrassed and fully aware that the man doesn't know anything. She could still save this, but she doesn't

"You know what, can I get a rain check; I've been a little under the weather." Anne doesn't know why she says it, or maybe she does. Now it's his turn to be disappointed in her. The 'disappointed in Anne Carter' line is getting to be a pretty long, much longer than the line to get her signature for damn sure. He tells her his name is Steven, so she can sign her book. Anne takes his number and puts it in her pocket with all the other things she should have done, right next to the list of casualties and innocent bystanders whose only connection to each other is their own independent level of derision for Anne Carter.

Mental Note: It would be nice to find someone I don't let down.

Chapter 8 The escape revisited

The hotel room is a mess. A Pizza box and the melting remnants of a pint of Hagen Das Raspberry sorbet litter the desk and drip onto the carpet, while the biohazard top blanket was the first thing Anne threw on the ground. *Really who would use one of those? It's just gross and unacceptable.* Towels are hanging over every chair; it would amaze anyone that Anne could have used that many in just two days. The clock says she is only two hours late for the second day of the Convention. She assumes they have figured out that she's not coming, but they are Trekkies, so maybe they haven't. She just couldn't get herself to go again. Today needed to be a true recharge. Since the end of the convention the day prior, all she had done is sleep, sit, vegetate and shop for clothes online. The TV is still on, its constant drone of moderately entertaining programming filling the space which might otherwise be filled with self-assessment and personal loathing. Anne isn't prepared for that right now, needing some time to heal, or at least bind those wounds to continue the journey. *Or is it your escape? Is the road simply a physical extension of your refusal to deal with the reality of your life?*

Tim fixed the bike, it turns out the '44 War Indians used a system of points inside a distributor cap. Anne thought those were only for old cars, but anyway, apparently the bumps dislodged the point cover and caused some marring of the points which caused the bike to die. He cleaned it up and the bike is running fine. He called three more times saying he found a company in Canada that makes a similar distributor cap for a four cylinder, that can be modified by a machinist to fit and will work better. His kindness and over the top service merit something more than just money. The tow and repair charges should have been several thousand dollars, but he rolled it under the AAA coverage. Anne sat in my room licking her wounds and wondering what she could do for him. She could send him a big check, she could send him a first edition, signed copy of all her books, but nothing seemed quite right. She pulled out the laptop, promising herself that the next time she pulls her out she will write something that matters, and searches the great wide world of the internet until she found the perfect item. Sometime in the next week UPS Freight will deliver several crates to Tim's house. Inside are a frame, a motor, and enough ancillary parts to build two Indians. It won't be the General, but with his mechanical skill and passion, something good will come of all that mess. Maybe in the great scheme of the universe this makes up for the mess Anne made. *I still can't believe you porked the heifer. Please don't say that.*

Collecting up the items that have been strewn across the room, each item is packed as neatly as possible so it all fits into the bags. The extra day also allowed her to have an expedited cleaning done on all her clothes, except for the ones she threw away. Socks and underwear on a road trip should just be disposable. *Maybe that's a new invention, adult diapers for those long road trips, hell anything that helped pad my bony ass and absorb some butt sweat would be a welcome addition.* Gold Bond Medicated powder has become an old friend, riding through the Southeast. *Isn't that Monkey butt a bitch?* The laptop is the final item to be packed; it goes directly against the lower back. That seems like the safest place for it, although for the last three months instead of being her instrument of creation, it has served for little else than shopping for clothes on a hotel Wi-Fi.

The check out happens with less drama than the last one, or the check in for that matter. Anne makes no comments about how shitty their town is, or how glad she is to be leaving. That was earlier Anne, later Anne just wants to hit the road.

The pack is already tied on and the saddlebags are filled. The tank's full of premium and the buckskin gloves are totally dry. It's late morning so it's still cool, but not unbearable. Looking at the kick-starter, Anne changes her mind since she's all geared up. With a press of the starter and after a slight grinding sound the engine roars to life. Inside the parking garage the echoing is almost deafening at idle, as they pull out and the RPMs climb, it becomes a deep throaty scream. The General is bellowing that he is coming forth. Lock up your sons, hide the good booze and draw the shades. Anne Carter has risen from her grave of sadness and self degradation to ride forth yet again.

Finally the impenetrable hymen of the Missouri state line is within sight. With no small sense of escape and fulfillment Anne crosses the line officially into a new state and new attitude. There doesn't seem to be any exact measure of where exactly the General is taking Anne, but it feels west. The long flat miles of Kansas roll by and soon she needs a diversion from the monotonous hum. Syncing the Bluetooth in her Iphone to the helmet communicator on an abandoned off ramp, a second later there are the smooth sounds of Kenny G. *Who put this shit on here?* She scrolls for a Genius setting that's to her taste, British Rock, no, Classic Rock, no, Mark Kozelek, yes, that's the one. This playlist has Red House Painters, Sun Kill Moon and the disc of AC/DC covers. His music just seems like it was made for traveling flat country. Now this leg has a soundtrack. Kansas is a lot of flat, with eighteen-wheelers rolling by at a near metronome timing and a whiff of hot diesel exhaust. Day turns to afternoon and still she's riding. The wind and her perspiration have reached an understanding, an equilibrium of evaporative cooling. Anne is glad she didn't wear her jacket, which would have been too much. The General sounds great as they pull into some little gas station and grocery, a few heads turn. The gas tank gets filled and her stomach gets filled, then more riding.

Anne stops trying to force her mind to a specific subject as the infinite possibilities of solitude and inventive thoughts blossom. She wonders what happened to the guy from the Wonder Years, writes a song that the guys from Alice in Chains would be awesome for, if they weren't dead; and solves the innumerable political problems of our time. There are arguments, after all how could she adopt a free market model without considering the Capitalist ideals of Ayn Rand? She attempts to stay away from memories; those are dangerous. Stopping for gas again and she notices her hands have a tingling feeling, where tapping her fingers sends a warbling shock up her arm.

It's time for a break. A spot of grass just a few hundred yards from the gas station looks comfortable. It's probably where people take their dogs to shit. Anne looks for a spot without a tootsie roll to lie down. Nothing feels better after a long ride than getting horizontal and closing your eyes. Sure your ass and hands take the most abuse, but it's harder than most people think to pay close attention to what's happening on the road ahead for hours on end without a break. Driving a car is nothing; you can find people texting, eating cereal and watching a movie without any ill effect. Miss a golf ball in the road on a bike and they'll scrape up your remains with a squeegee.

Above the Universe unfolds in a breathtaking display of grandiosity that always helps her remember her true insignificance. *To sense, not understand, but just sense the enormity and duration of Space and Time is to truly see yourself as a speck on a speck for only a speck of time. We are truly no more or less important than an ant or a case of amoebic dysentery. This is what Astronomy should have been in College, instead it was all books and PowerPoint slides. That's because teachers want to feel in control, as if all the necessary knowledge is in their book, at their disposal, but it isn't. If the world has taught her anything, it would be that the more sure we are of something, the more ignorant we become. I bet ants think they understand the universe too. If you think you know it all, you're deluded. Staring into the abyss of everything else helps us realize that what we know isn't anything. Our knowledge is the most arrogant ignorance that can be imagined. Any self proclaimed expert is really just a scholarly bullshit artist.*

This would be a great place to do a hit of acid. Are you fucking nuts? *Okay, so it's not a good idea, but it would be awesome.* Well that goes without saying.

It's been a while since the skies have been this clear above, the stains of progress visibly reducing the stars in the night sky. She is most of the way through Kansas now; must be getting close to Colorado. Anne's mind goes to the man from the Convention, Steven. The timing was unbelievably bad; if only she could have changed how that all played out. *You always want to change it.* If she had met him the night prior, she might still be in Kansas City. *It's always 'what if' with you.* She pulls his number out of her pocket, she tried throwing it away, but he bought her book. Not the book everyone else buys, but the one she wanted people to buy. That book has her in it, veiled and with names changed to protect the innocent, but her nonetheless. No one could like that book and not like her, after all, she lived the book. It was the first complete novel and it was about what everyone's first novels are about; her own individual experience. When Anne first sat down to write a novel the advice that was repeated over and over were four simple words, write what you know. *Steven knew me, he must.*

But just as a sliver of hope shined through, the flood of negative possibilities comes as sure as anything and she stuffs the paper back in her pocket. *Still not ready. Besides this is nice, just alone here with my thoughts. Don't involve me in your bullshit.* There was always the stalwart companion, the General. The darkness has brought a chill and she is forced up from the siesta to dig through her bags until finding the wet weather jacket. Wetness isn't the problem, but it also kept those cool night breezes away. Moving around Anne notices a little rumble in her middle section. As any good woman would do she tries to imagine that the hunger pangs are really only suggestions, she doesn't really need to eat.

A building across the street that seems to be made of glass block and neon beckons her to it. The smell of burning meat and rendered fat float across the parking lots, a great sign. A medium burger would slide down just right. The General completes the two parking lot journey in short time. The place looks like the 50's exploded in a mixed metaphor Carhop and diner conglomeration. Waitresses in pink skirts and roller skates dance from car to car in a dizzying display of acrobatic prowess. It's like they're painting a picture of what young people probably assume every second of the fifties was like, roller-skates, the beach boys and Drive Inns. You might expect some fleet of '56 Chevys to pull up, lead by the black one with flames painted on the side. Maybe John Travolta will be there, him and the T-birds, she is ashamed of herself for knowing all that.

Leather jackets and white T-shirts on the clientele would complete the picture of a 1950's carhop, but instead there are fleets of minivans with overweight soccer moms and children spilling out, many already in their pajamas. *This is what's wrong with this country, people going to dinner in their pajamas.* There are a few cherry old cars huddled together, with owners intermittently lifting the hood or showing some detail to an admiring passerby. The General does his part; several of the men are drawn to it and its rider, moths abandoning their castrated lives to live vicariously, if only for a minute. *Who wants to be me?* One particular fellow with only a retreating wall of hair above his ears comes to look, but within seconds he is called like a bad dog and reprimanded by his behemoth of a wife. *Well, that guy must want to be anybody but him.*

Histories and stories and all sorts of free advice are given readily, which would be great if Anne knew anything about motorcycles. Bill bought the bike cause it was cool and throngs of admirers is just what he would have loved, but Anne is starving and these fellows are about to risk any outstretched limbs. It's time to get some food ordered and these guys are blocking any number of waitresses who have eyed checked her as they went by. At a certain point Anne yells through the man telling the same story he told a minute before to a waitress across the asphalt. The balding gentlemen telling her about his totally restored Honda 90 has to break his story off, *tragic*.

The girl that comes up is hot, not beautiful, but hot. What would cause this distinction might confuse some, but basically she looked like the kind of girl that a man wouldn't take home to his parents, but he would love to take her home. She has bright pink streaks in her sandy blonde hair that are pulled into pigtails. She's about five foot two and maybe just a little on the chunky side. What is most drawing about her however is the massive black eye and bandaged arm. Anne is tempted to tell her 'I would leave him', but notices the number tattooed on her arm with "Pinky" under it. She must be a Roller Derby girl. That or she's the most bad ass stripper ever. Either way Anne is intrigued to say the least. Looking around, all the girls here look similarly hard and hot; must be a cult or something. *Can I join?* I order my burger, *come on medium well*, with fries and a Diet Coke. Anne asks about a bathroom and she points inside. Anne only has to fend off one more curious party before the waitress comes back with the food. There's an extra drink and Anne tells her that she didn't order that. She smiles pleasantly, however not seductively and says the shake is on her. A hearty thanks is coming, but she's already spun and headed away.

She points to the corner and says, "There's a table over here if you don't want to eat on your bike." Good to know. Anne gathers her food; that will work out a lot better than eating on the curb. The table is filthy, but given the layer of road grime Anne has accumulated in several hundred miles, the table should be the one protesting.

The burger is still slightly pink in the middle, prayers have been answered. Really the doneness of meat is the closest thing Anne has left to religion. Most girls wanted their meat ruined, this was one of many things that separated her from the typical girl. The burger is perfect, served with sautéed onions, shredded lettuce and a tomato that could have come out of someone's garden. This is exactly how Anne would make the burger. Leaf lettuce freaks her out, and raw onions give her the shits. This burger is like someone stole her recipe. It is superb and is gone grotesquely fast. She is basking in the afterglow of grease and cooked onion belches when she opens the shake. It looks good, nice and thick. The first spoonful forces her to set it down. This shake is a marshmallow and heath. *Somebody's punking me right now.* This is beyond coincidence. Looking around Anne doesn't see anyone she knows. No one is even really looking at her. Suddenly she is not alone any longer. "Pinky" is sitting across the table from her. This is a pretty impressive feat considering the table is on the grass and she's wearing roller skates. The Roller waitress gives Anne an appraising, but not really finding anything she likes, kind of look.

Anne is wondering if she might have slept with her husband and doesn't remember when she says, "So you're Anne Carter?" Well, it doesn't look like I slept with her. She knew how her name comes out in that instance. It's more like, "So ANNE CARTER, guess you don't remember me." That would be the signal to run, but this is less confrontational and more playful.

Anne retorts, "And you must be the infamous Pinky."

She laughs, "You can call me Janice." *Hmmm, that's underwhelming.*

"I prefer Pinky, although I will admit to picking up names I would rather not," Anne responds with an ultra serious look.

"You can only call me Pinky if you've taken me on in the derby, and Fuck Rush Limbaugh." Anne smiles to laugh, she assumed she was joking, but she looks very serious now. Thinking long and hard here, Anne is no aficionado of Rollerderby, but she knows these bitches hit hard. Her black eye isn't from bumping into a wall.

"I think I could take you," Anne says half heartedly. *That may be the stupidest thing you ever said, you couldn't take her with two friends and a crow bar.*

"We can find out, pretty lady." Now she's messing with Anne. She sounds serious, again Anne wonders if she's setting something into motion that she would rather not.

"I take it I have you to thank for the burger and shake?" She nods. That still doesn't tell her how she knew.

"How…" I start.

"The article in Maxim had you list your favorite guilty pleasure." Oh, the long miles had made Anne forget about that. Making the final slurping sounds with the shake while nodding agreement, hopefully Anne is showing the appreciation not only for her attention to detail, but also chicks who would read such fabulous garbage.

Chapter 9 Roller Bitches

What was I thinking? These are poor choices like you read about in a transcript of Jerry Springer. Is that show even on anymore? Jesus, find a new reference. Pinky has done as promised and taken her out with her fellow Girl Power Roller Derby enthusiasts. The Kennedy Junior High school gymnasium is sparingly populated with fans for a match against the cross state rivals, the KC Power Posse. For her part Anne couldn't be more against the whole thing at this point. Of course that may have to do with the fact that she is wearing hot pink short shorts and lacing up a pair of skates that were obviously meant for a girl half her age. *Are you really sure about this?* Looking up Anne sees the answer staring her in the face. The blue team has a bruiser that must be almost five eleven and at least two fifty, maybe two seventy five. She has a huge pudgy face that makes her look like a gigantic baby, but with enough eyeliner and glitter to look like she either ate a fairy or a Goth chick, probably both. She smiles at Anne like she's on the menu and slams her fist into her other palm. *I think I just got served, whatever the hell that means.* She is rethinking the whole line of decisions at this point. *I should have called her by her Christian name; Pinky is obviously reserved for better people than me.* The sound of the buzzer seems to indicate things to people; it means nothing to Anne, possibly that she is late to math.

Pinky comes over to help her get on her feet. To say that Anne is uncomfortable on these skates and in this getup would be to under exaggerate by a factor of at least one hundred. She is wearing one of the thinner girls shorts, and although she couldn't say for sure, it sure felt like there was part of a butt cheek peeking out. The pasty white skin of her legs isn't exactly boosting her self confidence, but she's been on a cross country motorcycle trip, what do they expect. The only lucky thing for her is that they have promised to keep her identity concealed, some kind of Batgirl thing.

"The big baby looking girl with black hair was eye balling me," Anne tells Pinky, half jokingly.

Pinky looks at her seriously and says matter of factly, "She's a mean bitch, watch yourself. How d'you think I got this," pointing to her black eye. Anne makes one more look at Brunhilda, that's not her being cruel, that's what it says on her jersey, and she is laughing to another blue teammate while making the breaking stick motion. *That's just mean.*

"Is it too late to change my mind?" Anne is serious, but Pinky just skates on ahead with a Cheshire cat smile.

Skating around the hay bale lined track, Anne is starting to remember what it was to skate, just as the buzzer goes again. Everyone is off like a shot, leaving Anne feeling more like Prey than Predator. Anne tries to remember the last time she was on four wheeled roller skates. *Uhmm never?* Just then the announcer pipes in with the introductions for the Pink team. The skates have a rubber stopper on the toe that helps her get some momentum. Just as she starts to catch back up to her team she hears her name over the PA system. *What happened to the Batgirl thing? I'm supposed to be Batgirl. At least they didn't call me the Slut Poet.*

She is upset but just then Brunhilda and another girl from the blue team skate on either side. Anne is trying to keep her balance, trying to speed up to catch the rest of the team, when they each take hold of a side of her shorts and pull. Before Anne can even think to move her hands the shortest of shorts are around her knees. *Okay, game over, take me home. I need to get out of this thing.* Anne tries to pull her shorts up with as much dignity as an almost 40 year old woman on roller skates with her shorts around her ankles can muster. They introduce Brunhilda and her team, as a fun thing for the fans she whips one of the pink tassels from Anne's shorts out into the audience.

The tall girl on the Pink team with Baby Doll written on her arm, skates up to her and says, "You're making us look bad old lady," and skates off.

"Well it wasn't like I requested it, YOU know. And I'm only thirty seven," Anne yells after her, only then wondering if she was referring to the pantsing incident or the size of Anne's posterior. Baby Doll motions a body push, points to her and then Brunhilda and Anne spots her shot. She skates as hard as she can; it's getting easier now, catching up with Brunhilda. She is flying and ready to hit into the beast's massive frame, possibly killing them both but somehow regaining her wounded pride, when Brunhilda somehow moves that massive body from Anne's sight and suddenly she takes a hay bale full in the face. The crowd is roaring with laughter. Video cameras are all pointed at her and she knows Elizabeth is sick right now; somehow she knows. Anne seriously considers jumping the bales and skating her way to freedom when Pinky gets body checked right next to her. She winks and grabs Anne's hand to help her up. The rest of the field is chaos with fast skating and devastating blows.

"You wanna get some payback, or you wanna lay there like an old grandma?" Anne shrugs apathetically, which results in Pinky punching her in the arm.

"Grow a pair will ya." *That seems unlikely.* Across the track Brunhilda and a teammate come together and crush the tall girl. They laugh and high five and that seems to be just the impetus to get Anne back into the fight. Her short shorts are flapping in the breeze of her pumping legs as Pinky and her race to catch up to the pack. *I sure hope those video cameras are focused on someone else.*

Pinky skates ahead, then signaling for Anne to come around her. Closing her eyes she does as instructed, just as she gets close, Pinky takes her arm and uses her own momentum to catapult Anne into the blue team leader. The girl is caught totally off guard and slams into the wall. Anne wonders if she's going to get up after that one. No time for concern now though, as the two start scanning the field for the big bitch that is Brunhilda. They spot her on the other side of the track; pushing hard to get to her before the heat ends. Finally they get close to her but she sees them coming. Anne lunges for a body check but she is amazingly dexterous and not only leaves her pushing air, but somehow gets behind Anne and pulls on her shorts, giving her an incredibly painful 'wedgie'. It also serves to unbalance Anne and a moment later she is plowing headfirst into the same hay bale she fell into before. Anne is just able to clear the debris from her eyes to see Pinky level Brunhilda with a hard shoulder, sending her somersaulting over the bales and into some chairs. Anne winces to think of the damage she might do to the poor chairs. The buzzer rings and both teams make it to their respective sides. Anne is sure she must be bleeding internally; certainly she looks like she has had a proverbial roll in the hay. One of the teammates is kind enough to remove several pieces of straw from her hair. After what seems like only a few seconds a buzzer sounds.

"Here we go", Pinky says.

"No, I'm not ready", Anne counters.

"Don't be such a girl".

"Are you serious", Anne yells back, but now only to the air as Pinky skates off. "This is bullshit", she fumes to herself and the discarded warm up suits left draping over their chairs. With a shake of her head and more trepidation than excitement she heads back into the meat grinder.

After the humiliation of the Derby, the girls want to make it up to Anne, so they took her to what they described as a local club. *Somehow I think I should have expected this.* Anne is sporting a beautiful black eye, Pinky jokes that they are "twinners". Anne gets the idea that they are going to a strip club, and that it was on the dance card long before she joined this motley crew. The General is safely tucked at Pinky's house, good thing, because she needs a drink to dull the pain from the various bumps and bruises. She is back in a shirt and jeans, but the girls are still fully decked out in their gear, sans roller skates. The place doesn't actually look like a strip club, lacking the garish neon sex lamps that they usually have. The sign says Brass Rail, but from its hidden nature to the rainbow stickers on all the cars, this place has the look of a gay bar. *This ought to be interesting.*

As Anne walks up to the door, some of the girls were still lingering in the car, the girl at the front door says, "Fuck off Breeder." Anne can only laugh, wondering just how she can tell that Anne prefers cock to vagina. *Is it my hair?*

"She's with us, you old dried out Vulva." Anne had noticed the Roller girls seemed to use various female anatomical parts generally proceeded with an adjective regarding bleeding, dried out or smelly.

She lets Anne in, but something tells her she wouldn't have to try hard to end up on her head in the parking lot. *Mental note: no groping the poor little Asian boys.* Once they get inside the building Anne is in a different place. *This sure as hell ain't Kansas.* This isn't a lesbian bar as she might have guessed, this is a full on gay bar. Couples of men and couples of women are dancing in various stages of dress and undress. It looks like a Roman Orgy must have looked.

A small Asian man runs screaming up to Pinky, "Oh my God, you were so fucking awesome tonight. Who's your friend?"

Anne realizes that she's the friend. Introductions are made and he steps his gushing up to the next stage. "Oh my God, you have to let her take her around."

He gives Pinky the naughty look and Anne starts to feel nervous. There won't be any, 'Don't touch me faggot' here, not and live anyway. She is lead away by her hand. *Really, we have to hold hands? You're a shit fag-hag.* Anne is introduced to some really fabulous people, about half of whom seem to know who she is and the other half freak out. *This is what I get for writing four guy on guy poems.* When she wrote the books she wanted them to have mass appeal, so she represented every group she could think of. They seemed to be very appreciative of the work, as if she did something for gay rights. It certainly wasn't that, she almost wishes it had been seeing how much they care, but it was simply a choice of economics and mass appeal.

Finally back at the table with the girls Anne asks Pinky, "Why does everybody seem so nice?" She shakes her head as if the answer should be obvious.

"You wrote Pandora's Lust."

I shrug, "So?"

"Your third biggest Character is gay." Anne is aware of this fact, but it still seems of distant relevance. People love Darian, but for the most part they looked at Anne as an impediment to the real character. They want to know more about him, less about her. These guys wanted to know about Anne Carter.

"Yeah, but he's not the main character, and there have been lots of gay characters in literature." Pinky looks at Anne like Anne used to look at her children when she tried to explain why you shouldn't draw on the walls with crayon.

"You wrote a best seller with a strong gay man. Not someone weak or frail, or as a secondary comic relief. You treated him equally. This isn't LA; let's just say that most the people in this place haven't had much of being treated equally."

There it is. Anne hadn't seen it before because it didn't affect her. Anne didn't see race struggles, because her race doesn't struggle. She didn't think about what she wrote in those lines, in LA or New York her work wouldn't even be on the radar for advancing the gay cause. Anne smiles and gives Pinky a hug and a smile.

She smiles back and whispers in Annes ear, "You know I'm not gay, right?" Anne feels embarrassed for a second, both the women's eyes searching the other for reaction and meaning. Anne assumed she was gay all along, from her reaction to her at the Car Hop, the roller derby, now it appears that Pinky thought the same of her.

Anne is still thinking when Pinky looks toward the door. It's Brunhilda and the Blue team. Anne looks for the bartender, ready to sprint over to call 911. Only there isn't any fight, all the girls hug and look like they're best friends. Brunhilda runs over to Anne, taking these absurdly Tinkerbelle steps and wraps her arms around her. At least six vertebrae pop as she hugs the air from her lungs. She lets go and Anne can see that she's a little teary eyed. This is in stark contrast to the girl that met her tonight on the track. She introduces Anne to her girlfriend Sheila, her name is actually Beth. *No shit. She seemed like a Brunhilda to me.*

The night progresses and Anne must admit that these guys know how to party. She is drug onto the dance floor at least twenty times, each time with the same expression, 'Oh my God, this is my song.' Most of the dancing is as a group, although there are a couple of slow songs she gets pulled up on. Anne doesn't get pulled up by a straight guy, no, it seems she is here mostly as a party favor, something for the fancy boys to tell their parents. Guess what, I danced with a girl.

The little Asian dude looks at her longingly on a Culture Club song, but she pretends to have something in her eye. She's all about equal rights and decency, but he's not going to grind his sausage with her while Boy George and the fellas croon on in the distance.

Eventually even gay bars have to close, and thank God for that, Anne is past tired. Luckily there were a couple of the most gorgeous boys near a bathroom with a little bump. It might be Thursday when they all stumble out into the parking lot. Anne is going in Pinky's car, which only has four of them now, the rest gone with various proclivities, more with men that one might think. Anne gets one more soul crushing hug from Beth, whom she really has affection for now, despite the face full of straw she suffered from her. They are getting in the car when two trucks full of rednecks pull up. They jump out of their trucks and move forward as a group. There must be eight of them at least. They are yelling and taunting a few of the boys coming out of the club. Anne looks over and sees her little Asian boy and two of his friends surrounded by four of the bigger redneck boys. Anne says boys, because no one of them could have been over twenty years old. She heavily considers just getting in the car. But either the experience of leaving MarJean alone, or because of the hospitality she was shown tonight she just can't walk away. Slowly and deliberately she closes the door and walk toward the situation. This just needs some adult intervention and supervision.

The window rolls down, "You don't have to get involved." Pinky's being nice; she can see that Anne is no physical threat to anyone but herself. *They wouldn't hit a woman right?* But for whatever reason, maybe because she didn't dance with him or just a sense that no one else would be willing to do it, Anne was not going to let anyone beat up on HER little gay Asian man. *I wish I knew his name now, this is awkward.*

"Is there a problem," Anne yells out. Her voice waivers slightly, but she still remembers how to invoke the mom voice. They back up a step, looking at each other. They're staring into the motion sensor lights from the club, so they can't really see her yet.

"Yeah there's a problem. Faggots and Lesbos like you shittin up our town. Beat it rug muncher before you get one too."

He might be on the right track, Anne can't remember ever being in a fight, not even a hair pulling match really, but she is sure that cooler heads and sobriety will prevail. Mentally she is trying to message Pinky to call the police before things get out of hand. *Although who knows what king of Roscoe Sherriff might show up and deliver a government sanctioned beating.* Anne realizes that Elizabeth is going to be pissed for the second time tonight, or should it have been three? Her heart is beating like a jackrabbit. She steps into the fray and now she is in the light, not behind it.

The leader starts to say something, but just then the one on the right says, "Hey, that's the chick from the Roller Derby, the one that got her ass handed to her. Should'a known you were a dyke." This just gets them all laughing and Anne looks somehow even stupider. Her face is red and hot, she wants to cry from the strain but she wouldn't give them that satisfaction.

"Yes, that was me. What da ya say we call it a night, no need…" is all she gets out. One of the boys goes for the small Asian and Anne steps in, just to try and break up any trouble. Unfortunately she didn't pick a great time as the punch was already being thrown and what was probably intended for someone else connects right into her eye. The world goes dark and sparkly for a moment as Anne drops like a fifty pound sack of shit. Once the momentary shock of it wears off she leaps to her feet and lunges at the boy who threw the punch. He may have been trying to apologize, but it was past that for Anne. Her hands were balled in rage and when he loses his footing she is on top of him in an instant. She gets two good hits to his face before being pushed off by another of the boys. At that instant all hell breaks loose.

Beth and the rest of the Blue team converge on those four boys like they are a plate of brownies. The boys are bent and bleeding and trying everything they can do to get back in their truck. The other four boys are already speeding off. Beth is hanging on the handle screaming at them to fight like men as they peel out of the parking lot.

Suddenly there are arms around Anne helping her up; she turns to find a very handsome young man pulling her up. It isn't until after a second that she realizes he is in a uniform. *Oh good, now I'm going to jail.* Officer Reynolds starts laughing and Anne breathes out happily, hoping she has avoided jail. Officer Reynolds is helping to dust her off and checking her eye. It helps that that eye was already black. Anne guesses that she looks like she needs to be headed to a battered women's shelter. At the car Pinky has resorted to filing her nails, seemingly oblivious to the whole event.

"I'm glad to see you were worried about me."

"Beth wouldn't have let them hurt you; if anything I was worried for them. Dennis, I see you met our new friend. Dennis this is Anne Carter." Hands are shook and Anne has a hard time taking her eyes off the young man.

"Would you ladies like to get some pancakes?" Officer Dennis asks.

"You can take me anywhere you like," Anne responds.

Damn those uniforms.

Chapter 10 Dismissed

After pancakes and coffee at the dirtiest diner in the history of diners, the group ends up back at Pinky's apartment that she shares with two other roller derby girls. Pinky tells Anne that she is relegated to the couch. She says it in kind of a bitchy way; her attitude seemed to change either with the fight or the addition of Officer Dennis. *And here I thought we were getting along famously?* Honestly, Anne is grateful to have a spot to crash tonight. The straight comment that Pinky had made that night in the club seemed to start a gap between them. Officer Dennis steals a glance, he's definitely interested. Pinky brings a set of sheets and a blanket, Anne's not exactly sure how to put a fitted sheet on a couch, but it's a sweet gesture. Dennis seems to be lingering, it seems unclear if he lives in the house, or if he's attached to one of the girls. Anne starts to wonder if he's attached to Pinky, maybe that's why the distance. She's so tired of trying to guess who's who and connected to whom, that she almost doesn't care anymore. Throwing the sheets on the couch, she wraps up in the blanket and lies down. Trying to convince herself that she's not too tired to sleep, she makes a slow and methodical catalog of all the items on the walls; someone is a talented photographer. The walls are filled with black and white studies of abstract nudes, mostly women, as it should be. Eyelids get heavy and Anne is asleep without even having to count.

Suddenly, someone is there in the dark beside her. Anne tries to shake the sleep out of her head, she can't see anyone, but she's sure someone is there. Whatever light was on when she went to bed is gone now and she stares into the yawning abyss. She puts her hand out and feels a hard pressed fabric, warm and with taut flesh underneath. The dark form lowers and in a moment she feels lips upon hers. Her head is dizzy with waking and now her senses are lost in the grey twilight between sleep and wake. It gives the moment a fluffy dream like quality, allowing her to ignore any pesky thoughts that might otherwise interfere with her pleasure.

The hands are strong and sure. They work at her clothes and their own. Soon the feel of warm skin is on her. The kissing is almost violent in its penetrating need. Anne is sure the interested party is Officer Dennis, but in truth she doesn't know for sure, which somehow makes this even better.

A second later she is totally naked and aching for him to be inside her. She whispers in his ear, "Fuck me." There is a moment of hesitation, the dark stranger pulling back for a moment, as if considering his options. Then his form presses even harder against her, almost devouring her mouth. The hands on her breasts knead her and increase the throbbing need below. She wants him, but either to tease and torture her or prolong the agony, he is not moving to finish the job.

She reaches her hand out to feel him, strong and ready. She pulls on him, willing him toward her. "I shouldn't", his voice is like a splash of cold water, but just startling, not refreshing. Anne knows it's Officer Dennis, but what is wrong eludes her.

"Stop thinking, just do it," her voice is as soothing as she can make it. Welcoming him to invade her most private of spaces, to share herself with him. She knows he has gone too far to stop now and a second later she is rewarded as he presses forward and the hollowness is gone. She is as she was meant to be. In this moment she feels totally complete, a necessary part of the world. As his motion speeds and builds she starts to push back, wrapping her legs around him. She doesn't think about tomorrow or next week, she doesn't think about thirty seconds in the future. She is totally lost in the moment and how good he feels inside her. Their sweaty skin on each other slides like silk. She pulls at him, she wishes she could scratch his back, but she has no nails. She is being loud, she knows, but she can't help it. Suddenly the world flashes and she feels dizzy again.

Dennis is panting heavily, arms around her. Anne pets his hair like someone might a small child. They lay there, him still inside her, catching their breath. She smoothes his hair and tucks it behind his ear. Suddenly he kisses her again and pulls away.

"I have to go, I'm sorry." She can hear him pulling his pants and shirt on. The rustle of his gun belt and then he is walking away. Anne knows a lady would say something, but obviously she is no

THE END OF THE ROAD

lady. It seems stupid to beg him to stay when she wants him so desperately to go. That was a horrible mistake with a veritable stranger, now Anne feels used and cheap. The evidence of their tryst is leaking out of her into another stranger's sheets. Anne picks up her own clothes and does her best to get dressed. She considers just leaving now, but she's wiped out tired. She looks at her phone and sets a mental alarm clock for three hours later. Officer Dennis walks back by, presumably on his way out the front door.

"Thanks, I mean, I would…." He is stumbling badly with his words. Anne wishes that he just hadn't spoken.

"Don't worry about it, it was fun." She lies and hopes desperately that he won't try and kiss her. Unfortunately he has to, some shade of chivalry that young men get from watching too many Prince and Princess Movies. The kiss is quick and he is gone almost before it's over.

Officer Dennis, I hope you have understanding roommates.

In the morning Anne wakes with a start. She meant to be gone by now. There are girls walking around in Pajamas, it looks like an 80's Sorority house. Anne smiles and nods, trying to get the sleep boogers out of her eyes. This is awkward, nobody seems to be talking. *Did I dream the whole thing?* Looking at Pinky, she looks as pleasant as ever, somehow it feels forced. Anne looks at the other two, trying to recall the vague details of dark encounters. *It had to be Officer Dennis.* She would like to just go, but since no one is saying anything she feels breakfast is expected of her.

Every kind of junk cereal on the planet is here, Anne would have never let her kids eat this crap. She finds the least repulsive sugar bomb, Cookie Crisp. Looking for the Almond milk, but only 2% is presented. *Oh how I suffer.*

The cereal does amazingly taste like little chocolate chip cookies.

Anne is trying not to stare at Pinky, who seems to be doing the same thing. That name doesn't sound so correct this morning. Anne wants to ask about Dennis, but there is something wrong here. She senses tension. She wonders if she was with someone's boyfriend last night. Technically that wouldn't be her fault. She is chewing wondering if she should be ready to defend herself. Maybe someone is going to come with a frying pan or something less comical.

"Well, are you ready to go? I know you need to get on the road if you're going to make good time."

Pinky said it, but either because Anne doesn't want her to have said it or because she can't believe she said it, says, "What?" Pinky gives her a sad and resigned look, but Anne's not sure what to say here. She doesn't want to embarrass her in front of her roommates.

Anne's mouth opens a couple of times without any words coming out. Pinky is looking intently at the cereal box label in front of her. Feeling slightly emptier, yet safer than she had a moment before, she stands up and walks over to get her phone and wallet.

"Thanks for everything." Anne tries to make it sound casual and light, but she can tell she doesn't mean it, everyone can tell. Then she goes, walks out the back door toward the General. Straining her ear hoping to catch a "come back" echoing in the distance, Anne knows she is bound to be disappointed. Nothing comes and she hasn't forgotten anything to run back inside to get.

I should have forced her to talk to me, but now I'm sitting in her garage, unable to come up with a viable excuse to get back into her house. Anne keeps looking to the back door, hoping it will open and Pinky will run out. She is sure if she checks just one more thing on the General she will have come to her senses and chase her down. But eventually it sinks in even to dim old Anne that she's not coming. *I know why, and I know why it hurts. I know I have done it to other people and I deserve it, but it doesn't make it hurt any less.* She sets the helmet on and selects the Blues genius on her Iphone. *It's going to be that kind of a day.* She tries not to peel out or make any grand statements on her way out of the driveway. Looking back at the stop sign and Anne swears can see someone staring out the window. In the rearview mirror the face fades in the distance as the General pounds down the road.

THE END OF THE ROAD

Mental note: Karma is a Bitch.

The End of the Road

Chapter 11 Pile it on

The Cookie Crisp is running thin. It wasn't much of a breakfast to start with, but its staying power and protein content is seriously in question when Anne needs to stop an hour and a half later. There's a truck stop ahead so Anne hits the turn signal to get over and takes the exit toward the smell of old grease and pancakes. Pushing through the doors Anne tells herself that it is a commonly held truth that truckers know where to eat; apparently they know a good meal when they get one. They also know how to spot a good lot lizard, slithering between trucks giving sweaty monkey love to the haulers for fifty bucks a shot. For any unfamiliar with the term "Lot Lizard", this is a prostitute that frequents truck stops, servicing multiple trucks of lonely long haul drivers. As one might imagine, it is not near the highest level of whoredom, more quite near the bottom actually. Anne can't remember where she heard that term first, but she's spent enough time on the road to know there is more than a little truth in some urban legends.

The 'please be seated' sign is the cutout oak lettering with polished brass accents, not a great sign. After waiting less than a minute she is led to a table by a most pleasant Hostess with three missing teeth and more blue eye shadow than should be allowed by Federal law.

When the waitress arrives, she calls Anne sugar and honey in the same sentence. *That seems excessive to me. Don't oversell it sweet thing. You're not getting a tip big enough to fix that broke ass face.* Anne peruses the menu, trying to keep her arms as far off the table as she can for fear of being permanently glued there by the spilled syrup and coffee cup rings. Everything feels greasy, in fact she realizes sliding her fingers together; the menu's greasy. She doesn't necessarily mind grease, it can be delicious, but you don't want to leak grease through your anus, that's unpleasant riding.

Finally settling on some French toast, the world's prettiest waitress makes it back with Anne's coffee. Apparently she is not actually Anne's waitress. She is at once tempted to beg for the toothless beauty queen to be her waitress. The she pig behind her now is forty-five pounds overweight and her hair looks like she washed it in lard. There is a zit on her forehead that you could take her pulse with. She wipes down the table with the dirtiest rag Anne has ever seen in her life. She tries to dodge it, but the corner flaps out and catches her arm. *This place is like a cornucopia of human garbage.*

Reminding herself how badly some of these episodes have gone she asks, "Can I get the French Toast and a pot of hot water?" The yard pig looks confused as she takes the menu extra slow. Her little brain is processing the unexpected information, and although she turns to go, she has to come back and ask, "So you just want hot water?" *Be nice, she's preparing your food. If you upset her too much that white pus factory on her forehead might burst on your French toast.*

"I have my own tea," Anne says pleasantly and holds up the bag of leaves. She still looks confused, but Anne just continues to smile and hope she can figure out what hot water is. Looking at the spot where the rag touched her arm, she tries to pretend that it hadn't really happened. At least now she can't see the filth on the table. It's an old table top, cleaned until they wore through the Formica top at the corners. Committing to the filth she lays her arms on the table top.

A phone starts to ring and with annoyance then shock Anne realizes it's her phone. *Maybe it's Pinky?* She answers the phone, not looking at the number to hear only silence, not even the sound of her phone speaker engaging. Looking at the phone, she realizes the call is connected, but her repeated answering is greeted with silence. Then she looks at the flashing blue light on her helmet. Sputtering profanities she grabs the helmet and jams it on her head. "Hello, hello," there's the other voice. With great sickness of stomach she realizes that it's the sound of her mother.

"Oh, hi Debbie. Sorry, I had the phone transferred to my helmet." *Even her silences sound annoyed with me.*

"You need to come get Jordan." Her matter of fact tone is in direct contrast to the court hearing where she told the court that her heart could not allow Anne to retain sole custody of her own son. *Where now is her testimony of my unfitness to be a mother?* The anger rises so fast and so hot that Anne can't really think.

"I can be there in two days." More silence, but now she can hear her mother thinking. *She wants to be shitty with me; she is desperate to be shitty with me.*

"Where are you now?"

"I'm not sure, almost to Colorado."

"We're putting him on a plane tonight, pick him up in Denver."

"I'm not sure I can," only she is speaking to dead air. The soft clicking sound and blank screen are all that indicate that the call has ended. *Case dismissed your honor.* Taking the helmet off, Anne should be embarrassed by all the chuckling truckers in the booths around the joint, but she is overwhelmed by this sudden turn of events.

"But I don't know if I should take him right now, it's not really a good time," she says to no one in particular, because no one is actually listening to her. Anne asks a trucker looking fellow that's walking by how far it is to Denver. He shrugs his shoulders and keeps on walking. *That wasn't much help.* Anne pulls up the maps app on her phone and plugs in Denver International. Dropping a pin where she is, she waits for it to calculate. It looks like she is about four hours out of Denver. *Mom's bluffing, she won't send Jordan to me. She might send her to one of my sisters, but never to me.* Just then her email buzzes and she notes that it's a forwarded itinerary from Expedia. She pushes her fingers against her forehead to try and push back the headache that is coming. Laying her head on the table, apparently she forgets just how filthy that towel was. *This must be what a panic attack feels like.*

She tries to remember that this is her little boy, maybe not so little now, but hers nonetheless. When Bill went back to school, Anne was working nights, so they wouldn't have to pay for daycare. Bill would lay him in their bed and she would hold on to his foot so she didn't lose him off the edge of the bed or accidently crush him rolling over. Sometimes she could still feel his little foot in her hand. This wasn't a punishment; this is what should have always happened. *My little boy is coming back to me.* She looks through the window at the General; there is one small fly in the ointment. She is lost in thought when the lovely waitress brings her French toast. She lays it down with a cup of steaming water.

"I couldn't figure out how to put your water in the register so I just didn't charge you for it." She says this as a whispered secret, something to be held within strict confidence. *Well it seems things are looking up.* Anne tears into the French toast, it is pretty damn good and she has to lend some credence to the "eat where truckers eat" line of thinking. The more she thinks about the General the more she thinks there might be an elegant solution.

Phoning Elizabeth, this time without the helmet, "I need a favor."

Liz replies how she always replies, "I need one too."

Chapter 12 Thus it begins

With heightened security regulations at the Denver Airport Anne is forced to wait outside the security checkpoint. She hopes she picked the right one; it's always possible for a late gate change. She waits ten, twenty and thirty minutes. A quick check of the arrival board indicates the flight has arrived. *I do not want to call my mother, this is bad. Why doesn't he have a cell phone like everybody else?* Anne looks down the corridor toward baggage claim. It's possible he made it past, and might be waiting somewhere else. Jordan is seventeen years old, but Anne still didn't like the idea of him wandering the airport all alone. This is how people get kidnapped and killed. She is at a loss for a good plan when she feels the familiar vibration in my pocket.

Picking up she can hear her son's irritated voice saying, "Are you here or what?"

"I'm outside the security gate, where are you?" Jordan exhales a loud huff that means she should have known whatever he is about to tell her.

"I'm outside the passenger pickup, level 4."

"Oh, okay, just wait there. Do not go with a stranger I'm on my way." That was over kill. Any doubt Anne might have had is relieved as she hears him laugh and snort. *Laugh and a snort? That seems a little excessive too.* She runs for the passenger pickup, only to realize that this is commercial pickup on level 5. Down a level she walks out onto the sidewalk, looking one way and the other. She is in the middle of the way pickup area, 50/50 which way, so she just picks to go right. People are waving and being met by loved ones. There are hugs and tears as she picks her way through the crowds scanning for Jordan. There's a gap in the people and she begins to think think she may have picked wrong, but at the far end there is a young man in a hoodie fully engaged with his phone or IPod, but definitely not looking for his mother. Anne wouldn't think it was him, except for the bag. He is carrying the dark brown leather messenger's bag that was Bill's. Bill had carried it to work every day of Jordan's life. The leather is beaten and abused; it looks like the plane drug it behind all the way from Salt Lake City. Sudden and with painful clarity Anne can see the corollary between the bag and her life since; well, since everything. She walks up slowly, taking her time to approach him carefully. It's like the Crocodile hunter approaching a rattlesnake. He has the power to wound or even kill her; she has to be very observant. Then he looks up and she can instantly see within him her six year old son's face as clearly as a summer day. That was the year they went to Disneyland for the first time. His eyes were so wide and his smile so complete that that picture has stayed with Anne through all the years and all the heartache. Only he's not smiling and his eyes aren't open that wide. *I want them to be, I want him to be excited, but he's not.*

He didn't pick this, and Anne didn't pick this either, a fact they both seem keenly aware of. She smiles with all the hope she can muster and he gives her a little smile back. *Maybe this will be okay.*

"Where's the car?" he asks.

"I don't have a car; we gotta run up a level and grab a cab." His smile fades into a sneer as he lifts the handle on his carryon bag and pushes past. *That's more what I expected.* They ride the elevator up and hail a cab. He opens the door for her, Anne tries to give him a hug on her way in, but it comes off as forced and horribly awkward. Anne informs the cab driver of their destination and he speeds off toward Denver.

It's pretty quiet in the cab, Jordan has his headphones on and Anne is not sure how to proceed; how to break some of this ice between them. Instead she finds herself staring into the life-consuming iPhone. *Maybe there's an app for awkward family moments.* She had given this habit up, pulling out an electronic distraction anytime she wasn't actively engaged, deciding that it was making her miss, well everything; but she feels such a profound loneliness in this cab that she can't help herself. Anne jams her phone back in her jacket, willing herself to be present in the moment. She looks out the windows at the mountains in the distance. Finding nothing of real interest, she refocuses her attention toward her son. He's tall and muscular; he must have gained four inches in height and more than thirty in weight. He definitely got Bill's build. She immediately wants him to change out of the grungy hoodie he's wearing, which sports the fashion name 'PornStar'. *I wish I could have skipped noticing that. That's not something a mother wants to notice.* He's wearing his father's watch; other than that there doesn't seem to be any other jewelry on him. *I wonder if she still wears the locket I got him after the funeral.*

Anne thanks God he doesn't look just like Bill, which would make her agony worse than it already is. As it is, she still sees little things, small similarities with his father, but she's doing a good job of denying them so far. They arrive at their hotel pretty quickly considering how far out the Airport is from downtown Denver. Anne pays the driver without getting out, Jordan already has his bag. They walk to the lobby, of course he's five steps ahead of her as if his mother's stink might weigh him down. *Now I know how Muslim women feel.*

At the front desk he turns on his heel and says, "Where's my key." Anne tries to respond coolly, "Do you need a key; I thought I would carry it."

His sneering look turns to full venom, "We are not sharing a room," this is painfully close to a shout. Anne is not sure what Dr. Spock would say here, but her first reaction is to tell him that he can damn well share a room with her just like they always had. *But we haven't always anything anymore.* The rules have changed and their situation has changed. The whole world changed, *so why do I feel just the same?* She considers it for a moment before approaching the front desk.

"I need another room that adjoins mine." The front desk girl is very helpful and the room next to her is vacant, so it is a simple addition. Anne can still see that this isn't what Jordan wanted, but he knows that he can't push her too far. *Does he now?*

The clerk hands the key to his room and he says politely, "Thank you sir." Bill would have been so pleased just then. They had preached civility and manners every day of their lives as parents. Even with all that happened, their kids turned out polite, well Jordan turned out polite anyway. Anne offers to take his bag but gets the sneer again. *Just imagine when I ask what happened between him and Grandma. We are in for some awesome talks.* Anne watches him go into his room, knowing that she should say something, but totally oblivious as to what that thing is. She has a distinct desire to run screaming down the hall and out into the street before plunging headlong into traffic. Instead she opens the door into her room and plops on the bed.

Doubt gnaws at her mother's mind. She seriously doubts Grandma Debbie sent him off with a full stomach. Opening the separating door she is faced with the blank back of his door. She knocks gently, nothing. She knocks again louder.

"What," Jordan's voice queries from the other side.

"Wanna go get something to eat?" No response, which means he's hungry. If he wasn't hungry he would have quickly dismissed her.

"Like what," he asks. *Like if you don't open this door and talk to me I'm gonna rip it off the hinges.*

"Whatever you want," Anne lies. *Let's get him out in the open, and then I stand a chance.*

"Sushi?"

"Yeah," Anne says and means it. She was afraid he would ask her to take him to McDonalds or Burger King. But then again he's not six anymore, some little child desperate for the toy and a chance to play on the slides, maybe somebody should remind Anne of that. A door opens, but not the door she's at. Peeking into the hallway, there he is, looking much like he did when she left him ten minutes before.

"Any chance of replacing the hoodie with something a tad more formal?" He looks at her venomously, but then he must realize that she's right and ducks back into his room. He is out a minute later in a collared shirt and more cologne than Anne would prefer, but she has to admit it's better than a hoodie. *He's quite the ladies man, or could be anyway.*

Jordan's chopstick skills have improved since the two ate sushi together last. Anne suppresses a smile remembering how the waitress had used a rubber band and the rolled up paper to create kid proof chop sticks. The restaurant is an ultra modern Americanized Sushi bar. They have rolls with Kobe beef and tofu, which scares her a little, but everything they get is excellent. Anne tries to ask about school and get the minimum answer, although it sounds like he is doing well. She is surprised he's a senior. She thought he was a junior. Anne does her best to play it off that she really knew, not exactly a major contender for mother of the year. After finishing their main rolls the waiter asks if we want dessert. Anne says yes and orders a dessert roll. Jordan doesn't want one, but Anne needs a minute to talk to him and she didn't want to ruin the meal.

Anne opts for the Blitzkrieg or 'lightning war' campaign, hoping to catch him off guard, "so why did your Grandma have you deported?" Suddenly and instantly the civility that lasted through dinner is gone.

"It's none of your business." Anne reels from the blow but she expected it.

"I'm afraid it is my business, you are my son."

"Since when?" *He goes for the knockout.* Still upright, she is still in this fight.

"I have always been and will always be your mother."

"You can say whatever you want, but the truth is I don't have any idea who you are anymore. And you sure as hell don't know who I am." With that he stands up and walks away from the table. He turns coldly to the front door and out into the street. Anne fumbles with her wallet to get the bill paid so they don't gang tackle her at the door; in a panic she just throws a couple of hundred dollar bills on the table. *That was pricey.* She busts through the doors and spies him about a half block up the road. She ignores the 'don't walk' signal, dodging traffic through the intersection. Jordan has stopped a little way ahead; it appears he wants to be caught. There's an opening and Anne darts between two cabs that blare their horns and try to pinball her between them. Jordan has taken to looking stoic. *So I guess this makes me the jerk? I had to ask, didn't I?* Anne approaches softly to put her arms around him. His arms unclench and he puts his arms around her. She realizes that he has gotten softer in the last couple of seconds. A slight shaking makes her realize just how pivotal this moment may be. Boys don't cry often, humiliate them and they may never speak of it again. This is a touchy operation. "Why did everybody just go away," Jordan's voice is breaking.

"Honey I didn't go anywhere, I'm right here. I'm always here for you." His shaking is less but his grip on her hasn't lessened. Then his arms go slack and she tilts her head up to look at him.

He says without malice or venom, without any twinge of emotional manipulation that Anne can sense, "But you're not."

Chapter 13 Conventions can be fun, but not for you

Breakfast was provided in the hotel lobby so it proved to be easier to get Jordan there than it had been to coax him to dinner the night before. Anne is finishing her delicious muffin with a glass of apple juice when he comes up. Anne points out the cornucopia of breakfast treats laid out across the room. They are staying at the Marriot near the airport and really Anne thought this was one of the best hotel breakfasts she had tasted in years. Anne points out the omelet station and suggests the bacon and mushroom. He doesn't look real excited about any of it. *He should have seen some of the 'included breakfasts' at previous hotels.*

Anne rediverts her attention to the newspaper she was reading when Jordan came in and he wanders off to get something. He comes back with two plates piled as high as they could possibly be. *At least he's getting our monies worth.* Jordan eats with the social graces of a long term prison inmate, his arm around his plate as if someone would try and steal his sausage. Anne doesn't want to disturb the calm they have here, but she has to know what happened with him and Grandma. Anne gives herself a moment to develop a game plan. *Run man, just run.*

"I don't want to make you mad, but can we talk about what happened with your grandma?" She says it as pleasantly and unconfrontationaly as she can.

He immediately clams up, but Anne can see by the way he's eating his fruit that he is going to tell her. He probably wants to tell her, it's got to be hard to keep whatever it is a secret. Anne lets the question ride, asking it again gives away power, or so she had learned in a leadership course in a prior life. When no answer is immediately forthcoming, she looks at him intently, but says nothing. *Now it's a game of wills.*

Almost too quiet for her to hear, Jordan makes a soft statement, "Grandma caught me doing some stuff." Anne tries to remain calm.

"She caught you doing what?" He doesn't answer and Anne starts to guess that it wasn't his homework or a science fair project. Anne looks around because for the first time in months she doesn't want to be overheard.

"Were you having sex?" Anne can't believe she gets it out without throwing up. *Well I lost my appetite.*

But his answer shocks her even more, "No." *Oh my God it's drugs, we're fucked.*

"Was it drugs?" she asks. He reaches across the table and hits her.

"No MOTHER, it was not drugs. We were just fooling around, but we did not have sex." Well now Anne just doesn't understand. Debbie kicked him out for making out? *I knew my ultra religious Mother was crazy, but this was extreme. I thought she had found a severed head in his closet or something the way she shipped him off.*

"So just making out," Anne does her best to wrap up the pieces.

"Pretty much, kind of." His answer is as elusive as his use of verbs.

"Was it with a boy?" This question floors Jordan, quite visibly.

He is almost shaking when he replies, "No, it was not with another boy, mommy, I have a girlfriend if you would ever listen to anything I ever tell you."

He gets real quiet and leans in, "I was going down on my girlfriend Jessica in grandma's room." The world gets fuzzy for a moment. Anne becomes the mother from Leave it to Beaver. She longs for a return to old fashioned values. She is swooning, literally swooning like Aunt Bea in Mayberry. *Did he just say that?* She is ready to yell and chastise, but her hypocrisy kicks in. She had a boyfriend that was younger than Jordan is now; and she did a lot worse than that. *Where was Rush now, he should be standing behind me laughing.*

Anne just cannot get it in her head that he's not six years old. She starts to ask if they used protection, but she doesn't want to have to explain what protection is in that instance. *I don't know if I could tell him to use saran wrap or not. Really I don't want to talk about it.* She doesn't want to know and she doesn't want to talk about it anymore.

Slapping her hands together, she attempts to clear the air of all that, stuff.

 "Okay, what do you want to do today?"

"Aren't you gonna lecture me about how premarital sex is wrong?" Anne looks hard at him to see if he's ready to have the talk from her. In their former life it was always Bill who dealt with the boy stuff and most of the sex education the children received. Anne was just too blunt and honest. When Jordan got his first wet dream Anne was there, Bill was out of town. She went into exquisite detail about how his body worked. She had dealt with it then, what the hell, honesty is the best policy right?

"I'm your mother, so secretly, in some deep down place; I didn't ever want you to have sex. I could have had you die a virgin with fifty cats and been totally satisfied. I hope I taught you why to get physically intimate with someone, because I'm thinking it's a little late now. But honestly, I think it's awesome, you're seventeen, and it's about time. Eighteen would have been better, twenty one better still. I hope you're being safe; Gonorrhea is remarkably resilient with teenagers; and there are more girls wanting to get pregnant out there than you can imagine. But most of all I hope you're doing it because you are in love and want to express that. Even if that love doesn't last, every tryst you have with someone that's for the wrong reason leaves a little scar tissue on your heart that never really goes away."

Anne means every word, there are things she doesn't say, but this is what she has to say to her son about it. She can't condemn him for something she has done and still does every chance she gets. From his story Anne reads that he's smarter about this than she ever was, and probably will ever be.

He looks up from his empty plates, "how about a movie?"

It's Anne's turn to look disappointed, "I was hoping you were going to suggest going to the Magic and Fantasy convention. I'm speaking there in about an hour."

He looks perturbed, but not too, "No, that wouldn't have been my first choice. Why would they have an Erotic Poet there?" Anne rubs her temple to consider the same question wordlessly. *Elizabeth seems to like the idea. But, just wait til you see what we get for it.*

The payment for spending a day this way is waiting outside. The guy delivered it this morning, according to the front desk. Anne tries to cover Jordan's eyes, but he's not having any of that. They walk out and there is the General, with a matching sidecar.

"Where's the surprise," he asks.

"Look at the side car on the General."

"How is that a surprise for me?"

"Surprise, you don't have to ride on the handlebars." Anne walks to the bike to figure out how exactly they are going to fit on this thing when the time comes. The two of their bodies is not an issue, but she's not real sure about their bags.

Jordan is standing behind her. "I don't think that thing's safe."

Anne gives him her own disgusted look and tosses him the helmet that was bought for him. He gets in the sidecar, but Anne notices he's sitting all scrunched down, as if he could hide in there. Anne thought he would like it. Instead it looks like he's embarrassed. Oh well. Anne fires up the General and he sounds strong as ever. She goes to push them back out of the parking space, but it's kind of uphill and there's no reverse. She can't do it from the bike.

"Hey, how about getting out and giving us a push."

"Are you serious?" Anne nods. He gets out and Anne can almost get them out now with the reduced weight, but when he pushes it does help. Anne has them going in the right direction now. Jordan gets in again, this time somehow sitting even lower than the last time. They tear across town, people waving everywhere they go. Nobody cared about the bike before; Anne guesses the sidecar is enough of a novelty now that everybody thinks it's cool. The convention center is just ahead and being the person she is Anne heads for the valet entrance. She stops with about six hundred people watching. When she pulls off her helmet they give a small but noticeable cheer. Anne throws the valet the key and helps Jordan out. He stumbles a little bit getting out. He is mad, Anne can tell from his hurried walk. She follows, hoping he gets to like it more; they're going to be riding it for a month.

Inside anxious fans quickly mob them. This isn't like the Star Trek convention, these are hard core fans. There are more questions than Anne can count coming faster than she could ever hope to respond. Her first mistake is trying to answer any of them. Once people can see that she is responding, they start to push to get closer and make their question heard. Only seconds later there is a scuffle and a portly boy in a grey cloak and staff is getting his face pummeled by a blonde boy in elf ears. Security is on them and finally a worker rescues Anne and Jordan, pointing the way to the green room. She has seen this before, they don't mean any harm, and it's just that it is real to them. Like fans at the Adult Video Awards, these guys are really lonely. They were paying for Anne's indulgent lifestyle, she really shouldn't complain, but Jordan seems shook up by the whole thing. Anne tries to talk to him but he isn't speaking right now. This is why Anne never wanted a teenager. She and Bill used to joke that they would lock the boys up in the closet until they were eighteen. Only there isn't any locking him in the closet, he might be able to take her; in fact there was a real good chance of it. Anne sense's there's something he wants or needs to say, but he's trying to say it through silence. *He wasn't like this before.*

Jordan had never been known to suffer silently, so why the change? Was this the dreaded teenage angst Anne had heard so much about. Or was she finally seeing what the accident had really cost? Was this unending well of silence to be her punishment? Were they to be locked together in a cycle of self indulgent sulking or punitive shouting matches? Anne hated it when Jordan wouldn't talk to her, what was she supposed to do with all this silence?

The conference room is ready and the staff comes to gather her. They seem disappointed that Anne didn't dress up in lingerie. *Are they fucking serious? As if I would sell my integrity and self respect to help bolster sales in the West.* Although, Anne must admit, it is entirely possible that they are under the impression that this would be an act to increase the esteem in which her fellow humanoids held her.

Sometimes a person might get thinking that the staff are normal people, but ask yourself; who would voluntarily staff a Fantasy convention?

The room is filled to maximum capacity. She pulls out her rehearsed speech. No impromptu stuff here, give these guys a chance to shout questions out and there will be another brawl. Anne notices that the pudgy wizard and zit faced elf are in the crowd, albeit apart from one another. She starts the reading with a naughty but basically clean little poem titled, Cum as you are. Afterward she talks about her inspiration and writing process for a few minutes. *I would just once like to tell people how I really came up with the idea. How they would react to hearing that I wrote the book as a joke, with what I thought was an almost comical approach. My characters were grandiose to the point of ridiculousness. There was no subtlety, no development. They ravaged each other, sexually and physically, until the brainless masses had what they wanted, dripping erotic poetry.*

But this was for them, so she spoke about the dreams she had, the world she saw in her mind. She spoke about the greatness of the fans that helped her make her dream a reality. She is on fire; she is giving them just what they want. She is telling them that they're a part of creating this world. They're hanging on her every word. Except one, he's standing in the back against the wall. He looks as disinterested as anyone could ever be. He isn't holding a copy of the book, or dressed up as a character. Unfortunately he's Anne's son. Like a fine crack that spreads out of control, knowing he is there is distracting her, making her stutter and miss her marks. The crowd starts to murmur, which makes her falter even worse. Luckily she is saved by the bell and the video presentation for the Movie adaptation of Pandora's Lust is ready to be shown. She goes back to her chair and looks out; he's still there, intent on showing her how miserable he is. Anne doesn't know if she can take him like this, something has to change.

Walking up to him afterward she expects more silence. Only he grabs her arm and pulls her close to hear his harsh whisper.

"You know everyone thinks we're here together. Like together, together." His words startle her for a moment, but just then a young man walks by, giving her a wink and a small arm tap to her son. *Disgusting, these people have problems. We have to get the hell out of here.*

Although, the illusion probably won't do any harm to book sales. Shut up!!

Slut Poet.

Chapter 14 - How to crash your motorcycle

They're pulling into Cheyenne and the General needs gas. The long stretches of Colorado have inconsistent gas stations at best. Of course they have done their best to stay off the main highways, which makes the station frequency even worse. These long stretches of brown earth speckled with sage brush remind her of home. Jordan gets out of the sidecar and stretches. He pulls his helmet off and Anne suppresses a laugh at his disheveled hair. Their relationship seemed tenuous at this moment; any disruption to the status quo threatens to rip a hole in any common ground they might have made. Plus Anne is quite aware that the helmet won't be doing anything wonderful for her hair.

As he passes her by, he is doing his best to pretend he doesn't know her. Anne casually notes, "Nice hair."

With a quick turn and a little smile he notes, "Look who's talking."

Anne had always wanted to have a relationship with Bill like this. Where there was a playful back and forth, but he had been too traditional for that. He wanted meat for dinner, and for it to be served at 5:45PM every night. He regimented everything in their lives, so much that Anne quite often felt like she was suffocating.

She pays for the gas and talks to the checker for a minute, who is a moron. She has no idea where she is, how to get across her state, or where is good to eat. *Is there anyone working a cash register that can tell you anything? With an ass that big, how do you not know of a good place to eat?* They decide to press on. Any place mostly known for a rodeo is not a good place for them to linger. Jordan is doing the thousand yard stare when she gets back to the General.

Eventually she gives in, "What's the matter honey."

Of course the response is what she should have expected, could have written, "Nothing." He throws his helmet on his head and plops himself in the sidecar with as much enthusiasm as a dead rat. *You're making this miserable for him. If you don't do something different, something he wants to do, you might lose him; and this time it will be forever.*

"Wanna learn how to drive this thing?" The words are out of her mouth almost before she knew they were coming.

"I don't think that's a good idea," he says back with the dripping sadness voice. *For once we all agree on something.*

Then she is using bad words again, "come on, I'll help you." He gives her a sideways look as if wondering whether or not to laugh at a joke. He stands up out of the sidecar and steps on the Generals hand tooled leather seat before plopping down on it.

"The first thing is that you don't ever step on the seat," she scolds him without trying to sound too stern. *Thank God I had them add the starter; that would have been thirty minutes of frustrating hell.*

"Now what," he says excitedly. Anne realizes that she's excited too. *How bad could it be? Oh God, it could be the end of all things and all people! Calm yourself, you'll be right there in the side car.*

"Do you remember how to shift?"

"Yeah, mom, I had a motorcycle." Anne gets sad for a second, but moves on to shifting.

"Okay you shift just opposite from your bike, use your foot as clutch and this you shift with your hand...," the instruction lasts for about ten minutes until she thinks he has the basics. Plopping herself down in the sidecar, helmet between her legs; it's not as comfortable as she had thought it would be.

"Okay, put it in neutral and start it up." He nods hesitantly as she hears him testing the clutch with his foot, pushing the bike back and forth until he can find neutral. Anne refrains from correcting him or taking over. She has done this in the past and it never helps. He presses the clutch in and hits the starter. The General fires right up but he keeps the button down until Anne's hand reflexively reaches out and smacks his.

"Sorry, you need to let off the starter as soon as it starts." He revs the motor and everyone's heart is pounding.

"Okay, put him in gear, easy on the throttle." There is a subtle click as the bike engages in gear.

"Now, slowly let out the…," the bike jerks forward and Anne's head slams back against the seat. The bike is moving faster than the sidecar and they make a small circle smashing into the gas pump ahead. As they crash into the gas pump, Anne's head slams forward and smashes her nose against the top lip of the sidecar. She is not sure whether to staunch the flow of spurting blood or kill the bike. Luckily Jordan had panicked and forgotten to pull the clutch so the General dies and Anne can hold the blood pouring out of her face.

Twenty minutes later they are sitting in a Cheyenne Emergency room to get her nose stitched.

Jordan has hardly said a word other than the repeated "I'm sorry, I'm sorry" that he did all the way there. Anne jokes with him that wounds heal and men really love a girl with deep scars, but it isn't helping. In looking at the design of the sidecar Anne can now see that this was not really intended for safety, more to look cool. The shop that's going to pound out the front fender is also going to install a safety pad along the rim of metal that she bashed her face into. Looking at Jordan she is glad it was her, not sure if she could have lived if it had been his face forever sketched with a long pink scar. *Although, I don't think dudes appreciate scars the way chicks do.*

They stay in a crappy little hotel that's close to the shop; who said they could have the bike repaired by first thing the next day. They go out for pizza and Jordan is really making an effort to be nice. He fills her drink and even goes for napkins. He is trying to make her feel better, but as always she is lacking the right words to say to convey that it's not his fault.

"I want you to try again tomorrow." He shakes his head no and they continue eating. "I really want you to try again tomorrow." He shakes his head no again and they continue eating.

"I really, really want you to try again tomorrow and we'll start in a wide open parking lot." He looks at her and Anne recognizes that look. He doesn't want to give up; he's stubborn just like his father, but he feels as protective of her as she does of him. He'll do it Anne realizes and they can finally finish their disgusting pizza. *What kind of barbarian puts pineapple on a pizza?*

Chapter 15 - We need to talk

Tensions are running high as they take another try with the General. Jordan has been bucked off once and Anne's nose looks like someone beat her ass. Anne grasps the new leather padding reassuringly; it's time. He does everything right getting it started, just like he did the last time. Jordan comes to time to let out the clutch, but this time there isn't enough gas and the bike stalls. Jordan immediately shuts down. *This boy is just too damn sensitive.*

"Honey, it's fine. You just have to develop a feel for it. Listen to the bike and what it's telling you. You can feel when to shift and how fast to let out the clutch."

He looks up and says in near defeat, "Kaden would have done it by now." Shards of glass puncture her inner organs and she tries to focus on what he's doing. *Listen to the bike and help him.* He starts the bike and gives it a little gas while letting out on the clutch slowly. Anne closes her eyes, hoping for the best. A second later they are rolling along the parking lot.

"Now try shifting into second gear." It's a jerky motion, but he's getting a feel for it by the third time. They continue around the parking lot, shifting and practicing their turns. Twenty minutes later he seems to have mastered the stop and go.

"Alright my young pilot, let's take him out on the road."

He turns on her, "Are you insane?"

"Best place to learn." Anne knows he has been driving for the last two months and she hadn't gotten any phone calls about dead bodies, so what the hell? *Let's live this life. Dum Vivimus Vivamus.*

The roads are empty of traffic, but he is still looking both ways as if they were in downtown New York. Anne looks at him and gives him a confident nod, ignoring the small voice in her head that says 'we're about to die'. Slowly he pulls out onto the road. They're heading along the roadway, the wrong direction, but Anne realizes she should have been more indicative of which way to go. He is getting better.

A few stop signs later and a series of two rights and a left and they are on their way. He slows slightly as they pass the parking lot, but he doesn't say anything and neither does she. This is too awesome to come up with some complaint. Anne's son is driving a motorcycle. He explores the power of the General, playing with up shifting and downshifting. He's a natural really. He should be; motorcycles are in his blood. Anne and Bill grew up on dirt bikes. Bill's father died next to one. Not exactly the precedent you want, but it wasn't his fault. Benjamin Carter had been working on his 1967 Harley Davidson on the road next to the cemetery when a drunk driver struck the parked motorcycle and him, propelling him over fifty feet into the air, his body finally coming to a rest across a branch in a nearby tree. He was killed instantly, his life snuffed before Bill even got to meet him. Bill would have been just a lump in his mother's Uterus. But this is Jordan's moment; nobody can take that away from him. He looks so serious, but Anne can see the smile hidden underneath. Suddenly they are going really fast, as if he wants to check out the top speed on the General. Then he lets off and they coast back to 55. Anne can't stop smiling; she sits back and releases her death grip on the padding. She allows herself to close her eyes and trust, it feels so good. She can't hardly think of the last time she trusted someone. When she opens her eyes some minutes later it seems someone else is driving the General. *Bill?* Her eyes fill up and she gets a hard knot in her throat. Raising the visor the warm air blows over her and dries her face. *I hope Jordan didn't notice anything.*

West across Cheyenne is the great wildness of Wyoming stretching out like an unpainted canvas. Brown land cut with ravines and peppered with sagebrush. It's wind country and as they pull into Rawlins Wyoming they can taste a fine grit on their teeth from a solid helping of that Wyoming dust. This is the kind of town riders live for. The antique storefronts make it feel like they just stepped into another time. They are able to overlook the few franchise restaurants when Anne spies a little hole in the wall place on the historic main street. Jordan wants to go to the Chile's, but not on her dime. There are too many times when they will get forced into a place like that to choose it when there's something more unique.

Rawlins must serve some of the oil country because many of the men look like they just came off a rig. Dirty stoic faces piling into large dirty trucks with various oil subsidiary names on them. This is a real blue collar town; nobody comes here antiquing, although there are probably some great old stories to be found. They walk down the main street until they come to the Bluebird. It looks a little old style diner, a throwback to the late 1800's. Inside the entry foyer looks like an old apothecary, complete with glass jars of various candies and antique ointments on the back shelves.

The oldest hostess in the world greets them with, "Howdy, jest the two of ya?" Anne looks around, there is no one within fifty feet, but she confirms it for her. She takes them to their table at the slowest pace imaginable. She fidgets with the utensil and napkins, her hands have skin so thin you can see her tendons moving with each action. Her blue hair is done in marvelous old lady style.

"Where y'all from, California?" she asks.

"No Ma'am, we're from Utah," Jordan tells her. *Oh no, don't say that. I'm not from Utah anymore, I'm from, elsewhere.* She has relatives in Utah and asks if they know them. All Anne can do is blink. She starts to tell them all that's going on in Rawlins. There is an outdoor movie tonight, with costume contest. She was horrified to find out that it will be an Adam Sandler film, Happy Gilmore being shown. In the following days there is to be a duct tape fashion show, Anne personally would love to see that, the highlights include vendors, a bouncy house, coloring contest, bike and classic car parade, clogging performance, old-fashioned races, ice-cream eating contest, volleyball tournament, "kids and pets" parade and the famous outhouse races. The old woman stares at the wall blankly and Anne wonders if she's had a stroke.

Suddenly she yells, "Well that's all I can remember," and she's off. They never see her again, but it was sure fun while it lasted.

Their waitress is more of the young girl who dreams of 'getting out' type. She's pretty, if too thin with a weak chin. Jordan is immediately smitten with her and Anne smiles to see him fidgeting and trying to sound worldly.

"Yeah I'm driving my mother across the country", he tells her.

"On like, a motorcycle? That sounds like so much fun."

"It's pretty cool, I guess."

Jordan notices that as he's talking to the waitress, Anne is smiling and has her glance locked with a handsome cowboy type across the room. He waves his hand in front of her.

"What the hell?"

"What do you like that guy or something?"

"I don't know, we haven't even met, it's kind of hard to judge from here."

"Well, it's embarrassing."

"I let you flirt with the waitress without making a scene."

"That's different."

"How and why is that different?"

"What about dad?" Anne feels the dagger.

"I loved your father very much."

"You wouldn't know it." Just then their food comes and Anne does her best to stuff food into her mouth instead of letting words come out. It seems Jordan would have her in mourning for the rest of her natural life. Anne hopes this conversation will pass without further comment.

"How come you don't ever talk about Kaden?" Lancing pain goes through her bowels.

"I talk about Kaden." *Liar.*

"No you don't, any time I even mention his name you get all sick looking." It was true; Anne could not deny that it caused her great pain to think of Kaden. Even then with a delicious meal sitting in front of her, the mention of his name made it impossible to eat. What she can't tell Jordan is how close thinking about him almost brought her to losing her mind. She can't tell him about the pills or the ER visit, she doesn't want to burden him with all that. He thinks Anne had him stay with his grandparents because she wanted to go on some whirlwind tour of the world with the books, but for a long time all she could think about was him, not eating or bathing or paying the bills, just him. The home movies Bill had made years before became her fix and allowed her to wallow in the sweet misery of a picturesque past she could not reclaim. Even now she knows where in her wallet is the small picture of him she took that Fourth of July. He was about four years old, holding an American flag.

Jordan can't know what that does to her; she can't let him see how close she is to losing it. Anne holds her sanity by the thinnest of strings and she doesn't dare tell him. Mothers are supposed to be strong and Anne knows she's not. *I didn't deserve to be his mother or Kaden's.* She stirs her pot roast around her plate to make it look like she ate more than she did. They don't speak again at dinner. She pays the bill and tries her best to ignore the batting eyelashes from their waitress. They walk out to the General and it's his turn to mediate. Anne gets in the sidecar, but Jordan won't get on. She nods toward the seat. He shakes his head and suddenly they're lost in a world of miming and gesturing. Anne gets out of the sidecar to drive the bike when Jordan wraps his arms around her. Anne wraps her arms around him, noting the subtle shaking.

"I miss him so much mom, I miss both of them so much." Anne is trying to keep herself numb, but her tongue is getting big and her chest aches. Big wet tears roll down her face.

Chapter 16 –The Ranch

The miles roll by through Wyoming and once again the sun is directly in Anne's eyes. In addition to being unpleasant, it is also a poignant reminder that they will need somewhere to hold up for the night soon. The cell signal is as sketchy as the road maintenance is here. When they get signal, a quick search for a hotel ahead reveals very little to make her optimistic. The one place that they could make by dark is called the Twin Creek Ranch and Lodge, in something called Lander Wyoming. Anne marks it on her map before the cell signal drops again. This is desolate country, long expanses of brown with grey-blue mountains in the distance. Any near ravines have started to show the red rock that hides beneath them, indicating they seem to be in what Anne calls the real West.

For every pine forest out here there is a thousand square miles of God forsaken Taiga. The humidity is much lower which makes the riding more comfortable during the day, but it's amazing how cold it gets when the sun hits the horizon. Sunburns come faster and the amount of grit on your teeth after a long ride multiplies exponentially. This is home for Anne, even when she wishes it wasn't, the stark open country just feels like home. Lying on a beach in St. Thomas is a heavenly moment, but not for one second did it feel of home to her. Anne sees the turn coming up so she taps on Jordan's arm and signals him to slow down. He stops in the middle of the road, not a big deal since they are pretty much alone.

"Your turn to drive," he says sounding very tired. Anne feels tired as well, physically tired as if the energy was wrung out of her like a dirty dish cloth. Crying does that to her.

She hops on the General and can tell that the man of metal and gears missed her. This seat is more comfortable, that much is certain. It might have something to do with improved suspension in the bike. *I ought to have someone look at adding some shock absorbers to the sidecar.* Looking at the map on her phone she takes one final bearing, and then starts down Twin Creek Road.

THE END OF THE ROAD

If Rawlins was a step back into the seventies, this place is a step back into the 1870's. Cattle are everywhere, seemingly all wanting to cross the road at random intervals and for seemingly no reason or predictable pattern. This must be one of those "working" ranches, where people pay to come pretend they're cowboys. She is trying not to scare the cows, imagining with horror what a stampede would mean to the three of them. The herd must be several hundred cows and she knows enough to know cows are ignorant unpredictable animals. They're not going to attack, but they might run in front of her, or directly into her. She slows down to a crawl, which allows their dust cloud to catch up. There is a cabin ahead and just as its windows appear, so does the beautiful panorama of their ranch.

The General grinds to a halt and Anne steps off. The poor old bastard is covered in dust so thick one might suspect they had been on dirt roads for a hundred miles. *It's been a while since they had a good rain here.* In sharp contrast to the barren lands around them, the ranch has a small stream running through it, feeding a verdant green oasis.

"I hope they have a room," Anne says to Jordan, noting the three vehicles around the main house. Jordan shrugs his shoulders and they make their way toward the main door. Before they hit the first step a tall man in full working cowboy regalia, and real stuff, not midnight cowboy style, walks out.

"Speed limit is ten miles an hour on that road," he says in an unemotional tone, more informational than scolding.

"I'm sorry, I didn't see a sign."

"Well," he says in a more pleasant note, "you might be able to see better at ten miles an hour. Name's Tony." He reaches out a massive hand and crushes her in some Western show of man dominance. His hands are rough and calloused, he obviously works this land.

"I'm Anne and this is my son Jordan, we're hoping you can put us up for the night." He looks her over like he might inspect a side of beef, then rubs his chin, in what looks like a mannerism developed mostly for tourists.

"Rooms are all full up, havin a family reunion a sorts." Anne nods understandingly and starts to turn around.

"Problem is, I don't think you're gonna make anywhere else by midnight. Course you could just crash on the couches." His voice is gruff, but Anne understands the hospitality he is extending to them. This is unforgiving country and nobody knows it better than him. It immediately makes her like him.

"We would be much obliged." Anne reaches out and shakes his hand again, this time putting as much strength into her grip as possible. He smiles and beckons them inside. Anne laughs to herself. *Just imagine what the Lifetime people would say if they saw this whole thing.* They follow inside where a group of random eclectics sit on couches and stand around in various poses. There is a flash of someone in the back kitchen moving quite hurriedly.

"That's Janae, ma Wife." She waves from a distance, shooting her husband a scolding look and beckoning him with a quick gesture. "Make yourselves comfortable."

Anne takes their jackets to hang them on a deer antler coat rack. Inside the house is decorated in might be referred to as Western Charm. The walls are chinked pine logs with some bark left on. The furniture is almost formal English. There are delicate white china pieces around the room and on the walls. It reminds her of a settler's cabin, or at least what one would expect a settler's cabin to look like. As if someone brought their finest things along with them from back east and made the rest from the ground. Anne finds an empty couch to survey the people in the room.

There is a man in his late fifties who obviously instigated this 'family reunion'. He looks like the Midnight Cowboy. His boots are very shiny and his hat is ridiculous, not to mention the faux pas of having worn it in the big house. His wife is sitting in one of the chairs with her pressed jeans tucked into a pair of pink and turquoise boots. Her western shirt has silver buttons and her hat looks like something out of the old TV show Dallas. The kids were obviously drug there; they range from twenty to probably almost thirty. Two boys look just like the dad, the two girls don't look like either and Anne can't decide if they're daughters or girlfriends. One of the girls is blond and other is a brunette. The brunette and the boys are totally absorbed in their phones and one laptop. The blonde steals the occasional glance at Anne and Jordan while listening to the mother.

Suddenly the man stands up and walks over to Anne and juts his hand out. Anne stands up.

"I'm Ted. This is my wife Anna and our daughter Katie. That's Thomas and Ted Junior. This is Junior's girlfriend Elise."

He immediately walks back and sits down, as if knowing Anne's and Jordan's names was inconsequential. He stares at her, but she's not entirely sure if he wanted to know about them or not. He never does ask the question.

"What brings you here Ted?" It's hard to tell if he wanted to know about Anne, but he definitely wanted her to ask about him.

"We've come from Chicago to get back to nature. We're going to help move the cows tomorrow." At this there is a low whine from both of the boys. Anne looks over but they are just staring at their portable electronic devices.

"It's gonna be great," Ted says to some unknown recipient and far too loud. Anne nods reassuringly.

"Yep, we bought the whole place out so they could be together as a family." *Oh, here they get to the meat and potatoes.* She is interrupting their family joy-joy time. Anne just smiles and looks off into the distance. After a moment she can feel the 'rent a cowboy's' glare on her, or at least on her tits, so she excuses herself to go out on the porch. The sun set a few minutes prior and night is just in the process of settling. Everything looks red now. It's just her on the porch. It doesn't appear anyone is coming outside. *I thought maybe Jordan would come out, but I think maybe he's excited about seeing someone other than me.* Anne makes it over to the General to look in the special pouch, inside is a small pipe and a pill container full of Purple Haze.

Purple Haze was the medicinal marijuana recommended to Anne by the Director for Pandora's Lust. She takes them and heads over toward the barn. With the light failing and hidden from the house she fills the chamber, lights it and takes a long hit. *That's so nice.* Just as she exhales the sweet smoke someone is poking her in the back. Coughing and sputtering she turns around to see the son Thomas.

"You gonna pass that shit or what?" Anne hands him the pipe without really thinking. He takes it and the lighter, drawing a long slow hit.

He blows the smoke out and says, "nice." Anne does another, might as well be killed for a sheep. As she exhales Anne notices that Thomas's looking at her. Only he's really looking at her.

"Oh my God."

"Don't tell your dad," Anne bursts out.

"You're…," he says. Anne nods yes and uses her hands to gesture for the boy to be quieter. Anne is awfully high, but in retrospect she is pretty sure that this is the moment Thomas threw himself at her. This might have been hot but instead it's insanely awkward. Anne has the feeling she's becoming a checkmark on a list. But Thomas keeps kissing her, reducing the intensity while sliding his hand up to feel the contour of Anne's breast. Anne kisses him back as her blood starts to come up, hands drifting to the boy's strong shoulders, which are firm and surprisingly ripped. Anne's hands are migrating south when she hears, "Mom," yelled from the porch.

They break apart and scatter like cockroaches in the light. Anne looks for Thomas but he's gone. It feels a little ridiculous to be hiding in the bushes from her own son, but she doesn't want to be the one to blow their cover. *Thomas must have come from the back of the house.* Anne walks toward the house and now it's pitch dark. Motion sensor lights kick on and suddenly Anne is in the spotlight.

"There you are, where were you?" his question has a lengthy draw out at the end just like his father's used to. *Don't judge me.*

Anne walks up the steps, "just catching the last of that sunset." Jordan's looking her over like a first rate detective, then he sniffs and shakes his head. *I'm pretty sure he can smell the weed, but he might also be able to smell Thomas's cologne, it was pretty strong.*

"Dinner's ready," he says in the 'I know what you did but I'm not going to say now, but we will talk about it later' tone. They go inside and the family is with Tony and Janae at a very large table. There's room for at least four more people. Janae gets up and gives Anne a hug; this really is a step out of an older time. They find their seats at the end.

Anne waits for the signal to dig in when Tony says, "I'll say grace." This really is just like home. As everyone bows their heads Thomas looks at her with a wry smile. He looks around to notice that everyone has their eyes closed and it makes him bolder. He flicks his tongue out. This would be super hot, but now the paranoia is hitting Anne. Thomas must be nineteen or twenty, but still. He continues to show her interest until his father coughs. *I guess somebody didn't have their eyes closed like they should.* Thomas's eyes close and Anne looks at Ted. He is purple with his eyes closed. *Maybe this will be more fun than I thought. Might be a poem or two here, Redneck Son or Forbidden Farm Tales.* Only just then Anne gets the kick in the shins she deserves from her own son.

Does the sanctity of the dinner prayer mean nothing anymore?

Chapter 17 Like a Rhinestone Cowgirl

Bill was looking directly into Anne's eyes, a sad smile on his face, as if he was disappointed in her. His hand held out to touch her cheek, to show that tenderness that he so rarely showed. She had so many things to say to him, she needed to say she was sorry, but no words would come out. Again he touched her shoulder, now shaking her. Suddenly Anne snapped awake.

A deep voice whispers, "Anne, you or your boy done any ridin?"

"Uhmmm," Anne tries to clear the fog and understand why he would wake her in the middle of the night to ask this. "Like a motorcycle?"

"No, I saw your bike, like a horse."

"Uhmmmmm, yeah. When I was a kid anyway, why, what's happening?" Her eyes have adjusted and cleared some and she can see that it's actually early morning. The light is just starting to filter through the windows.

"My help is sick and I got a bad feeling about this group. I could use your help if you'd be any."

"Let me get my clothes on." Only then she realizes that her clothes are already on; they're still on from her little midnight rendezvous. *What I need to do is wash my hands.* She stands up and tries to stretch out her legs. Jordan has pulled the blanket over his head, as if he knew there would be an early morning call to arms. Anne considers waking him, but decides against it, putting her boots on and walking outside with Tony.

Her breath is clearly visible in the morning cold, odd because she knows in three or four hours it will probably be Ninety degrees. They head to the barn to pick out horses in the near darkness. The corral has probably twenty-five horses standing in it. Tony squeezes through the fence and starts culling them out. Over the fence sit several lead ropes and halters. One by one he picks the horses he wants for the day and leads them to the gate, where he hands them off to her. Anne notes that he seems to be picking the oldest and calming looking horses he can. He pulls out the sixth horse, a big bay, and walks out with the horse behind him. This doesn't seem like the right number to Anne. They venture into the tack room and she is amazed by the assortment of saddles and bridles on the walls. There are some English, some standard, high backs and a few that have so much silver she is surprised a horse can carry it.

He points to one of the silvery ones, "Put that on the big bay out there." She is not pleased, the bay is large, but he also looks like he might fall over dead just putting that monstrous saddle on him. "It's for Ted, he'll want that saddle, trust me." She shrugs and takes the stupidly heavy saddle outside. Tucking the stirrup onto the horn she heaves the saddle onto the horses back, it is all she can do to get it over. The old bay doesn't even move. Anne tries to remember how the strapping works, the belt in the back is simple, but it takes her a minute to remember how to tighten the cinch strap. The horse is pushing his chest out, it's a pretty common horse thing, they don't like it tight, but riders don't like it loose, lest they be sideways. She tightens it down, and then walks away for a minute. When she comes back he's stopped and she can tighten it properly. The bridle is really garish, silver everywhere; this horse looks like it could venture to Argentina to ride in some Gaucho competition.

Most of the horses are ready when Janae brings us out some coffee and biscuits. Anne passes on the coffee having had ranch coffee before; luckily Janae brought water, because the biscuits are a tad on the dry side, even with butter and jam. A few minutes later people start streaming out of the house.

Ted and his wife are in their finest, him fully cowboy and her in her English hounding outfit. *So that's why we put the English riding saddle on the palomino.* To say this group made a less than awe inspiring presence would be an under exaggeration of epic proportions. Ted and his wife, his daughter Katie and Thomas joined the ride today. Junior and his girlfriend were apparently not joining for whatever reason. Ted still felt the need to stare at Anne's chest, or scowl at her, each alternating based on some arbitrary factor.

Anne shows Thomas to his horse with a smile. She helps Katie into the saddle, pulling a stalk of straw from her hair. They smile at each other. *This just gets better and better.*

Ted walks his tired old horse over to where Anne is trying to get her own affairs ready, "Are you going to ride like that?" Anne looks at her own clothes, long sleeve hoodie, jeans and hiking boots. She has her riding jacket tied up on the back of the saddle.

"Yep."

He snorts and walks his horse over to Tony. There is a heated exchange for a second, with Ted steering his horse away in a huff and Tony shaking his head. Suddenly Ted is off his horse and inspecting his saddle.

Anne walks over to ask, "Is there a problem? I put your saddle on myself."

He sneers at her, "Yes, I know. The front strap's loose." With that he raises his knee hard up into the old bay's chest, causing it to exhale sharply. At the same time he pulls the cinch strap tight as he can get it, which makes Anne wince. His three hundred pound frame can pull a lot of tension. She has seen this technique before, usually by shitty owners who had no business on a horse.

"That strap's too tight," she informs him. He doesn't even respond just heaves his fat ass into the saddle and rides off. *Well at least I didn't have to help him up.*

"What an asshole" she says to her own horse, rubbing his muzzle.

Tony is up ahead telling the group what their jobs will be. They are going to move a group of cows from the western slope to the North Slope. They move the cows occasionally to keep the vegetation from getting totally stripped. Tony has two old dogs, some kind of inbred heelers one might guess. One could also guess that they could probably do this without the human interference. Tony takes the lead and the rag tag fugitive fleet is off.

Anne's allergies are going crazy with the horses stirring up dust and pollen with every stomp. She wishes she had her allergy medicine. Normally a toot in the nose of Nasonex and a pill would fix this issue. The motion of the horse walking starts out feeling really bumpy and jarring. She tries to get in rhythm with the horse, swaying her body with his and it gets better. Anne is in the back trying to keep everyone together. Tony spots the cows up ahead and he instructs everyone to fan out into a large V shape. He points to where the cows are supposed to go.

"Slow and steady." Anne is on the far forward left of the formation, just here to keep cows from escaping sideways. Katie is the other side of the formation, Anne might try and talk to her, but several dozen cows are in the way. She turns around in her saddle and she is shocked to find this is working as well as it is. She knows that a cow's flight reflex is a pretty known quantity; Tony would obviously understand this perfectly. Everyone is exactly where they need to be to keep this herd moving in a straight direction. Occasionally cows get moving the wrong direction, to escape between the gaps, but the dogs are on that, flanking them before they reach this imaginary line. *This is nice, I could get used to this.* Suddenly the cows start mooing more and Anne hears Tony's voice. She can't hear what's going on but looking back Ted is badly out of formation, causing the V to become tilted. He is moving faster than the group and has not kept his line consistent. Anne looks around for his wife and she is nowhere to be seen.

Katie and the Thomas are doing fine on their side until they notice that their dad is doing something different. This is when all hell breaks loose. Ted sees the direction of the herd changing, Anne doesn't know if he thinks there's a cliff somewhere or what but he puts the spurs to his old bay and the horse starts to trot. What he fails to understand is that the cattle would sense the movement and in the same predictable pattern, move to avoid the closeness of his horse. Suddenly the cows are running as well and this time straight at Thomas, who stopped to see what's going on, halting his horse broadside to the now onrushing herd. Tony is trying to catch up with the herd to push then left, but it doesn't look to Anne that he's going to make it.

Ted starts screaming, "GET OFF YOUR HORSE, RUN, RUN."

Anne screams across the void, "Are you fucking retarded? STAY ON YOUR HORSE AND RIDE WITH THE HERD."

She hopes he heard her. Anne doesn't dare ride toward them; that would only further panic the herd. Either because the boy heard her or Tony yelled something he turns his horse and starts trotting with the herd.

Tony's yelling, "Turn em left," over and over and to the boys credit he does just that. He slows to a walk and the herd finally slows down.

Everyone is looking around; Katie has ridden over to Anne and exclaims, "How exciting." Anne tries to smile back, because that's the polite thing to do, but she desperately wants to throttle the girl's father. Speaking of which, the old Rhinestone cowboy is nowhere to be found. Tony's looking around too, but based on his shrug Anne guesses he can't see him either. They abandon the herd for a moment and regroup.

"Where's my dad," the son says, sounding genuinely concerned. They start to retrace their steps back and find his wife walking her horse, as if she were on a Sunday afternoon pleasure jaunt.

"Something's wrong with this saddle, it's not very comfortable." Tony's head is almost purple. Still they can't see Ted. The group spends almost ten minutes until Katie spots a waving cowboy hat in the distance. They ride to find that Ted is walking without his horse. His silver jewelry is all-askew and he is drenched with sweat, even in the early morning hours. *And I thought I was out of shape. This fat bastard is about to blow his valves.* Tony throws him a bottle of water and he drinks it down.

"Where's Tonto?" and everyone assumes Tony is talking about the horse. Ted points further over the ridge, seemingly too out of breath to speak. They ride that direction, Ted riding bitch behind his wife.

There in a lump is Tonto, legs sticking up in a very 'unhealthy horse' position. Tony jumps off his horse and runs up to the horse, putting his ear to the beast's chest. He looks up and back at the horse. He feels the saddle front strap and furiously rips it loose. With a great heave and yaw the horse breathes and jumps to its feet.

"Who cinched this strap?" Ted is looking awfully abject right this moment. Tony knows who did it.

"Let's get back to camp."

Ted starts to let himself down, to presumably get back on Tonto, when Tony says, "I think you're in the best scenario now, Mr. Brewster."

Kachow!! Anne is quite happy. They walk the horses toward the barn. Once there, everyone dismounts. Ted and his wife walk briskly toward the cabin. *I guess they are not going to help put the horses away.* Anne takes the saddle off Tonto while Tony looks after him.

She is working on the other saddles when Tony says, "We still have to get those cows into the right pasture." She leaves the saddles on their horses with a third saddled just in case. Suddenly there is shouting and Ted and his wife are dragging suitcases through the dust toward their vehicle.

Anne makes a worried face and Tony laughs, "Don't worry, Janae'll set em straight." Sure enough she was right behind them, helping to put their luggage into the dirt. Anne and Tony are both laughing as the family scrambles into their vehicle and leaves in a cloud of dust.

Janae looks at the two, "What's so damn funny, you know they're gonna leave a shitty review on Trip Advisor?"

Janae shakes her head and laughs a little, scowling and smiling simultaneously, "Lunch is ready in a half hour; and there's plenty NOW."

Anne looks at Tony and he looks at her.

"You laughed first," he says.

They laugh again; it feels good after almost losing the big bay and the stress of the herding incident. Tonto looks better, but Tony will have to have a vet out to look at him soon, unless he dies of old age in the meantime.

They tie off the bridles, "I'm gonna miss Thomas though," Anne states with a smile.

Jordan comes out with a stern look at his mother.

"What?"

He continues to give her the look, as if to say, 'I know what you did.'

Everyone sits down to a monumental meal of fried chicken and mashed potatoes. This is the closest Anne has been to a family meal in several years and she does her best to bask in the momentary radiance of a great moment and some embarrassment that wasn't hers.

Chapter 18 On the road again

It's time to go, Anne hates to admit it to herself, but she realizes that to stay longer would be to wear out the welcome of some great people. Tony and Janae were happy to have them stay after the family that had blocked out several days left, free of charge even. Anne offered to pay, but once they had refused once she knew it would be insulting them to offer further. With that gift however comes the caveat that you can only abuse their hospitality so long. It had been great when Jordan joined them on a few rides. After all herding cattle is a pretty manly thing; this was something Bill would have done to 'man' him up.

As a way of saying thank you Anne makes breakfast while shirking her dark time chores. She has everything prepared for French style omelets. The eggs are at room temperature and all the ingredients are precooked, save the cheese. Once everyone is sitting she starts each one, only letting the mixture cook for about 50 seconds apiece. Everyone seems happy with the omelets and the potatoes she makes, however the tea is receiving a mixed reaction. For all the teapots throughout the place one would have thought them to be more tea minded.

"I just don't get it, I need something with some kick" Janae says.

"Maybe tea's not for everybody. It's a roasted tea with notes of caramel and Irish whiskey. It reminds me of an old leather jacket my father had and the smell of pipe tobacco in an old private library, built out of Walnut and brass. It's a smell of a different time."

Janae looks at her with a weary smile and drinks her tea like a good girl. *Maybe she can be taught.*

Saying goodbye is harder for Jordan than it is for Anne. She can see he is on the verge of tears when he goes in for a hug from Janae. They say to come back anytime and Anne wonders if that means come back when they don't have clients to scare away. Tony and Anne shake hands and it's done. He walks off toward the barn while Janae waves them off. Anne tries to show her good guest policy and drives as slow as she can on the dirt road out. Luckily it's fairly early in the morning and it must have sprinkled some; because the road doesn't coat them with any dust at all. Taking one last breath of the crisp clean pollen-filled air before plunging back onto the highway, Anne decides that it definitely rained a little last night.

She hadn't asked Jordan if he wanted to drive, but that was by design. She needed to drive right now. It helps to keep those pesky thoughts and feelings at bay. Like any high attention activity, motorcycling was most valuable for its ability to capture the riders focus, keeping it off the messes in their lives. *I wonder if that's why riders, climbers and adrenaline junkies were always shitting up their lives?* She could only hold the thought for a second, as a sweeping turn ahead demanded her attention. Anne settled in to listening to the engine thump, the pace of the drumming speeding and slowing in time with her turn of the wrist. The whistling of the wind on her helmet sounded almost ethereal, like the spirit scene from Raiders of the Lost Ark. She thought of that for a moment, until an oncoming truck brought her back to the road, speeding through the high desert plateau toward their next adventure.

The cool morning ends abruptly as the rising sun beats down relentlessly on their backs. *Today's gonna be a scorcher.* Anne is hoping to make it to Jackson Hole today; it's only about three and a half hours. Not far out of Lander they're pushing hard north and the high desert plateau yields to Alpine meadows and patchy pine forests. They're getting into the Tetons now, their jagged outline in the distance indicating why the temperature is starting to ease up some. Reaching her hand down to feel the air coming off the General; it's warm but not uncomfortable. The engine isn't running with as much power as it was, the elevation probably has something to do with that. Anne finds a nice vista and pulls over. Jordan looks at her with alarm as they come to a complete stop just barely off the road; actually the General is still mostly in the road.

"Why are we stopping," he asks.

"To look around."

Anne pulls out a bottle of water and takes a long draught. She offers him some and he takes it, Anne notices that he wipes the rim before drinking. Anne starts walking, Jordan finally running to catch up with her.

Crossing tall grass and wildflowers it appears they are following the remnants of an established trail. Anne wonders if she locked the bike well enough, but trusts to fate as they plunge deeper into the forest. Suddenly the pines open and a small lake appears, no bigger than a small house, it looks like a studio backdrop with the purple mountains in the distance and surrounding wild flowers.

Anne looks at the lake and back at Jordan. Giving him a slight push and yelling "tag, you're it," she is off and running toward the lake. She can hear Jordan behind her laughing and breathing hard trying to stay up with her.

Anne tosses the keys and her jacket on the run but leaves everything else on as she jumps off a rock and into, ta da, thigh deep water and mud. *It's a good thing I didn't dive; I would have broken my neck.* She works to pull her feet out, nearly losing a boot in the process. Jordan is a moment after her but was slightly smarter and waded out. The water is freezing cold; it must feed from a glacier somewhere.

"This is Teton water Jordan," as she splashes toward him. He splashes back and Anne becomes lost in the moment. It's like she won the lottery, only it's better because she gets to keep this treasure all for herself. The gravity of the moment stabs at her, as if drawing her undivided attention to the perfection of itself. This is a moment she hopes to remember forever, a story Anne will use to remember a perfect moment with her son of spontaneity and defining for them what their family will be. She tries to capture the feel of the cold water on her skin, the smell of pine and reeds, the sound of the wind in the trees, the taste of the cold clear mountain water her son splashes on her. *Let him save this moment, let him remember it in all its majesty and perfection and let him forget some of the bad.*

"Okay, it's freezing. I'm getting out," he says and it's over.

Now they can relive it, recount it and write it in their memoirs, but the moment has passed and the experience becomes memory. Standing on the bank trying to figure out how to dry her socks she can see where it happened. She thinks maybe she ought to take a picture, put it in a scrapbook. *But what else is left to put in there?* Everything from before today is locked up in a storage unit in Layton, Utah. Movies and books and pictures of a lifetime of moments just like the one that happened in that lake. Moments that torture her with the knowledge that the people that made those memories possible can't make more with her, knowledge that some of those people didn't want to make more memories with her. If only she had been able to soak in a minute more of the lake, that might have been enough.

The reality of their situation looks dire from afar. They are soaking wet, on a motorcycle, in the mountains. But they're only about twenty minutes out of Jackson and Anne has an idea. Wrapping their dry jackets around themselves they ride, hoping they can endure the cold. Screeching dust and rocks behind, they tear onto the highway. The canyons approaching Jackson Hole are an awesome spectacle, pine trees so thick they look like carpet. When they pull into town Anne is almost dry, but so chilled it's hard to swing her leg off the bike. Jordan looks cold and miserable.

"New clothes party?" Anne asks.

It's a question and although Jordan, and every son, hated shopping with their mother, the chill of the fading daylight seems to make him more accepting than he usually would be.

He throws his jacket in the sidecar and gives her a wink, "New Clothes party it is."

There is maybe nowhere better on earth to buy a crazy outfit than Jackson Hole Wyoming. It is a town made up of people desperate to show their down to earthiness while also displaying their obscene wealth. The stores sell tourist items like outhouse model kits and rich tourist items like ten thousand dollar boots. They settle on a place with antler handles on the door. Jordan picks out a Hoodie and low riding jean ensemble that makes him look like the tour guide to the Snoop Doggy Dog museum. Anne goes conservative with black pants and a white blouse. Jordan gives her a sour look; she hasn't gotten crazy enough, but she hasn't accessorized either. She finds a belt buckle the size of a Texans ego and a belt with silver dollars. Ostrich skin boots help to complete the picture, but the hand tooled leather jacket is the piez de resistance. Finally she gets the thumbs up from Jordan.

Jordan is trying on an assortment of cowboy hats, "I don't think that's quite going to match" Anne adds. Jordan gives a crooked smile, seemingly coming to the same conclusion. A cute young sales girl comes up just then.

"What about your old clothes?"

"Burn them" Anne adds without a second's hesitation.

They walk down the street to a salon and instantly Anne knows this is the place. A very tall blonde woman with almost as much hair as bosom welcomes them at the door.

"Can I help you," it's not real friendly.

"My son is looking for a makeover."

Her face just lights up. She does a little dance and moves in behind Jordan to tussle his hair and play adult Barbie, or Ken as it were.

"I'm gonna go find a Hotel." Anne turns to leave, with just a twinge of uncertainty about the enthusiasm this woman was showing her teenage son.

After finding a ridiculously expensive Hotel room Anne returns to the scene of the crime. Jordan is coming out and Anne hopes her credit card isn't melted. He walks out of the salon and her initial reaction is to cover him with a tarp, he's no boy, he is strikingly handsome, almost beyond words. The long greasy hair was replaced with a mid length cut with stark highlights. The blonde streaks somehow set off his blue eyes, for a moment he looks like a grown up version of Kaden. Tears well in Anne's' eyes. *Don't do that, this is about Jordan.* Jordan looks shyly toward her, his humble look seemingly hoping that she will approve, but the memories keep flooding her and it is all she can do not to think of his brother and cry. It is as if the new hairstyle draws attention to the wonderful thing that Anne had been able to keep for herself. It would be very difficult from now on.

"Did you have fun," Anne asks.

"Yeah," he says in a Cheshire cat fashion that makes Anne suspect something.

"Did you leave with a girlfriend?"

"Uhmmmm, not exactly"

She is about to ask for clarification when he says, "You do know that was a guy, right?"

"Who, the stylist? She looked like all woman to me."

"Other than her gargantuan Adam's apple," he says as if that should have been obvious.

"She was a little tall," Anne says as if that should have been obvious.

"Don't feel bad mom, it's a whole new world out there. A gentle poet like yourself is bound to be a little lost."

Anne is still a little shocked. She had such great shoes.

With one final shake of the head they are both able to laugh at it. Anne is surprised that she missed it and that Jordan caught it. But she is more proud that he caught it and that it didn't seem to bother him. That's what she would have hoped her son would do.

THE END OF THE ROAD

The End of the Road

Chapter 19 This place is haunted

Jackson Hole has a couple of excellent dining options, the finest being Bubba's Barbeque. This was one of the finest smoked meat stops in the West. It is as unpretentious as a name like Bubba's makes it sound. The help is pleasant if not amiable, but the food is delicious. Your arteries literally clog just looking at the barbeque sauce dripping off a rack of ribs. They should have a cardiologist on staff, that's how good it is.

They finish their meal, which was at the old person hour, but lunch was skipped after the big breakfast with Tony and Janae. Anne ordered well and ate admirably, but left enough on her plate to feed another person. A fitter her was quite proud, usually the remnants on her plate were green and starchy, rarely meaty and delicious. Jordan has a huge glop of barbeque sauce on his chin but Anne doesn't want to say anything, she tries giving him the nudge and hand signal. He looks at her like she's slightly retarded. *He's the one with sauce on his chin.* Anne reaches over with her last remaining corner of clean napkin, dipped in her water to remove the offensive smear. Jordan smiles and laughs, going just a little red. This has been great. *We're really bonding, I feel like all the crap that happened just vanished, the past is off my radar. We are forging ahead with a great life.*

Heading out into the night air it all feels possible. Anne isn't sure what the future holds, but it's gonna be a whole lot better than what she was doing.

"Wanna go to a sports bar or something," Anne asks.

Jordan shrugs his compliance and the General tools around the old west streets until they find a place that looks family friendly.

"You know I could get in a real bar," he yells over the sound of the wind as if that would ease her mind.

"Great," Anne says to the wind. Then she spies a place and makes an awkward corner triangle into a fantastic parking spot. "You can have a sip of my beer if you're good." Jordan chuckles.

Inside there is a mix of every kind of white person you could imagine; rich and old, young hippies, even a few Mexicans for flavor. They find a little table and Anne orders a Chardonnay for her and a Shirley Temple for Jordan. The waitress looks at her as if she might turn her in to DCFS, then looks at Jordan.

"Make mine a Roy Rogers."

What the waitress doesn't know is that Bill used to make these for the boys sometimes. Anne would buy maraschino cherries for an adult party and make Shirley Temple's and Roy Rogers' with the leftovers.

"Do you remember how much Kaden loved Shirley Temples," Anne asks.

"No, Kaden liked Roy Rogers'. He was always trying to figure out how to scam you into letting him have a Coke."

"That's right."

"Do you remember the time we lost him at Disneyland and by the time we found him he had guilted some poor Disney worker into giving him a Coke?" Anne had forgotten that.

"And we called him lost boy all day. Ooh was he mad." This hurts, but not as much as Anne had feared it would. This feels like how you should remember someone you loved, instead of just wallowing in the comprehension of their permanent absence.

"Do you remember the time we went hiking in the Uinta's? And the moose that stomped through our camp, everybody thought it was a bear. Remember your dad and his little pistol? The hike that we took after setting up camp, watching the sun set; that was a perfect moment for me. I tried so hard to save it, to hold onto it. I just wanted it to last forever."

Jordan looks at her smiling, "Of course I do."

They sit for a moment staring past each other, trying to pick through the trash heap of their lives and pull out the lingering sweet moments to share.

"What happened to the video from Disneyland? The one where we got to open the park, Kaden was five, I was seven."

"It's in storage," Anne confesses.

"I'd really like to see that sometime."

Anne doesn't have the heart to tell him how she has tortured herself with that movie. How many times she let it play while she slept, hoping that in her dreams Kaden would be there, where she could hold him, feel his little arms around her, squeezing the air from her lungs. She missed the way his feet used to stink horribly after a long day and he would chase Jordan around the house with his sock. The feeling she got watching him from the stands in his football games, yelling to encourage him and hoping she wasn't putting negative pressure on him. She missed the way he made them waffles, how he would serve them up to everyone with such a look of pride.

"Remember his waffle skills," Anne asks, realizing for the first time that she is crying.

"Yeah mom, I remember." Her chest feels like it's in a vice and she tries to swallow hard to get her voice back.

"Mom, I have to go back for school in a week."

This shocks her from her haze, wiping her eyes and trying to regain her composure.

"I thought grandma was done with ya?"

"I haven't talked to her, I think I'm gonna stay with Aunt Jane." This was Bill's sister, but at least she was the one Anne loathed the least in his family. She had a daughter about Jordan's age.

"Ok, so where do you wanna fly out of."

Anne is hurt, so hurt she doesn't dare talk about it. Somewhere deep she knew this would come, but denial can be a drug too. He wasn't going to spend his senior year with his mother, riding shotgun on the General. Hell, this time couldn't have gone better.

"Dad always talked about Seattle, how about there?" Anne nods yes and takes a long draught of her wine.

Anne had always loved Chardonnay, somehow the sharp flavors combined into a clear note of summers finest moments. She is not sure what to say to Jordan so she says nothing. She wants to go back to the best times stories, but slowly she becomes aware of something happening. People are pointing at her and Jordan, chuckling.

Looking up on the television there is some paparazzi/Reality TV show on. Her picture is on the screen and she is forced to do a double take. Maybe it's something about the show. Then she sees the video, amateur video of the roller derby match. Someone got a perfect shot of them plowing her into a hay bale. The scrolling header below says something about adult entertainment. Anne looks at Jordan and he is purple. No one likes being laughed at, but a teenage boy feels stronger than just about anyone on that subject. Suddenly his drink topples to the floor as he storms out. Now people are quiet, as the judgment ratchets up a notch. Anne is trying to figure out how to pay quickly when the waitress comes up to the table.

"Don't worry about paying the bill. We have a reputation to uphold here. He's young enough to be your son!!"

Anne is so startled by her words that she can't say anything. *He IS my son. Say it, don't tell me, I know.* But then the waitress is gone and Jordan's gone, and Anne's night is shattered. How did this all happen in less than five minutes?

Outside Anne expects him to be waiting by the General, but he's not. She yells his name up and down two blocks, but she can't see where he's gone. Anne straddles the bike, firing it up to roam up and down the streets. She sees lots of people, but somehow none of them are him. Finally she pulls into the hotel and parks the General. She asks the front desk if they have seen Jordan, but they haven't. Opening the hotel room she hopes to find him sitting on the bed giving her a stern look, but no luck. Instead Anne sits on the bed and looks sternly at herself. Minutes turn into hours and the next thing she knows someone is shaking her.

"Mom, wake up."

"You're back. Honey, I'm sorry, it wasn't what it looked like."

"I knew Dad was divorcing you."

His simple statement hits her like a sledgehammer. No one knew that, they had agreed to keep it quiet for the kids. None of Bill's family, especially his family, or their friends knew. The accident had happened just days before his lawyer filed for divorce.

"And I know why he was leaving you." This is worse; Anne had hoped he wouldn't ever know this. Tears start to flow from her eyes. *Is this where I lose him, all that I have left?*

"Things aren't as easy as they seem when you get older," Anne says clutching at straws hoping to buy a minute to clear the fog.

"Well it seems pretty simple; don't sleep with other men if you're married. Apparently that was too hard for you. Poet or not, that's a rule." Now he does sound like his father.

"I could sit here and try to explain myself, but in truth I don't have an excuse. What I did was inexcusable. It might have been a manifestation of some innate desire for divorce, but it wasn't right and I can't defend it. I loved your father in ways I can't even explain. I wish with all I am or ever have been that it had all gone differently."

Jordan's shoulders shake as he starts to cry and wraps his arms around his mother. This is going to be a long night.

Chapter 20 - The Prison I built

Slivers of sunlight pierce the room. Anne had hoped to close the drapes tight enough that the impending sunrise wouldn't wake them, but dawn comes and shoots a piercing ray almost directly into her eye. She and Jordan had stayed up talking for hours. Regardless of the intrusive nature of the sunlight and the lack of sleep realized, Anne actually feels unburdened. As if a huge proverbial weight has been lifted from her shoulders, last night's revelations proved the old adage that communication is paramount. It had shocked her that Bill had confided to Jordan about the affair. The way it had come out was not pleasant or pretty for anyone, so Anne had assumed he had taken those pains to his grave unspoken.

Pandora's Lust was the phenomenon Anne had always dreamt of. In just over six months of writing and editing she had the first three sections in a series of erotica that could extend indefinitely. Her previous failures had shown her that what she thought was good was unpublishable; so in a fit of anger she had taken every cliché and overworked premise and put them all together in one weighty tome. Earlier manuscripts had lain on desks and gathered dust for half a dozen years before this, but this book sold itself. Soon she had offers from three major book houses. Suddenly her ego was getting the boost it so desperately needed. Over a decade of bored housewife syndrome and repressed sensuality vanished with her popularity. Her sphere of influence was no longer just a small bubble within Bill's dominating world. She was her own person; someone people wanted to talk to, to listen to, and to be near.

She quit being everyone's maid and cook to go on a book signing tour for six months. When she got home she hardly recognized everyone, but in reality it was she who was the most changed. She wore chic fashion, she had lost twenty or more pounds and she was so full of confidence Bill could hardly look her in the eye.

She was only back a few days when the people at Knudst Publishing said they had the deal of a lifetime for her. She boarded a plane by herself and went to New York.

First class tickets and limousine rides brought her to a glass skyscraper she could not see the top of from the ground. Every person who met her acted like they had just met a movie star, she was hooked like a junkie. The main people at Knudst had taken the liberty of speaking to a friend at the Lifetime network and they already had the basic framework for a miniseries event.

Suddenly Anne wasn't just going to be a published author, but an Executive Producer on a hit Lifetime series. Who could say no, certainly not any mortal woman? When she signed the contract, her financial problems went away; she paid the house off, bought new cars and updated the kitchen. Of course this was all for the family she mostly left behind. She had far more pressing matters to attend to than homework and a Wednesday night romp with her old man. At home the power dynamic was totally different. When Bill complained that the house needed cleaned, Anne hired a full time maid. Her decade of servitude had left her with so much resentment, almost hatred toward Bill. His touch made her skin crawl, he seemed so small and dirty in comparison to the light of her new world. She could only just tolerate to have sex with him, so sad, because before she had lived for him to come in from working on his motorcycle. Most of all she resented that motorcycle. It had stolen any money that could have paid for a gym membership, but worse it had stolen her husband's time almost every night. She dreamed of buying it from him just to set it on fire.

Anne got an agent, Elizabeth, who became a stalwart friend and really helped her negotiate the muddy waters of literary fame. Pretty soon Anne was calling Elizabeth with her issues and questions. Bill was left to carry on what was left of the life she abandoned for the world Anne had always dreamt of. Signings and conventions with an ever growing audience fed the beast of her inflated self worth. Like a swimmer caught in a riptide her old life faded into the distance, less clear and seemingly less important as the currents of the world pulled her.

The book was everywhere, even on Oprah's recommended list and pretty soon Anne found herself giving TV interviews and that led to people recognizing her on the street. Book sales were unreal, the executives at Knudst were begging for the fourth installation of slutty sappiness. Anne knew she would be distracted at home so she took two months sequestered inside a hotel in New York. She became a machine, page after page flew from her fingers and when the two months were over, she didn't have a book, she had two. She kept one in her pocket, not telling a soul that the book was written, even Bill or Elizabeth. Anne took Bill and the kids on vacation; they laughed and spent money like she had always dreamt of. She bought Bill the Sports Car he could have never afforded, but despite the dazzling brilliance of it all, what Anne saw were the cracks and rough spots.

As the winks and subtle gestures from beautiful young men who had been ensnared by her words came and were registered by her mind, she began to question her relationship with Bill. She began to focus on what was wrong with their marriage, on what she might gain from someone else. Every harsh word from Bill was a justification, a realization that she deserved better. In retrospect she had nothing to be unhappy with, and in the end that may have been her undoing.

Casting was ramping up on the series and they wanted her out in LA to help the screenwriter to truly capture her words. On the set she was a God, the woman who had dreamt all that would be built by their hands. Tables of food were laid out, and people demurred to let her ahead of them. It was in one of those lines that a young Production Assistant had sparked a flirty conversation. Bradley had been a professional surfer from San Diego. As if by some witchcraft, Anne felt drawn to him, feelings stirred that she had hidden away years ago. His curly blonde hair and infectious smile had her swooning. She began to watch for him and time their exits to coincide. He was obviously interested in her by the way he smiled and the nervous glances that darted about as they spoke. He never asked about the wedding band and Anne never brought it up.

Bill phoned late one night with misbehaving children and Bradley thought it was his phone. There was no denying a male voice at 2AM; and the foolish Anne of that passed time didn't want to. That foolish girl told Bill he needed to understand her needs, told him that he had surely done the same. She told Bill how much they had grown apart, all the things she had been taught to say to push someone away. In truth they both said a lot of things, most of which

Anne is unwilling or unable to remember sitting on the edge of her hotel room bed. Eventually Bill hung up the phone and over the next few days Anne only received stabbing texts and finally a phone call from an Attorney. Production was in a critical phase and so she contacted an attorney to delay the whole thing for a couple of weeks. Bradley was living in her trailer now full time and Anne wanted it over with, but the series had to come first. Screaming phone calls ensued and the world became hot and cold, hot from her nights, cold from the daylight view and realities of what she was abandoning.

They were rewriting the sixth episode when her phone rang again and she noted the area code from Utah. Anne excused herself and prepared for another screaming phone call. If she had known whose number it was she wouldn't have taken the call. Pressing the green button revealed a crying voice and her father in law almost in midsentence.

"Anne, there's been an accident, you need to come home."

Anne quickly realized the crying wasn't from him, but someone in the background.

"What's wrong, what's happened?" There was a long pause and she wondered if they had a sick dog, the wailing in the background was unbearable.

"Anne sit down. Bill and Kaden were in an accident, they're gone."

Suddenly the world shrunk, all she could see was the display on her phone, ticking the seconds of the call, the little voicemail indicator telling her she had a voicemail.

"Are they in the hospital, are they alright?"

"Come home."

And then the voice was gone. As if she had suffered amnesia and now it was miraculously cured, it all came back. The things she had forgotten were back. The way Bill brought her soup when she had the flu, holding her hand when Jordan had his tonsils out. But what she could not think of, what left her curled on the ground was the lingering picture of her son running toward her with arms raised. Only she would never see that again, she would never pin his boutonnière for prom, never give him advice on his college entrance exam. As if instinctively, her abdomen ached, dull pain from the place she had first felt Kaden's presence.

When news of the crash hit the papers, it took only days for the political forces to capitalize on her loss. Evangelicals said she had earned her sorrows. Rush Limbaugh gave her the infamous and unfortunately sticky nickname. Her own mother was so humiliated she took custody of Jordan. Anne had not fought any of it, like a boxer too tired to lift her gloves, she had taken each blow, sure she deserved them.

From the edge of the bed Anne looks over to marvel at Jordan's ability to sleep through the piercing morning light. *I still have him, I can't lose him. But you almost gave him away.* Anne stands up and puts her jeans on. The bathroom light flickers before blinding her. In the mirror is a silly girl she has known for some time. Sometimes she hasn't been able to look her straight in the eye, but today she can and what she can see is a well of sadness. Anne feels pity for her, the stupid arrogant ignorant bitch that she has turned out to be. She remembers her as an innocent child, a young woman and even an adoring mother.

She remembers seeing herself in a mirror changing Jordan's diaper, *I was meant for more than this,* she had told herself then. Anne wonders if that motherly woman would be happy with her reflection today, or would they both wonder how the other could possibly be so miserable, given the tremendous things in their lives. The visible wrinkles are there, even her youthful charm can't hide that forever. What is not apparent on this inspection is exactly how deep those cracks go; how deep into the flesh they really go. Suddenly Anne doesn't want to look at her anymore, so she turns the water on to brush her teeth. Afterwards she splashes water on her face as the image does the same thing. She wonders if there's redemption for that poor lost soul; maybe, maybe not. With a strong resolve she stares her in the eye with a motherly intensity.

"Get it together Anne."

Jordan says something from the other room.

"Nothing honey, just stubbed my toe." Anne gives the girl in the mirror one last stern look and makes her way out into the world wondering if she's the hero or the villain in this story. *Everybody should be the hero of their own story, but I'm really starting to doubt that I'm being true to that role.*

Chapter 21 On the road again, literally

Packing their gear onto the General Anne realizes how great and awful this city was to her. She had started with such high hopes and the promise of a great adventure and fun bonding with her son, but the city has left her feeling hollow, though less burdened. Last night's tearful exchanges wrung her out like an old bar rag. She and Jordan seem to be in a better place for it, but she could easily go right back to bed. Lugging their bags from the room she wonders how much stuff they bought yesterday. The sidecar has made packing the old beast much easier, but as she fights to leave room for a rider, it looks like they may have gone overboard. Before, every fold of a garment was critical to having it fit in the saddle bags and pack. Now the space behind the seat of the sidecar provides ample room to store their essentials and needful things. As Anne tries to adjust her feet in the new boots she questions the wisdom of having the shop throw her old gear away. *I should have saved the boots anyway.* Oh well, she is sure they are littering the bottom of some trash can somewhere.

"Why don't you drive," she asks Jordan.

"Yeah, I noticed you started skipping my turn lately."

She is glad he's joking again this morning. Serious talk can at times be contagious and pretty soon every comment you make to someone has to be about some heavy topic. They start out and Anne notices some hesitancy in Jordan's driving. From her angle she can hear the engine marvelously, the thumping sound of the heavy cams and the slight catch during shifts. They're strumming along the 22 through Victor, which Anne is surprised to see has grown since she was here last. Usually the route to Idaho Falls over the pass mostly constituted seeing a few ranches, but now several subdivisions have spread like a bad case of Chlamydia.

The highway is as picturesque as anyone could ask for, as they head up the mountain toward the pass at a pretty good clip. It's making Jordan nervous, or Anne's nervous for him, or he's nervous that she's nervous for him, something like that. He slows way down and looks over. He wants to quit, to hand the reins over to Anne. But today Anne needs him to see this through. She gives a punch in the air, meant to convey that they shall conquer, but he continues looking at her and putting along. "YOU'RE DOING GREAT, KEEP GOING," she yells over the wind and the Generals gravelly voice. He shakes his head, giving in to her demands, and raps out the engine to kick it up a gear or two. Anne sees him checking the mirrors and now a couple of cars have stacked behind them. Anne shakes her head as if to signal, 'no big deal'.

From her audio vantage point she notices the engine stumble more and more the higher they climb. Occasional pops let her know the extra fuel not getting burned on its correct cycle is getting ignited further down the superheated pipe. Suddenly she can smell hot engine, of course she is right next to it. Anne watches it, searching for some visible problem; there is a skim of oil on top of the cylinder that she thinks may be hot enough to cause the smell. She's not sure if the oil got there from the last oil change or a small leak, but it doesn't seem to be a huge concern. Suddenly they are over the top and coming down the backside. Now the engine is slowing them, along with occasional heavy braking; Jordan is really struggling to find a gear that gives him the engine braking he wants without standing on the brakes. Suddenly Anne can smell brakes over the burning oil smell. She touches his knee and motions to let the bike go a little faster.

He lets the bike have another gear and suddenly they are moving faster than Anne intended. When he corners left it's not that big a deal, the bike just strains against the sidecar and at enough centrifugal force the tires squeal a little. On the rights however Anne gets the decidedly uncomfortable sensation of lifting off the ground. Her butt is puckered so tight she is surprised it's not holding them to the earth. Now she signals to slow it down a little and she feels the brakes, but Jordan's afraid of that front brake as all motorcycle riders are at first. She looks back to see that he's actually got the back tire skidding occasionally, which is not good. Anne looks at a corner ahead; deciding that it is the spot where their remains will be found to have launched from in the accident report. She closes her eyes and braces for impact, but it never comes and when she opens her eyes, the beautiful city of Victor stands ahead of them. Anne would kiss the ground if it weren't passing by at sixty miles an hour.

At the gas station, Jordan pulls in for gas. Anne is almost over the trauma of it when his helmet hits her straight in the chest.

"What?" she asks.

"How could you let me drive that, you knew I wasn't ready."

He's right, Anne had done that pass many times, but she really thought he was ready. He certainly did it admirably.

"I thought you did great, we made it didn't we?"

To this he says nothing just stalks off toward the station. *Maybe he's headed to buy a new pair of underwear? Who are you kidding; you need a clean pair too.* Anne sits on the bike waiting for him to come out. It takes a few minutes, just long enough for the engine to stop making that tinking sound, but eventually he comes out and sulks into the sidecar. Anne doesn't say anything, because she's afraid if she does, it will go badly for everyone.

Anne fires the engine to life and they continue their route to Idaho Falls. This area is what one would describe as high mountain meadow. Pine trees ring large expanses of lush green grass in the late summer months. In a dry year this area gets brown and fire reigns supreme, but this must have been a good water year because the area is as green as Anne has ever seen it. Ranch houses sit off in the distance, each trying to capture some lost sense of solitude and self reliance.

Ranches here are owned typically by the kind of people who were great at business, but always dreamt of the day they would retire to that thousand acre ranch and herd cattle. The bitch about it is that those ranches aren't in pretty places like this; they have all been bought up by dentists and lawyers who want to dress up and play cowboy down at the Starbucks. Rusty antique farm implements litter their front yard as if to protest these facts and prove their country fried credentials, but the fact that none of them has any hay and only a couple even have horses tells her that this is the next step in suburban planning, sort of the mini ranch. It smells like dress up and disingneuine douche baggery to her.

They press on past the ranches and now the smell of pines reign supreme again. Their strong clean smell and the cold mountain air are about the most beautiful thing she has ever breathed. The General seems to approve as he pushes them steadily onward up the mountainside. Anne has to downshift twice; *we must have more weight than I thought in the sidecar.* They have most of the road to themselves and she is glad as she swings a couple of the corners wide. They crest the hill and Anne wonders if they should pull over before beginning their decent. As they pass by the thought is gone and they start the steep downhill. She is glad she's driving on this part of the road. Jordan is definitely not ready for this. Anne has to up shift, the bike won't hold second gear and there will surely be cars behind her at some point. She notices Jordan is really watching what she's doing, either out of fear or a desire to learn. Anne had hoped he would, sometimes a bad experience like that can really help motivate someone to learn. Third gear is humming along well, but a series of turns has her on the brakes pretty hard. She considers downshifting, but the difference between third and second is a lot and she doesn't want to damage the engine.

The road gets steeper and she is on both breaks to keep their speed under control now. Anne knows she can't keep on the breaks like this all the way down, so when they come to a straight section, she lets it run for a moment. The road continues straight for a while now so it seems like a good place to let the General flatten out. Anne looks over at Jordan and gives him a confident smile. When she puts her eyes back on the road she sees that she has made a poor series of choices. The road is turning sharply to the right and now she can see why there haven't been many cars on the other side. A large cargo truck has been holding up traffic, there must be twenty cars trailing behind him. She feathers the breaks until she can feel the rear tire slide. They're still going too fast. The addition of the sidecar has changed the dynamic of turning, without being able to lean they are forced to rely on the surface tension of their tires on the road at a ninety-degree angle. This makes the ass end really squirrely. However as they slide toward the long line of cars, Anne begins to see that they are in greater danger of flying off the cliff than hitting the cars. Using the brakes until the last second she throws her weight, leaning into the turn. She can hear Jordan scream as the sidecar lifts off the ground, but miraculously they stay in their lane. Anne doesn't have any time to congratulate herself as the road twists the other way and now there is a solid line of cars on her left. She is feathering the brakes, but in a surreal moment she feels the tires lose traction and suddenly they are sideways. Time slows down and her field of view narrows down to a small tunnel. She turns into the slide while pulsing the brakes and suddenly they are back on the straight path. She smiles because she knows she has it under control now. The adrenaline letdown makes her arms feel tired and her heart sounds like a machine gun in her head. The front brake is pulling really well, so she downshifts to second. There is a small break in the line of cars in the opposite lane. The speed comes under fifty miles an hour and she looks over at Jordan for a just second.

She smiles and he smiles, because neither of them notices that a Buick Skylark has pulled into their lane hoping to pass some of the cars ahead of it.

The Skylark driver tries to get back into her lane, but there's a big truck there and she can only give Anne part of her lane back. Things slow down again; Anne sees that it's an older lady with some shopping bags in the passenger seat. She has time to notice how much she likes that color of white in a sedan. She tries to calculate the distance from the lady's bumper to the edge of the drop off. She thinks they can just squeeze through and as Anne passes the driver's window without collision she thinks they're in the green. Until her rear end comes over and clips the General about where Anne's leg is and she hears some really awful sounds coming from her lower body. *Crunching sounds, that's probably not good.*

The impact spins the bike and before Anne knows it they're pointing the opposite way driving backwards, until they stop abruptly, and the world tries to straighten out. The bike has stopped as the sidecar wedged itself against a Jeep Grand Cherokee. *I love those things, all leather inside and they handle like a dream.* Everything gets woozy until Anne looks over and she can't see Jordan. *Where is he?, Somebody find my son, I need to save him.* The pictures start to go like a slideshow of someone else's vacation and the voices she can hear sound like Charlie Brown's teacher in the background.

Anne looks down at her leg and something doesn't seem right. *Isn't my foot supposed to point forward?* The lights dim, but finally Jordan's face is clearly in front of her. Strangers pull her off the bike and something feels wrong. Her left leg feels numb, no, now it's hurting. No, maybe it's numb. The ambulance takes what seems like an eternity of people stuffing jackets under her head and asking her if she's okay. Anne asks over and over about Jordan, but they can't really hear her through the helmet. For some reason they refuse to take it off. She thinks maybe Jordan's holding her hand. After the ambulance gets there she decides its okay to pass out.

Mental Note: Maybe you're not as good a driver as you think you are.

Chapter 22 - So a Doctor, Agent and my Son walk into a room, stop me if you've heard this one

When Anne finally wakes up it's like swimming out of a deep well, she wonders if like Rip Van Winkle she has been asleep for decades. She almost expects to find a long grey beard below her. *That might be a good look for me.* Anne vaguely remembers some crazy dreams but she's having trouble clearing the cobwebs from her mind. Looking around she quickly realizes it wasn't all a dream, although the pink Llama was definitely part of some really crazy dream. She is in a hospital room and the whole thing seems kind of fuzzy. She remembers the accident, at least the first part. She remembers the x-ray and signing something, but the rest seems like a dream or nightmare. Her leg is in a sling, raised up just like the movies. Her hand is also bandaged. She looks around the room, but no cards or flowers from anyone. She looks for the nurse button, but doesn't see anything. She sees someone walking by and asks her to come in. Apparently she is just a visitor, but does help by informing her that the nurse call button is on the side rail of the bed. Anne gives it a press and in a moment a short brunette in the most garish pink scrubs walks in. She is five foot nothing with a deeply perturbed look on her face along with a thick coat of lip hair that would put most men's moustaches to shame. Actually really looking at her, it's as if her entire face is covered in a downy coat, kind of like the Grinch.

"Do you know where my son is?"

"He just ran down to get something to eat; we've been waiting for you to wake up for an hour."

"A girl's gotta have her beauty rest." The nurse smiles weakly, patronizing Anne just enough.

"Hey, help me up I need to use the bathroom," Anne tells her.

"Just go," she replies.

"I'm not going to pee on myself" Anne replies back with a surprising amount of spite. The nurse just looks at her sternly and she gets the feeling that arguing with her won't help. So after a moment of hesitation she lets it go and the warm sensation courses over her leg, in a thin and direct line. Anne pulls the blanket up to see a yellow tube disappearing into a hideous pair of granny panties. Nurse Ratchet just smiles smugly and checks the IV bag. Anne is still in shock when Ratchet tears the blanket back to expose her poor violated womanhood.

"Looks good," she says before turning to exit. *Oh God, did that just happen? I wonder if there's a camera somewhere, maybe this is a practical joke.*

"What about my leg," Anne asks the air.

Ratchet pokes her head back in, "I'll ask the Doctor to come talk to you about it."

She is left in the unknowing haze that is the modern day privacy act morphine drip. Luckily Jordan walks in a few seconds later.

"Hey, you're awake again."

"Again, have I been awake since the x-ray?"

"Yeah, but you did seem kind of out of it."

"Are you okay?" Anne asks. She can't see any bandages on him.

"Yeah, I was tucked down in the sidecar, remember?" Anne shakes her head.

"Dr. Radcliffe says you'll be fine. He said the bone was broken in like six places and they used a nail or something like that."

"A nail, like they build houses with?"

"You already used that joke mom."

"Did it get any laughs?"

"The doctor seemed to think it was amusing."

"Well it's important to be appreciated." Somehow just this short exchange has left her tired. The cast on her leg is pierced in several places with long silver pins, she is guessing they extend into her leg and just the thought of it makes her hurt. No, it really does hurt; sort of a distant ache like some big fat bastard was sitting on her leg.

"I think I need something for the pain," Anne tells Jordan who is still wearing his semi-concerned parent frown.

"How much do you remember," he asks, ignoring her query for additional drugs.

"I remember the car pulling out and hitting the truck, then it's hazy, a little of the ambulance and getting the x-ray." Jordan looks surprised, almost bemused.

"Just so you know, that was almost four days ago." *Now I feel woozy. It couldn't have been four days ago, where have I been?*

"The doctor said that the anesthetic might cause some amnesia, but we've talked every day, you don't remember any of it?" Anne shakes her head no and wonders if she will remember this. Maybe she can only exist in the current moment like the guy from Memento. Jordan looks concerned again. He smoothes her hair back and walks out into the hallway. Hopefully he's going to get more drugs; Anne would even take Ratchet at this point. Instead a young man in a white lab coat enters the room.

"So, how are we today?" Anne isn't sure what to tell him. He acts like she knows him, and there is a vague familiarity, but really she doesn't have any idea who he is.

"Do I know you?" Suddenly his very amiable nature changes to concerned Doctor.

"You don't recall us meeting?" Anne shakes her head no and he starts scribbling on her chart furiously. Then he has his light out and shining in her eyes. He's having her track his finger through an imaginary path, while he tries to blind her with his little flashlight.

"Okay, everything looks okay, it might just be lingering Midazolam levels."

"That means what exactly?" He looks at her with a serious face.

"Mrs. Carter we admitted you with multiple open fractures to your left lower leg. When you got here you had lost a lot of blood and had to be rushed into surgery. Part way through the surgery your vital signs went too low for the anesthesiologist to keep you fully under. We had to bring you partially out and perform the tibial nail under partial anesthesia. Because of the traumatic nature of the surgery and your reaction we administered Midazolam to cause you to forget the surgery. I believe you had residual levels in your bloodstream that caused your current memory lapse."

Mental Note: Get a prescription for that the next time you send your life into a tailspin.

"So what's the story with my leg," she asks pointing to the white mass with steel pins in the place where her leg should be.

"Your Tibia was fractured in four places; we placed a titanium rod down the length of it that should have you back on your feet in a few weeks. The fibula was broken in a spiral pattern and fixed with a stainless plate and screws. We can take the hardware out in six months, if you like, or you can amaze the TSA people at the airport, it's up to you. You should be able to go home in a couple of days, if we can get your memory working."

Where do we go if I don't have a home? Her guess is that question is out of the good doctors' scope and certainly not covered by insurance.

"Can I get something for the pain?" The Doctor squints again and pulls up a small cylinder with a red button connected to some machine.

"This is your pain medication, just press the button when you hurt." He scribbles some more notes. Anne presses the button six times or so, nothing. Apparently he doesn't understand the needs of those who use chemical engineering for recreation on a regular basis.

"What are the pins for," she asks.

"Those are called K Wires, they help hold some of the fragments in place until they heal, then we just unscrew them out." He sounds so upbeat, Anne wonders how upbeat he would be if he were in this bed. She feels unusually angry, she's not sure why, he has been nothing but nice and informative, but the pain has gone from an ache to a pulsing throb. Then as fast as she was angry it's gone. The room gets fuzzy, Anne knows she needs to stay awake to ask more questions of the good doctor, but when she opens her eyes again he's gone and Jordan is watching TV.

"Any decent channels on that thing?"

He looks over and smiles, "Not really, no."

Anne takes a minute to look around the room, there are flowers on the night stand now, and she guesses they are from the Agency. Elizabeth must be sick worrying; she's about the last of the people that worry about Anne as a person, besides Jordan. Watching him watching TV Anne realizes how fortunate she was that he didn't get hurt. She wouldn't have been able to live with herself if he was gone. She wonders if he knows that.

"Guess I should have let you drive," Anne jests.

"It wasn't your fault; it was that stupid woman in the car. She did send you some nice flowers though."

He points to the flowers Anne thought would be from Elizabeth. "No flowers from Liz?"

"Who's Liz," Jordan asks finally looking away from the TV.

"My agent, the one that takes care of everything."

"Oh, her. She's here somewhere."

Anne looks around as if using her name might bring her running.

"Liz is here? Wait, why did you say it like that?"

"She's just worried her golden ticket might not be able to churn out another hit book for her. She doesn't care about you, you're just a paycheck."

He looks resentful, almost defensive. Anne wonders what has happened in her mental absence. The good news that no one seems to care about is that she remembers her conversation with Jordan and the good boy Doctor from the morning.

"Elizabeth has done a lot for our family. She's more than just an agent she's been a good friend." Jordan looks at her and a second later stands up as if to attack.

"Then she can take care of your crippled ass," he yells and storms out into the hallway. Now Anne is alone with her confusion. *What the hell just happened?* She turns the television off. She only has a minute to ponder before Elizabeth walks in.

"Hey Anne, how are you feeling?" She's trying to give her the mother routine.

"Better I think?" Liz nods as if to stymie the conversation about her. "What happened with Jordan?" Liz looks intently at her shoes now changing roles from worried mother to petulant child.

"I may have overstepped his bounds, I'm sorry. I'll talk it through with him."

Anne smiles, because she knows how Liz is. She came in here trying to reorder the world to help Anne and ended up making Jordan feel marginalized. Anne should have guessed it, but she thought these two knew each other better.

"Don't you two know each other, I always assumed you talked; you always know about him."

Liz bites her lip, the sign that a woman has lied to you and now must come up with the truth.

"Actually I had never met or spoken with him before two days ago. Actually I didn't even know who he was when I got here; I thought it was some boy toy you picked up. The only photo I have ever seen of him was from when he was like eight."

"How is that possible?"

"Your mother is who I always speak to. She tells me what Jordan's doing." Whether it's the pain or the anger over this stupid situation Anne is suddenly raging. *That old bitch has overstepped her bounds for the last time.*

"Cut her off."

"Cut who off?"

"Debbie."

"Your mother? You mean, from the money?"

"Yep." Elizabeth looks nervous, but Anne knows she'll do it if told firmly enough.

"See if Jordan is in the hallway. I wanna talk to both of you before I hit the pain button again." Elizabeth looks anxious, but again, Anne knows she'll do what is asked of her, that's why she's her agent.

A minute later a red faced Jordan and a humble looking Elizabeth come through the door. Anne is lucky Jordan didn't have his own money or he might have split.

"I want to apologize to both of you," Anne starts. Jordan suddenly doesn't look quite as mad and Elizabeth doesn't look quite as anxious. *Women love an apology, they live for it.*

"Jordan, Elizabeth has been my proxy in dealing with my mother and your grandma since I left. She makes sure the checks go out, that your birthday present comes, that you're doing okay in school. Because I was too scared to deal with my own mother, she has been there. Don't be mad at her, she's been taking care of me, the big adult baby that I have become, for years. It's important to me that you two get along, you're the only people I trust."

Anne feels the beginning of tears on her cheeks; normally she wouldn't get this choked up. It must be the drugs, or the need for more drugs.

"What checks?" Jordan asks.

Now Elizabeth goes from anxious to confused. "I send a check for four thousand dollars to your grandparents every month."

"No you don't, how can you lie like that?" Jordan is red faced again.

"I sign the checks," Anne tells her. He looks confused.

"But grandma says you don't do anything for us, that you abandoned us?"

"And she's right, I have been at best a delinquent mother, but they have cashed those checks monthly regardless."

"But I couldn't even get a car because they couldn't afford it." Now he's mad, but finally at the right people.

"I'm sorry," he says under his breath to Elizabeth. She shakes her head and gives him a playful punch in the arm.

"Why don't you two go out and get some dinner, I'm going to zonk out if we're done here," Anne suggests. They both shake their heads; this is a fantastic first step. Jordan grabs his jacket and they head out of the door.

"Hey, while you're out, bring me back something edible, this isn't gonna work," Anne yells while lifting the lid on the hospital dinner surprise in front of her.

"You got it," Elizabeth says with a wink. Jordan looks back at her just before passing out of her sight, as if he was looking at her for the first time. A smile spreads across his face and he gives her a little wave before turning and walking after Elizabeth.

Sitting alone with just the constant beeping of her own heart on the monitor behind her, Anne is still angry. As she presses the pain button, she plots her horrible revenges against her mother. *Although in truth she was there when I wasn't. She gave my son what he needed when I couldn't give it. But they should have told him about the money.*

Staring at her useless leg she states to it categorically, "We got to get the hell out of here."

Chapter 23 First Woman on the Moon

The long miles of road between Idaho Falls and Boise pass by without a breeze or drop of rain hitting them thanks to the fully enclosed interior of the Chevy Malibu the rental car they gave them. Anne hasn't been able to get herself to look at the General yet, it's too soon. To see it would be to acknowledge what she had done to Bill's dream. After all, why was Anne driving the General, but the fulfillment of Bill's unlived dream?

She knows they crated up the parts and pieces and have them in a storage building awaiting her directions. Right now she is trying to enjoy the moment. Jordan is driving, singing like he thinks she's still fast asleep in her Demerol haze. The best photographs are taken when people aren't looking and this is much the same. This is one of those moments Anne wishes she could bronze in her mind and save for prosperity. She's not even sure what he's singing, something too new and hip for an old timer like her. Looking at his profile reminds her of the time they had Jordan and Kaden's silhouettes done at Disneyland. It was the small shop on Main Street that most people just walk by without a second glance. There was an old lady with a pair of small scissors in there that churned out such a masterpiece Anne was shocked there wasn't a line of people waiting. She had figured that like caricatures the details would be lost and it would end up looking much like anyone, but either a trick of her mind or the skill in the old woman's fingers, Anne could see her children in that small black scrap of paper. That same scrap of paper was now sitting in a box on top of a stack of other boxes in a storage unit that hadn't been touched in two years. She packed those pictures away with all the things she should have said and things she should have done. That storage unit contained the remnants of her life, the life she walked away from.

"Welcome to the craters of the Moon," Jordan interrupts his singing to announce.

I guess he did notice I was awake. Outside the car it does look remarkably like the surface of the moon, very little vegetation grows in this volcanic dumping ground. The sharp spires of stone poke up and it looks like the kind of place you could really wear out a pair of shoes fast. Also, either from the residual haze of the drugs or the slightly foggy and overcast weather, the place feels otherworldly. Anne wonders if this is all a dream, maybe she'll wake up, Bill at her side and everything all better. *I could see Kaden again.* The thought instantly causes a crushing pain in her chest. *How much money would I give to see his smiling face in the rearview mirror? I would give it all.*

"Pretty barren, huh?" Anne says to break the silence.

"I think it's beautiful, kind of a stark contrast sort of thing," Jordan comments, reminding Anne of exactly what she was just thinking.

That's exactly what Anne said to everyone who commented on the barrenness of the West. People from the East always complained that there was nothing to the west but sagebrush and distant mountains. Anne always thought the West exposed you to itself. It laid one bare to God or whatever power you believe in, stripped you of your arrogance and self delusions.

Now with the stereo off and the mist of a late summer storm around them they might be the last people on the planet.

"Pull over," Anne tells him.

"You can't walk on that leg you know."

Anne keeps nodding her head toward the edge of the road until he pulls onto the shoulder. Reaching into the backseat, she secures her crutches. Jordan is protesting, but Anne ignores the good sensible advice and starts picking her way into the field. It's like a vacuum of sound envelops the place. No cars coming and no industry of any kind around them.

"If you fall over and kill yourself I'm just leaving you here," her son informs her.

"I'm not going far, just right here. You know all the times I've been through here I've never stopped and walked around. I'll bet I've been through here a dozen times, but never had the time to stop.

That's a tragedy." Jordan picks up his feet as if looking for a safer place to set them than the black spiked terrain below.

"Yeah, I believe it."

The place smells like rain on the rocks, such a clean and yet dirty smell. No, not dirty; it was freshly tilled earth and rainwater. Anne closes her eyes and tries to take in the smell, the look, the essence of this moment.

"Mom, I have to get back to school."

"I know," Anne closes her eyes, trying to linger in the moment of her all too quickly running hourglass.

"I had Elizabeth book me a flight out of Seattle day after tomorrow" Jordan confesses

"I know," Anne admits sadly, realizing now the spell is broken.

We're here and we're starting to say our goodbyes. This is the beginning of the end, the words that can't be taken back. Anne knows she should be glad that Jordan and Elizabeth are talking the way they are. She should be enjoying the last couple of days with her son. She should be happy knowing that their next reunion can be happier and easier from the start. But she is burdened with the knowledge that tomorrow always comes, but quite often not in the way you thought. She is aware that just because someone is here now, doesn't mean they will be here in an hour. She knows too much and she is always wishing she could forget.

"We better get moving if we're gonna make Boise tonight," she tells him.

He smiles at her; he knows Anne doesn't want him to go. But this is what boys do, they leave. Jordan is glad she's not making it any harder than she is; and Anne's glad he stayed long enough to finish their time in Seattle. Anne's not really sure when that became the goal, but it has. Bill brought Anne there once upon a time, a lifetime ago if she really put her thoughts to the miles between now and then. Bill and Anne had been married ten years and they had never really

THE END OF THE ROAD

had a vacation for the two of them when he surprised her with a trip to Seattle. Kids and being broke had a way of forcing them into local kid friendly activities.

Now picking her way through the sharp stones of the craters Anne wonders, if they had taken more time for the two of them, would things have ended differently? The crutches pick their way through easier than her good leg and her bad leg is throbbing and feels like it weighs a thousand pounds. Pick, pick, shuffle; pick, pick, shuffle. Anne can hear Jordan behind her and he's laughing, she's sure of it.

"Nothing funny here young man," she informs him.

"I'm laughing with you, not at you," he throws her famously overused words back at her.

I used to tell him that when he was little. Finally with much effort and amazingly some sweat Anne makes it back into the car and slumps into the passenger seat. Looking at the boot style cast she thinks, *at least I don't have the metal wires sticking out.* She pops two of the pills and downs them with one of the partial bottles of water littering the floor of the car.

"You sure take enough of those pain pills," her son informs her.

"Well, I am a huge rock star."

He nods knowingly and starts the car. He looks for oncoming cars and Anne laughs to herself. *We haven't seen a car in a half hour but that would be our luck to pull out in front of a speeding semi.* Of course no semi pulls out and soon they are rolling along the poorly maintained highways of Idaho. Anne unplugs Jordan's iPhone and put hers in to launch a Willie Nelson tribute. Now it's Anne's time to sing. Jordan is gritting his jaw, as if that would help close his ear drums from the violent intrusion of her singing. Of course Anne only has about six Willie songs so before they even get a chance to bring out the Zippo's it's over. Anne's eyelids are heavy, but before she goes out she swaps the phones again so Jordan can listen to his music. The moon surface starts to yield to yellow fields of wheat. *Where the hell are all the potato farms?*

Anne feels like she's swimming in tar. Trying to wake up from a Narcotic induced sleep takes a lot of effort. She tries to get her eyes open, but it's like they're glued shut. Something's wrong, she can sense it. She wipes her eyes to help open them. Jordan has his head on the steering wheel, something has happened.

"Wh…What's wrong," Anne tries to get herself out of it. He looks to be on the verge of tears.

"Honey, what's wrong?"

He looks over at her, "you'll be mad."

"No, I won't."

"I'm lost." Anne tries to look around, but she barely understands that they're on Earth right this moment.

"I don't know what happened, I followed the signs but somehow we're in Ketchum."

"Ketchum, how the hell did we get there?" Jordan again lowers his forehead onto the steering wheel.

"It's no big deal. Let's get some dinner and we'll figure it out."

"Really?" His eyes are tired looking and when he looks over at her with the guilty face; she can see him at four years old, cookie frosting covering much of his face, denying he had been the one in the jar. *Where did it all go?*

Anne shakes her head yes. She looks around and sure as hell they are in Ketchum. The legendary Sun Valley Ski resort lies ahead up the valley.

"Turn around; I know a great little place your father took me to once."

Heading back south toward Twin Falls Anne realizes that she needs to buy a damn GPS. She has a map and knows her basic way around this place, but that doesn't mean her son does. Just a few minutes down the road lays the Brick house. A locals restaurant, this is where Bill had taken his clients to dinner when he was up here. There were more expensive places, but this one was a genuine classic he said. Stepping inside Anne realizes it has been years since she has been here; it might have changed hands two or three times for all she knows. A pretty young girl seats them and she looks around. It looks updated, but maybe it looked updated the last time she was here. Their waiter is a guy named Chris, *is it just me or is about every fifth person you meet named Chris*? He takes their orders and they have a moment to reflect.

"Thanks for not being mad about everything." Jordan smiles awkwardly.

"It's really no big deal, maybe your misdirection lead us to a fantastic dinner, your dad used to take clients here." He smiles and Anne is amazed how far they have come from their first dinner. It seems like the miles between this little spot in Bellevue Idaho and Denver did them a heap of good, Anne's not sure exactly sure what the quantity of a heap is, but it seems like it's a lot, maybe a truckload, more than a buttload for sure.

Their meal is very good and Chris doesn't have any other customers being so early, so they have a chance to chat with him. He is a handsome guy in his late thirties and Anne asks how he came to work there. It turns out he was a framer for ten years, but with the down economy he wasn't staying busy so he started waiting tables. Anne laughs, because he's been one of the best waiters she has had in a long time, prompt drinks, he took no notes and their order was perfect. A good kitchen helps with that obviously, but he wasn't out smoking while their meals cooked under a heat lamp either.

"So what brings you two out this way", he asks. Anne looks sheepishly toward Jordan, afraid to embarrass him. She gestures toward him.

"I'm driving my mother on her book tour. She's a famous, uhm, Harlequin Rhymester. Ever heard of Pandora's Lust?" The waiter had certainly heard of it and asked just the appropriate questions;

which Jordan answered politely and thoroughly. Anne could hardly speak, it seemed she had reached a balancing point, where her son was willing to accept her and she was terrified of blowing it.

When they're done Anne pays the check and leaves c a decent tip. She really wishes him the best of luck in whatever worthy endeavor he pursues and with that Anne hobbles out to the car, Jordan following. Anne turns suddenly and pushes her hand out.

"You can't drive, the Doctor said." Jordan tries to protest, thinking this will stop her.

"It's my left leg; I don't drive with that leg."

"You take too many pills to drive."

"I won't take any."

Stubbornly he hands over the keys and Anne savors the sweet victory of not having to endure any more passenger seat time, for a while anyway. She has to put the seat almost all the way back, but once again a piece of steel and rubber is under her control. The pain is manageable with the pill she secretly and discreetly took. The drowsiness is manageable with the other little pill she took when Jordan used the restroom. After all, what is a Rock Star 72 hour kit for if you don't use it? Onward to Boise!

Mental Note: This cast is starting to smell like ripe ass. Buy some Febreze or something.

Chapter 24 – So, what have we learned?

The car door closes not very loudly but leaves a deafening silence in its wake. *He's gone. Maybe he'll turn around to wave once.* Luckily he does and Anne gets to wave him off. Anne still misses walking someone to the gate and seeing them fade into the jet way, even after all these years of 'heightened security'. Now he doesn't fade so much as she passes through the doors and gets in the line at the ticket counter, still quite in her line of sight. Now she's the helicopter parent, hanging out in the no parking zone of the Sea/Tac Airport looking at her poor incompetent son. Anne feels the now regularly occurring pain in her chest as she lets her foot off the brake and signals her way out into the frantic Airport traffic.

It seems like everyone drives like a maniac at the airport. *How can every single person be late for their flight?* Anne finds the exit lane and finally makes her way onto the Five. Finally there is no battle for the stereo and she indulges herself with some Nirvana. It feels slightly touristy this close to Seattle, but what the hell. The GPS is bringing her into the city by a route she hasn't taken before. Anne would almost say that this is the back road in, passing all the industrial buildings and businesses that keep the city bustling, versus the scenic route that would probably be plagued with traffic. She rolls down the window once she is sure she's past Tacoma, far enough to escape the pulp mill smells anyway. Actually she doesn't even know if the city still smells like that. When the air hits her it's a cool mix of pine and ocean breezes.

She can hardly imagine a better smell. It smells like home, although Seattle has never really been her home. Maybe all the rain here makes it the kind of place where you realize just how important shelter is. What is most noticeable for her today however is just how green the city is. The light blue sky and tan expanses of the West end abruptly at the Snoqualmie pass. From there on it's true Pacific Northwest grandeur. The skies darken and mix in shades of grey, while the evergreens and ferns mix with the dark brown of wet wood to create a patchwork of decay and renewal. That's the other smell you get here, there is a lingering smell of death and decay. This is the kind of place where you can almost watch the cycle of life if you sit still long enough. Trees fall and rot and become soil so fast it seems like the whole place is on fast forward.

Driving between the buildings of downtown Seattle she's glad she didn't get a car with a clutch. As it is she has to pull the emergency brake when moving her foot from the gas to the brake. Anne passes by all the places she tried to take Jordan, the SAM, Pikes Place market, the Wharf. The new GPS is constantly trying to redirect her, but now she's just browsing. She is all on her own now and cannot possibly sit at the Hotel and watch TV. First of all there are promotions for the Pandora's Lust Series Premiere about every other half hour and it makes her a little nauseous. How horrible to think that if she hadn't actually written this, she wouldn't watch it. Anne spots a couple of cool little places she assumes are bars. They kind of look like an Apple Store, but much of Seattle does.

The valet is out front of the Executive Hotel when she arrives. He smiles and asks if Jordan got to the airport alright. Anne says yes and thanks him for his directions. Of course she didn't use his directions, because she bought a GPS in Boise. But force of habit made her ask and then sit patiently as he uttered a string of words that would have probably led her to an early grave if she had tried to follow them or even the general sentiment of his rambling instructions. He is the kind of guy who should refuse to give directions; unfortunately, he's probably the kind of guy who offers directions to anyone who even mentions they don't know exactly where they're going.

She limps through the doors using both crutches as sort of a cane. Finally through the doors she separates the two and approaches the desk. The young man behind the desk is positively handsome. The cut of his suit makes him look like a model. His hair is a dark mess of curls that bounce slightly as he turns his head, the muscles under his jacket strain the material. *Oh man, it's been too long.* "May I help you Mrs. Carter." *Oh, he knows me.*

"Actually it's Ms. Carter. But tell me, where would a dazzling young urbanite like yourself find other likeminded individuals?"

He tries really hard to smile, but the forced nature of his small laugh tells her that she just missed the mark by a lifestyle. He tells her a couple of names and Anne tries to seem interested, but honestly she was probing his interest, not his knowledge. *I think he's batting for the other team.* Anne slinks away on her silver leg horses toward the elevator. Finally out of his judgmental and harsh gaze she presses the antique brass button for the elevator. She has always loved this hotel, it has a view of nothing, but it has all the charm of a hundred year old hotel, with the updating of a modern masterpiece. Inside her room she runs through her clothing choices, settling on a short skirt and a blouse.

She takes the elevator down and exits through the coffee shop, to avoid the unpleasantness of the Homo-unfriendly at the front desk. Anne wonders about food, but decides to find a bar with a limited menu. Only a couple of blocks away, good news for her abused armpits, she finds a bar with dark wood and brass fixtures. Anne pokes inside, asking for a high seat to rest her leg. It's still early, too early really to be at a bar. Anne orders a beer and some nibbles from the menu. There are about eight filled tables in the place. Five are couples or groups of couples, one table of girls who might just be hosting the world's most conservative bachelorette party, and two tables with single men.

Anne gets her food and eats it, poor choice; Seattle has great food, but not what is put before her. Anne orders a Chardonnay and hopes that she can garner some vitamins and nutrients from its grape ancestors. People are coming in now, she smiles coyly and they look away. Pretty soon she feels like the pariah that smiles at everyone. *Maybe I'm a serial killer looking for my next victim?* Unfortunately she can't shake the feeling that she is out of her element in this place. Sometimes you can walk into a bar and you own it, men fight each other to pay attention to you or buy you a drink, you're on top of the world. But sometimes you get under the thing and the more you feel under, the more you look under, and pretty soon you're the untouchable who needs to be shooed from the bar in shame.

Out in the open air walking along it doesn't seem to get any better. Anne smiles at people walking by, but either they just walk on or they're listening to their iPods so intently that they don't even notice her.

Then the worst thing happens. The group of girls from the bar having their bachelorette walk by. Nothing in the world can make a person feel lonelier than being in close proximity to a group of close friends laughing and having fun with each other.

As Anne tries to clear the sidewalk for the group, she feels like Quasimodo, her cast and crutches feeling awkward and hideous to her. The group has almost passed by when one of the last girls takes a double glance at her.

"Oh, my, God. Are you Anne Carter?" she blurts. Now it's worse for Anne than if they hadn't noticed her at all. She now wishes she had stayed in at the hotel and ordered room service.

Anne nods politely, pretending to start to walk away.

"She's the one that wrote the Pandora's Lust book or whatever, the one they're doing the series for on Lifetime. THE POETRY SLUT!!"

The group squeals, nothing discernible to Anne, but suddenly she is part of their group. It seems that anything that offends Rush Limbaugh is of great interest to them. The group contains eight girls from the ages of twenty five to forty five. Regardless of age, it still sounds like a group of teenage girls to her. As she hobbles along trying to respond to the rapid fire questions in a timely manner, she isn't even really paying attention to where they're going. She could break away, but there is something instinctual keeping her there.

She has to change her initial judgment of the group as they move along. What had looked like a Mormon Bachelorette party from the bar, had certainly ratcheted up the action in the last hour. Penises were everywhere now, from binkies to magic penis wands to the brides t-shirt which revealed her to be 'cock crazy'. The combination of pain pills, camaraderie and wine is making her lightheaded.

Another block and they step into a darkened door with loud music. As if their party of woohooers was meeting its larger party of woohooers, the noise becomes almost unbearable. Once her eyes adjust to the darkness she can see that they are at a male review. An extremely scantily clad young lad is on the stage waving his package like he is trying to shake off a bad case of crabs. The women are going totally insane for it.

The group makes their way directly to the front and a table reserved under the name, Cock crazy harlot's. *Hey that's us apparently, isn't that great.* The waiter comes over in short shorts and is promptly swatted on the ass a half dozen times before getting the order for a half dozen shots of tequila. Most of the attention has been removed from Anne and now directed toward the stage. A very fit man in a police officer's outfit comes out. The music kicks up and he starts to dance his clothes off, literally. Anne is trying to have a good time, but it's bringing up bad memories. She can't help but wish he was there now, someone reasonable to talk to. The dancers were phenomenally handsome; each one looking like they were carved from stone, but it just feels ingenuine. She wanted to find someone who would flatter her and treat her. Now she was expected to stuff money into the man's panties. It just seemed surreal to her. This should be her thing. After all she was out here living for a dead man wasn't she? Wasn't she living his dream, because the reality of her own life and dreams were so vapid that she feared she would lose the will to breathe?

This wasn't good, she starts to get sad and that's the death blow of the good night. When the waiter comes she bellies up and takes a shot. When there are extras she takes another. She feels almost instantly better, once the tequila taste fades. She starts to see what's so great about being here. She starts to whoop and holler with the best of them. She pulls out a hundred dollar bill and orders another round. The waiter comes back and the shots go down so much easier. Her head gets light and her leg stops itching. A cowboy comes out and the whole building explodes in shrieks. When he comes close enough Anne lifts herself up on her good leg to push a couple dollars into his penis pouch. He gives her a little pee pee wave as if to salute her.

The night continues through a long series of men in various outfits pretty much running the gambit of blue collar career paths. She half expects to have a middle manager stripper come out at some point, but alas the lights flash and the music begins to fade. One of the girls whispers into her ear, "Want to get backstage?"

"Hell yes I do."

The rest of the girls seem to be sobering up and getting ready to head back to their lives of domestic tranquility, or servitude. They say their goodbyes and Anne follows the girl to the back.

It seemed to Anne unlikely that a man could walk into the dressing room at a strip club, but for whatever reason the men didn't seem that perturbed by the women's presence. Anne is severely drunk at this point, but she figures she can maintain. The girl seems to know one of the dancers, who immediately greets her with a long deep kiss. Anne is instantly so jealous she doesn't know what to do. She is now more alone than she has been all night, even when she actually was alone.

"Those two should get a room, huh?" she says to the policeman dancer from earlier. She picks him because somehow she figures the police owe her from Kansas. He smiles and looks at her appraisingly.

"Those two have a room; they live together."

"Well, that explains a lot I guess." Anne knows she's drunk and not making a great impression, but feels compelled to speak anyway.

"I'm Jeffrey"

"Anne"

"You wanna get out of here", he says. Anne is so shocked by this that she almost feels like crying. She reaches down and strokes his chest through his t-shirt. When he stands up, he is surprisingly short. He grabs a jacket off the rack and puts it around her. Taking her arm and one of her crutches, he helps her as they walk out the back entrance.

THE END OF THE ROAD

Walking is hurting her leg, so when he opens the door and eases her into his car, she fishes out the bottle of pain pills and pops two of the Lortab.

"So is this your fulltime job, teasing women?" Anne asks, summoning as much seductive prowess as she can in her current state of inebriation.

"Actually, I'm trying to be a writer."

"Oh, really?" Anne sits back in her seat, unsure about how to proceed. If she blurts something out, it might seem glib. Instead she decides to let the silence rest for a minute. Her head is actually spinning a little bit. She probably should have eaten something before taking her pain meds, but on the upside her leg doesn't hurt anymore.

"So, writer huh? You know I dabble in the writing myself?" *That seemed fairly cool, not too much.*

"Mrs. Carter, I know who you are. That's why I offered to take you home; I wanted to make sure nobody took advantage of you." His words take a minute to sink in fully, the Mrs. Carter part taking the longest of all.

"Actually it's Ms. Carter. There ain't no strings on me." She tries to smile, thinking the Pinocchio reference was quite clever, but the lukewarm response from Jeffrey leaves her questioning.

"Here we are", Jeffrey tells her. Anne looks and her hotel is directly across the street. She knows she should be thankful for the drive home, but obviously their purposes were on different arcs. She was attracted to him, but it was quite plain to her now that the attraction was not mutual. She smiled for a lingering second, hoping he would ask her something, or make some move, but as soon as she opens herself, she feels foolish. Taking the crutches out of the back seat she opens her door and pushes herself out into the cold night.

She feels foolish for hoping, selfish and embarrassed that she had not said thank you, and dizzy as hell. All in all, this was really turning into a shitty night.

THE END OF THE ROAD

The road's tilt made walking across it quite a chore with the crutches, compounded with the dizziness she was suffering from the alcohol and painkillers, she was really quite a sight. Negotiating the far curb, the crutch on the street starts to slip from under her. Whether from oil on the road or a bad placement, Anne has just enough time to wish one more time that she stayed in bed. As she braces herself for impact, suddenly there are strong arms around her. Jeffrey couldn't have been there a half second before she would have hit the ground.

His body is close to hers now, and in this instant she is more vulnerable than she has ever been, maybe in her whole life. This is a real knight in shining armor moment, as he helps her upright, she falls suddenly and immediately in love with him. She wants only to be near him and be protected by him. She would surrender anything to him in this moment. She wants to cry, wants to be comforted like a small child, but she wants him to take her also. She wants him to tear her clothes off and take ownership of his property.

As they walk through the doors she is trying to tell him all the things that are happening in her head and heart, but the alcohol and painkillers are combining to make her sound like a babbling idiot complete with tear stained cheeks and a running nose. Suddenly she becomes aware that tears are flowing along with the snot from her nose. A passing mirror shows a woman that looks like she is in the midst of a major breakdown.

At her room she realizes it is her last chance to really turn the whole thing around. She sniffs her nose and wipes her eyes. Jeffrey opens the door and helps her inside. She can tell that he is not planning on staying. *Time to change his mind.* With a more spastic than spontaneous move she wraps her arms around his shoulders and pulls him in. Her lips search for his, sensing a slight aversion tactic on his part. *We can still turn this around.* He is saying something, trying to press her shoulders gently away. Suddenly it is all too much, her head starts to spin and her stomach starts to rumble. Now she is pushing away from him, trying to get some distance. He seems to be afraid she will fall, so he is trying to support her, just as her stomach finally cannot hold out any longer and she vomits on her prince Charming. Her head clears for a moment, just long enough to see that the front of his shirt is totally soaked in a pink slimy mess. His face shows only

THE END OF THE ROAD

shock, she wonders for a moment if he is going to hit her. He stands up straight and turns before walking out the hotel room door.

Anne considers yelling after him, but at this point is seems that she has done enough. Maybe it's time to just call it a night. Without cleaning up the mess, she turns and plants herself face first on the hotel bedspread. Blessed blackness follows within seconds.

Chapter 25 – The Hangover

The tide of unconscious sleep rolls out and the first flecks of sunlight pierce her eyes, but a moment later the tide washes warmly over her again and it's all dark. The water recedes and this time Anne tries opening her mouth, only to find that it is so dry her tongue and lips are glued together. The dark water pushes up again, but a thin sliver of light still shines through. Anne tries to push her way out of the water, but the suction pulls so hard and her arms feel heavy. Anne struggles to open an eye to notice that the red numbers indicate that it's 7:15. Anne expected to sleep longer than 7 AM.

Then with a start she pushes herself up and looks around. *Is it 7 AM or 7 PM?* Anne tries to stand up but her leg feels wobbly and there's no sign of her crutches. Anne sits on the floor to get her bearings. *I need water.* Anne wonders where there might be a bottle of water, but all she can think of is the faucet in the bathroom. Shimmy and sliding across the floor she finally gets to the bathroom and pulls herself up, steadying against the countertop. Anne puts her mouth directly under the faucet and drinks heavily. The water tastes like it feeds from the toilet drains, but she can't get herself to stop. When her stomach starts to get queasy she splashes some water on her face and pushes her hair back.

The reflection in the mirror does not look healthy. She looks scary pale and red eyed. Anne finds the toilet and pulls herself onto it. The flow of urine takes a second, but once it starts Anne realizes how badly she needed to go. When she has finished the toilet water is dark yellow; dehydration. Anne flushes and moves back to the bed where laying down makes her feel like she might need to throw up. Nausea mixes with the heavy feeling. Anne lets the dark waters wash over her, wishing the waves would stop rolling her around, making her sick.

When the waters finally pull back Anne wakes up to look at the clock again. 8:25, this time it has to be PM because it's getting dark outside. She's thirsty again, but the growling in her stomach indicates she needs more than just water this time. Anne looks the room over and finds a pair of jeans. Sniffing them seems to indicate that they are not clean enough. Her shirts are still folded on the chair along with a dress she bought herself in Jackson. It is a beige color and longer, more conservative than she is used to, but it looked great in the store. After a quick shower she pulls her hair back and puts on the minimum amount of makeup. Slipping into the dress she looks in the mirror to be shocked, she looks like a nice girl. Usually there was a little too much leg showing, or too much cleavage, but now she looks like someone's mother. *I should have worn this when Jordan and I went out.* After giving a couple more glances she grabs her cards and room key to head out. Feeling woozy, she has to lie back down on the bed for a moment to collect herself. Her crutches are in the corner right inside the door; putting them in place she hobbles into the hallway.

Outside she sees the valet and he makes the face gestures to communicate asking if she wants her car. Anne shakes her head no, but motions him over.

"Where's a good place to get a healthy meal," she asks.

"Oh you are in luck; tonight Pike's place is having a nighttime food and wine tasting."

That was not exactly what she had in mind. Pikes is quite a haul from the hotel, especially on crutches.

He seems awfully excited to share this tidbit with her, so she asks, "Will you call me a cab?"

He smiles and runs back to his little hidden alcove. A minute later, before he makes it back, a cab pulls up and Anne looks around guiltily. There's no way this is her cab, they're fast, but not this fast. But she can't see anyone so she opens the door to get in. "Where to," a tall blonde female driver asks her from the front seat. Anne isn't used to a woman as a cab driver. She looks like a human version of big bird with a terrible perm on top of her linebacker frame.

"Pike's."

With that she tears off and the numbers on the digital display start to change. Trying to decide between watching her valiant efforts to mow down random pedestrians and her rapidly increasing bill is difficult and eventually she has to close her eyes to keep from getting sick. When Pikes comes into view, Anne's as excited to get out of the death cab as she is to get something to eat.

Pike's place is as lit up as she has ever seen it. Come to think of it, all the times she has ever been there this is the first time she can remember seeing lights at all. The far end entrance is blocked off with barricades, but a line seems to be forming at a mid point. Anne get in the line and after several long minutes she is prompted to buy a small mason jar with "Arcade lights" on it, a black bandanna and a handful of wooden tokens. No instruction is given to her, just a motion to enter the pavilion. Inside there are vendors lining both sides of the aisles, many of which were not here when Anne took Jordan through the day before yesterday. Each different booth seems to be tied to a local restaurant or catering company with their best couple of dishes out for sample.

Anne buys some oysters from the fish throwing people, some cake from a baker, some delicious wine ice cream, fruit and finally an excellent hot hard cider mixture. Anne balks at the two token price of the apple liquor; but the lady winks and tells her all secretively that "Hot Hara's Cider" is worth it. She hands her a small recipe card with the following ingredients, 1 quart hard cider, 1 quart apple juice, 1 cup Frangelico, 1 cup gold Rum, with a pinch of cinnamon and all spice, heat to serve.

It's so hot she has to sip it, it strikes her nose hard with alcohol vapor, but once it passes the midpoint of her tongue it is heavenly warm and surprisingly free of any alcohol flavor. It tastes like hot apple pie, plus booze. She is feeling much recovered now and so it becomes time to peruse what other activities the venue has. Several guitar players or musicians are working for tokens. Each one is good and Anne is happy to throw in a token. There is a sign directing people downstairs and shockingly she realizes that she has never been downstairs. Anne walks down, unsure of what to expect from a place under a seafood wholesaler. She is surprised by the cleanliness and blown away by the array of homebrew beers for barter down below. Anne does pass on the booze; the Hot Hera's Cider is getting her tipsy on its own; and after all she came here to recover not reoffend.

There's a small band playing on a makeshift stage. The first noticeable thing is the singers piercing voice. Soft and sultry, then loud and bold, she is mesmerizing to say the least. All the men are staring at her, hardly blinking. There's a chair up front and Anne is absolutely treated to the best part of the whole event. The singer is tall and voluptuous in all the right places, the kind of woman that everyone, men or women, would say is beautiful. Her pale skin stands in stark contrast to her dark red lips and heavy eyeliner. Her voice is smooth like velvet, like some old world mermaid she has Anne mesmerized. It feels to Anne like she's looking at her too, but dismisses it since any good performer would make you think that. She's almost what Anne would call a lounge singer; her sparkly form fitting dress would indicate that as well. When they take a break and pass around a hat Anne deposits the remaining tokens she has in. The singer's not just pretty, more accurate to say she's gorgeous. There is something in her sirens song that lingers, because Anne is trying very hard not to stare at her when the band takes a break. Their group sits at a table with various men and women, presumably friends there to hear them play. Anne is failing miserably at not staring.

Suddenly there are two hands on the small table in front of her and Anne has to catch her mason jar from falling on the floor.

"You're Anne Carter," the young blonde haired psychopathic boy in front of her states quite loudly. Anne wonders if somehow the kid from the diner in Missouri has bleached his hair and tracked her down for not friending him on Facebook.

"Uhmmmmm," she stammers, now that all conversations have stopped and many eyes point to the spectacle at her table. Anne isn't sure if she is going to have to fight this kid or what. He seems angry, his hands are shaking and he's seriously intruding on her personal space. Anne wonders if she did something to him, or his family or maybe his dog. Then he throws something on the table with a hard thud. *This shit is really gonna go down!* Anne is trying to figure out how fast her crutches will take her away from here. Probably not faster than he can run her down and bash her skull into the concrete. Anne feels in her pocket, looking for keys to stab at him, or a mace can that she never bought, but meant to, and finds nothing. Anne grabs her mason jar and wonders if she can throw it at him hard enough to knock him unconscious. Anne should have gotten it filled with beer, if only for its increased effectiveness as a weapon.

Then she sees it and breathes a sigh of relief, a book was what hit the table with such a noisy thud, its cover showing the house crest of Pandora. *He's just some crazy fan.* Anne smiles and he smiles. But now that her life's not in mortal danger she is just irritated at this little pimple factory. *Why tonight? I just needed a nice night. I'm going to punch him if he starts reciting poetry.*

Then he pulls out a pen, "will you sign this?" Somehow he has a copy of her book, it seems like odd timing. Maybe it was just a coincidence?

Oh God, why didn't I write a children's book, or a cookbook or something? Anne puts on her fakest smile and signs the signature that people love. Anne laughs, because her real signature doesn't look anything like this. But after numerous complaints from fans that said they couldn't read her scribble she went to a calligraphy coach and worked out a stage signature. *Yeah, that's where my life's gone to, calligraphy coaches and stage signatures.*

After she signs his book, his eyes get moist and Anne can tell he's about to tell her how the books changed his life. *Oh Fuck Nut, please just move on.*

"The Pandora's Lust books were great and all, but Hard Ride changed my life."

Anne has to stop dismissing him in mid sentence. Hard Ride was the second real book she ever wrote. There were only a couple thousand in existence and according to her figures only about a couple hundred had ever been bought.

"You read Hard Ride?"

He shakes his head yes and she has the feeling he's about to cry. He takes the seat next to her, Anne doesn't even protest because he's the first person she has ever met, well not counting the guy in Kansas City, that's read this book and loved it.

"It's you, isn't it?"

"Yeah, I'm Anne. Where did…" He looks frustrated for a second.

"No, in the book, it's you."

Now Anne is a little freaked out. She has never had a stalker before but she wonders if maybe this is what they're like. They warm you up by praising some detail that everyone else has overlooked, and then when your guard's down, they rape you. Or they stick you in a hole and eat you.

"Why would you ask that?"

"Because no one could write that story without living it."

That's funny, because those were almost the exact words Anne used with Elizabeth trying to get it published. How does Anne suddenly have this kind of connection with some kid in the basement of Pike's Place Market? She wishes she could decide whether to stay or run screaming for a policeman.

"More or less," she tells him.

He shakes his head as if to confirm the validity of some prior conclusion.

"Are you alone?" he asks.

Again, Anne doesn't know how comfortable she is talking to this kid, there's something unsettling about him. He looks familiar, like she's seen him somewhere; it's giving her a distinctly uncomfortable feeling.

"I was actually just getting…," she starts.

"Would you consider coming over to have a drink with us," he pleads and points to a table behind them, the table with the band and the extraordinary singer.

As Anne looks over the auburn haired singer waves them over and like Pavlov's dog Anne obeys without a single conscious thought.

Thanks brain, way to watch out for us. I'm suggesting they eat you first if we find ourselves trapped in a basement pit. It immediately strikes her, that's why the boy looks familiar. They are obviously brother and sister, but with her red hair, you wouldn't know it without looking intently at their faces. *It's their eyes.*

Anne gathers up her crutches and hobbles over to an outstretched seat that the fan boy hurriedly slides over. Hands are thrust out with shouted associated names faster than she can shake them and certainly faster than Anne could ever dream to remember their corresponding faces. It's about the most racially diverse group that could be had in this small a sampling. Asian, Black, Hispanic, Anne figures at least one of them is a Jew, just to keep it at maximum racial diversity standards.

Looking back over at fan boy, Anne mentions, "Actually we haven't exchanged names."

He looks shy but excited that she wants to know his name, "It's Tyler."

"It's a pleasure Tyler."

"This is my sister Matilda," he starts, finally revealing the name that Anne came over to discover.

"Mattie," she interjects with a sharp glance and juts her hand out to shake.

There is a small blue spark and they both laugh. Anne wonders if it was her dress or her plastic boots that got them charged up.

"Sorry, it's the dress on this concrete floor," Mattie says. Anne tries to mumble something but before she can consolidate any meaningful thought into words Mattie interrupts her with a squeal, "Oh shit, we're on."

With that she's off, leaving the large black keyboard player named Paul and the other two band members scrambling to follow. Mattie apologizes to the crowd and plows right back into the music. Anne watches entranced. Mattie's voice is amazing; sometimes stretching to the point where it sounds like it will break. Some songs convey such a sense of loss and agony that Anne feels tears welling in her eyes. During one particular song, Anne almost swears she hears her own words, a line from near the end of Hard Ride. Anne looks over at Tyler, but he is watching the band and doesn't return her look. *Maybe I'm crazy.* They do another six or so songs then wave goodbye to the crowd and join them at the table.

"So before we were so rudely interrupted," Mattie starts, but is interrupted.

The bass player gives an apologetic smile, "Sorry Mattie, they want us to get our stuff out of here."

She rolls her eyes and pats Anne's shoulder.

"To be continued," she says. Anne wishes desperately she were in shape to help them. Everyone seems to have a job, carrying some instrument or cables or something with them out the back doors. Without a word from anyone, they all leave. Anne is left alone in the quickly dispersing crowd, as booth vendors wrap their wares for the night.

Now she's alone at the table. It's just her in the center of the large room, the gal who doesn't get it that the party's over and no one wanted to take her home. *The unpopular girl with the crutches.* She is devastated without even really knowing why. If she hadn't been stuck with this bum leg she would have been able to help them load and endeared herself to them, but now she is just sitting here alone, discarded like an old band-aid. *Even fan boy left me, or Travis I guess.* Anne stands up to leave, hobbling around the table to her crutches when she hears a voice. It's Matilda or Mattie as it were.

"You comin or what?" Anne is immediately disgusted with herself at how happy and excited she gets in that moment, but tries to quiet her internal mind and just enjoy the turn of events.

Anne smiles, "you bet your ass I am," and she hobbles after that sultry singer with the fire engine red hair.

Mental Note: Find out where this Road ends before we get too far along.

Chapter 26 - There's something happening here

Anne hobbles the six blocks to Tyler's car. Mattie had to go with the band, or so it seems. Every other vehicle was full, or Tyler filled them by design, hard to say. Either way Anne is glad when he has a small Toyota Camry. Anne can't imagine a serial killer with a Camry. They speed through the streets of downtown Seattle, Tyler talking and Anne trying to listen, but also trying to find the brake on her side of the car. Anne keeps stomping the floorboard, sure that this time she will be able to brake the car and save their lives. Anne only screams once and closes her eyes three times.

"So what happened to your leg," he asks. Anne tries not to spasm as he asks her to recount the horrors.

"Got swiped by a car coming over the pass from Jackson Hole," she explains.

"In a car?"

"No, I ride an old Indian that I added a side car to for my son."

"I should have known that," he says and Anne was surprised he didn't.

"So where is it?"

"Where's what?"

"The Indian."

"Well technically his name is the General," Anne corrects. "And the General is crated up in Idaho Falls awaiting repairs."

He smiles at her coyly, "You ought to have them ship it out here."

"I would, but the only real Indian mechanic I know of is in St. Louis."

"I think we can get you taken care of," he says with what Anne might say is a smattering of foreshadowing. For the moment she just lets it go, Anne wants to get to where they're going and chat up his sister. In a moment they pull into the front gate of a property. He punches something into a keypad and the gate rises. Behind the stone wall bordering the property is a beautiful home nestled on several acres of lush foliage. The house is a Mediterranean with Modern sensibilities, and it's a beauty. There is an incredible amount of glass and lit up as it is, it sparkles like a Christmas tree. They pull into the back and when the garage door opens it reveals at least four high end sports cars and three classic motorcycles. Next to these classics, the Toyota and the other two normal cars look like tin cans. Anne steps out and walks right over to the bikes. One is an old Harley, but she doesn't know enough to tell what year it is, but from the shape must be a Knucklehead. The other two look more exotic, some kind of European bikes. Each one is as pretty underneath as they are on top.

"Come on, we're missing the after party," he yells from the far end of the garage.

"Who are you people?" she yells after him.

Inside, the band from Arcade Lights and about twenty more are mixing around possibly the most incredible kitchen Anne has ever seen. The range is probably eight feet long and the cabinetry is the most beautiful dark wood she has ever seen. She is checking out which of the cabinets contain the refrigerator when she feels a hand on her shoulder. Anne spins as fast as her leg will let her, it's her, Mattie.

 "Great kitchen," Anne blurts out stupidly.

"It's my parents, but I'll take credit for it." There's an awkward pause here as Anne tries and come up with a way to transition the conversation.

"I loved your band, or whatever it is."

"Thanks, my brother tells her you're some kind of writer." Anne's not sure what to say here, it doesn't feel appropriate to brag about some far away bestseller list. Anne wants Mattie to like her for the intrinsic value of Anne Carter, not some pathetic overstatement of fame. Anne can't imagine she'd be star struck by some little account author, but just to be sure Anne only shrugs her shoulders in answer to the question. *Don't say Slut Poet, say Harlequin Rhymester.*

Anne is trying to figure out how to change the subject when Mattie says with a laugh, "I think you just blushed."

Anne straightens up, "No I didn't."

"Oh yeah, pretty sure you did."

"So what do you do when you're not breaking hearts with your singing?"

"Is that a line?" she laughs at her again.

"No, did it sound like one?"

"Kinda," she says. "I'm a perpetually failing artist, hopelessly enabled in my self-destructive behavior by my fabulously wealthy parents."

"I doubt that very much," Anne tries to turn up the charm without letting it sound like a line. This is awkward, like a dance choreographed to unknown music. Only after you see their counter move, can you make your next move.

"Oh, I assure you, this house is full of bad paintings, sculptures, photographs and poetry that prove my claims."

"Show me."

With that they walk from the kitchen and down the hallway, pointing out her work. Anne tries hard to pay attention to what she's telling her, but in truth Anne is lost in the sweet sound of Mattie's voice. She would make a great TV anchor, her annunciation is superb. Anne wants her to sing everything she says. Realizing that might be slightly awkward, she chooses not to ask.

Anne runs through her mental notes to see how it's going. *Number one; talk about her, check. Number two; don't talk about me, check. Number three; be cool man, kind of check.* They're moving further and further away from the group now and Anne is trying to close the gap between them. Her heart is pounding like she's a fourteen year old girl. Anne tries desperately not to fall down as they make their way up the stairs. Huffing just a little she looks around with wonder. It is almost a museum of art pieces.

Beyond just trying to sound appreciative of her work for the sake of flattery, Mattie seems to actually be quite an accomplished painter. She's a little impressionistic for Anne's taste, but the colors are right and each piece leaves her with a sense of memory of a place. They move along a wall with pieces about every four or five feet and they just keep getting better. Then the paintings stop and the photography begins and Anne immediately think that this was her true calling. Everything is black and white. She shoots a lot of nature stuff but with some nudes and abstracts also. She has a real classical approach to her work; the models bodies are perfect, too perfect really. It's almost as if they were cast out of porcelain. Anne wonders how much time she took editing these photos. She's talking but Anne is not really listening. There is a photo of a swing set and a broken swing that to perfectly conveys for her a sense of lost childhood that Anne is hypnotized by it. It's almost a perfect shot. The weeds are tall indicating the area hasn't been used, the set is rusty and the balance and form of the shot are masterful. Anne turns to ask her about it, but Mattie stops any questioning by kissing Anne.

Anne forgets all about the pieces, she forgets all about everything that isn't Mattie and her mouth and her smell. Her mouth is at once advancing and retreating. The soft voluptuousness of her lips feel like warm silk. Her hand comes up and wraps around Anne's neck, pushing her hair back. She smells like orange blossoms and soap. Then she puts her hands on her chest and pushes her away.

"We better get back before we're missed." Anne's drive is fully engaged, she wants to agree to seem lady like, but she's not really used to pulling the troops back at this stage.

"Ok" Anne says, but doesn't mean. They walk back down the long hallway, but now Anne doesn't even see the pieces, just her. They walk down the stairs and Anne tries to mingle. Tyler introduces her to people, but she is constantly stealing glances at Mattie, quite often while she is doing the same. Anne meet Tomas, who is the family's' mechanic and she is able to stop stalking Mattie for a moment as they become engrossed in the details of getting the General back on the road. He asks about her foot, but she tells him that another two weeks in the boot; she should be in just a brace and weight bearing.

At his urging Anne calls Elizabeth and directs her to ship the General to her ASAP. She tells Anne she owes Jordan a phone call, he's worried. Anne tells her she will and hangs up. Now she is lost on this conversation. Anne excuses herself to call Jordan, knowing she should have earlier.

It rings once and he picks up, "Are you okay?"

"Hey. Yes, I'm fine, just sad that you're gone." He sounds worried; she should have called earlier.

"Okay, I was just worried. I had my first day of school today, officially a senior."

They talk for almost a half hour about how school was and how the move in is going with her sister. Elizabeth has been a champion about getting people out to get the house ready for habitation. She is so glad it's going well, Anne was afraid her sister would flake out at the last second.

Anne asks about the swimming pool, but Jordan just laughs and says, "We'll have to work on it."

When they're done, it's almost midnight in Seattle, so one AM in Utah, so she tells him to get his butt in bed. Anne hangs up and looks at the phone.

"Boyfriend?" comes the question from a voice immediately recognizable as Mattie.

"My son," Anne says and puts the phone in her pocket. Mattie looks radiant, she walks toward her in the cold night and she is immediately under her spell, Anne wants her so badly.

"Are you married?" she asks her abruptly.

"No," Anne says.

"Divorced?" she asks with a questioning look.

Pain in my chest.

"He died, actually in a car accident with my son."

Anne had never spoken that plainly about what happened, and certainly not to a stranger. But she keeps feeling there's something different about this girl, an implied friendship. She kisses her again, this time more sweetly, less lustily. It feels good and she is almost forced to sneak in a little tear, but doesn't. Anne wonders if she's shared too much. Anne should have said she had a boyfriend and played the whole thing off as a one night stand. But that's not what she wants, not really. Anne can play the game, she knows the rules and she knows how to win, but somehow she still keeps losing. Anne wants someone to ask about her. Anne wants to let her guard down, sleep in someone's arms, fart occasionally. She's looking at her, Anne has to say something. Anne could try to turn up the heat, but she knows exactly where that road goes.

"I need to go, but we should get dinner tomorrow."

"That was the right answer."

Anne laughs, "My second guess was, what is Liberia." She smiles and gives her a small friendly hug.

"Pick me up at six." *Damn right I will.*

Anne calls a cab and it meets her out front. Anne speaks with Tomas once more just before leaving, planning to meet him at his shop day after tomorrow to get the General back on his feet. Her cab is waiting outside and as they drive off she has a feeling that Mattie's up in a window watching.

Mental Note: Look in the mirror and try to save this feeling, this moment.

Chapter 27 - Well, now what?

When Anne arrives at Tomas' shop there is a large wooden crate sitting in the parking lot. With nothing else around it, it looks lonely, like some sort of abandoned step child. Anne knows what's in it, but now standing in front of it she almost doesn't want to see.

"Are you ready," Tomas' voice breaks in.

"Ready as I'll ever be."

With the hammer and pry bar in his hands he makes quick work of the metal straps and opens the end of the crate. Inside the crate is dark, but the vague form of twisted metal and the smell of oil do not bode well for any of them. Tomas calls for his assistant and they take the top and sides off the crate while Anne stands impotently by with her gimp leg. Anne feels numb, like she's been called to identify the body of a friend. Anne realizes in this instant that she had not realized fully what the General meant to her. She can remember when Bill got the bulk of the General delivered in a crate. How he had made love to her, promising that they would tour the country on that bike. She had hated the General for years, but in a lot of ways, it was all she had left of Bill. When she had returned to an empty house, she found the General sitting there in the garage, finished but not ridden a mile. She had gotten on it one night, not knowing what else to do, distraught and looking for some path to redemption. She drove off, intent on living the life she thought Bill had wanted to live. It sounded silly to state it like that now, but in the moment it had been the only path she could see.

The crating company removed the sidecar, so they pull it away. There under the straps holding it down is a twisted heap of metal with fresh scars and more rust than Anne remembers. Tomas is giving the bike a once over, pulling on parts, twisting the handle bars and eyeing it all with his accounting mind.

They had been speaking about this for the last few days and he had some idea what damage might be there and the prices for the parts he might need to fix it. Anne can see the calculator in his mind running totals as he finishes his inspection. Anne feels sick, physically sick. *Bill trusted me with this, I have to fix it.* Tomas looks over at her, "Hey are you alright." He grabs her arm and kind of shakes her back to reality.

"I have what I need for this minute, let's go inside and talk." Tomas is being extra gentle right now. He's not generally this way; in fact he's been a real ball buster up until now. But he seems to sense that this is more than just a motorcycle to Anne, even if she hasn't.

Inside his office he throws her a Coke, "Drink that, I don't want to have to pick your ass off the ground." Anne smiles and salutes him, the stinging cool sweetness of the Coke calming her immensely.

"I don't know if you're tall enough to pick up a full size adult like me." And just like that they're back to bantering. The moment of frailty and humility has passed and their masks are firmly back into place. Tomas smiles and they both have a small laugh.

"Okay seriously, we need to talk about your bike." Anne doesn't like the tone he's using, it's serious again. Hopefully this won't be the 'rip off the chick, cause they don't know better' sales pitch.

"It looks to me that your frame is bent where the car clipped the bike. There's a crack in the crank case somewhere, hence the oil in the crate. The starter that you put on is slowly destroying the kick start mechanism. The front forks are bent and the side car's wheel and probably shaft are bent."

That is quite a total of damage; really it is about everything they thought could have possibly been wrong, plus the starter issue. Anne knows what he's going to say next, it's what she would say if she was him. *But we don't leave men behind.*

"I just don't know if it's worth it to fix it, you could be talking about twenty grand or more to get it back into shape, even then it's probably only worth fifteen, we could sell it now for probably eight. We could look for you a…"

"I don't care what it costs, he gets fixed." Tomas' eyes narrow and he looks at her hard. They've been friendly, but he doesn't really know her. Anne might be a friend of the family that uses him almost full time, but there's no reason for him to trust her.

"Why?" he asks.

"We just have to." Big tears are rolling down Anne's face. Tomas' question is about more than just the money and it brings up things she would rather not talk about. It probably didn't make sense to fix him, but they were going to. She looks down at the walking boot on her leg. Anne knows that underneath it is a long titanium rod holding her together. *I can't abandon him, he's my best friend, however sad and pathetic that statement makes me.*

"The General is more than just a machine, he saved me. It's the least I can do to return the favor."

Tomas smiles, "You know, I hoped you would say that." He stands up and puts out his hand, Anne takes it in hers and with a handshake their deal is made. "I sure hope you got a big pile of rich white people money." Anne laughs.

From her pocket she pulls out a cashier's check for the down payment. Ten thousand dollars won't even get them half way, but at least he knows now that Anne is for real. He shakes his head and they head back out toward Anne's wounded comrade.

"I have one more question," Anne asks as they walk.

"What's that white girl?"

"How much would it be if I help?" He looks at her hard for a minute, then smiles and laughs.

"About double."

"Sounds like a bargain." *Now if I can just get a little functionality out of this stupid leg.*

"No time like the present to get started." He looks her up and down, shaking his head. Anne doubts she is exactly what his dream mechanic looks like.

"How did this chinga bike ever run at all," Tomas asks. Anne shrugs her shoulders in complete denial. They have been working on dissecting the bike for the past several days, at each turn finding something that needed fixing.

"Look at these heads, they're pitted. They did a really shitty job on these. They should have been machined, not just blasted. They shoot it with metal balls like BB's to take off the corrosion, but only a bendejo would leave these like this."

Looking at the upturned head Anne can see the rough texture but it takes another five minutes of lecturing until she truly understands the implication of a rough surface on the head.

Tomas has been giving her the advanced course on motorcycle maintenance and overhaul. It's amazing how little she actually knew about motorcycles considering how many hours she spent in the seat. Anne knew some of the peripheral stuff had been replaced, after all, how trustworthy could a sixty year old speedometer be? But they found that the rear cylinder head was from a later model Indian and the front wheel was from an earlier pre-1942 model without a separately bolted brake drum. The custom seat was not stock, but somehow the comfort of that should have made her aware. The head lamp, the horn with the face, and the exhaust system were incorrect replacement parts. *I bet Bill didn't want to spend the money, or he bought it with those parts.* When Anne shrugs her shoulders at Tomas he almost throws his wrench at her. The generator was new, but that was because of the addition of an electric start, which was also an abomination to Tomas.

Tomas and Anne had argued for three days on and off before he finally talked her into going back to the original kick start method. When he exposed the shaft they had machined to add electric start it was showing signs of stress fracture. The good news included the original Splitdorf magneto and a Schebler DLX-110 carburetor was in relatively good condition and still bolted securely to the engine.

Every time he found a loose bolt he would throw something small at her and tell her to buy some 'Chinga Loctite', whatever that was. The oil pump had taken a blow in the accident and had to be repaired.

Tomas makes a gift of a book by Jerry Hatfield, The Indian Motorcycle Restoration Guide 1932-1953. At night he expects her to study it and try to memorize some of the adjustments. In recreating the accident he has found a couple of items he recommends swapping out. First are the old front shocks, or lack thereof. It might look cool, but it really hampered the handling, especially in heavy braking situations. The second is braking; Tomas thinks he has figured out a way to add disc brakes to the old beast. It won't be classic to the bike, but he says Anne is such a terrible rider she needs all the help she can get.

Tomas's manner seemed a little boorish in the beginning, but she can tell from how upset he gets that he's very concerned for her safety. He has her adjust the carburetor and check the points about a dozen times so he can be sure she knows what she's doing. It's odd; that after this much time she finally knows something about the General. *It's almost like I bonded with Bill here.*

Sporadically Tyler comes to check on them. Anne can tell he's desperate for the two of them to be friends, she wonders how much he pressured Tomas to make sure the bike is right. Anne is always glad to see him, if for no other reason than that he always brings food with him.

The real problem is with his sister, Mattie. She has been filling Anne's thoughts an inappropriate amount of time. Somehow it just seems right with her, like a friendship so strong it hurts. Her companionship has filled a void in Anne that she had forgotten even existed. Anne thinks about her all day long, taking special attention to get all the grease out from under her fingernails before she sees her. Anne wants to touch her face, caress her hair; but she's pretty sure if she puts a streak of black motorcycle grease across any of these there would be dire consequences. She is a woman after all.

Most pressing on her mind at this moment however is the fact that Anne is expected in Los Angeles in just over a week. The time crunch has made her question everything, Tyler's hidden motivation, and Mattie's possible affection being fed from Tyler's desire to be her friend. Basically it's making her into some paranoid, co-dependent, relationship progressing psychopath; damn near like a woman. Anne knows she has to broach the subject with Mattie and soon. The fact that she is thinking about it when Mattie walks in that afternoon is a little spooky and leads her into more conspiracy thoughts.

"Looks like it's going well today," she says in her chipper voice.

"We're pretty much done here if Chica here could learn the proper technique for adjusting the air to fuel ratio in the carburetor."

Anne is shocked, she thought they still had days of work.

"How can we be done, the cylinder head is off," and Anne immediately regrets saying it.

Tomas shakes his head; "It's like the last scoop of ice cream on your cone. It'll be ready tomorrow."

Well that sinks it, she has to say something tonight and she's not even sure how to bring it up.

"What about the head, I thought it was too rough?" *I need another day. Elizabeth has been calling twice a day to find out when I'm leaving.* Elizabeth will press her to leave the second she can.

"Dinner tonight?" Anne looks at Mattie hoping she can somehow read her mind.

"I can't, you know I have a show," she says nonchalantly, she has no idea the bomb Anne needs to drop. Anne has never mentioned leaving, maybe because she didn't want to start their first fight, maybe because she knows no matter what it shatters the illusion of this utopian haze they've been living in. Other than the show tonight and one two weeks prior, they have been able to spend any time together they wanted. Shopping and laughing together, Anne was starting to remember what it was to trust someone. After all, it took a lot of trust to let someone put highlights in your hair. Humans just don't get to live like that; at least that's what her pessimistic mind keeps telling her. *And I'm right.*

Anne pulls Mattie aside; she doesn't want to hear it from Tomas, "I still want to see you tonight."

"Silly rabbit, you could come to the show, you know." That had not completely occurred to Anne actually.

"Come with Tyler, I'll have him come pick you up." Anne doesn't even have a chance to protest.

She leaves and Anne is left with Tomas' judging look and the knowledge that she is going to have to display a prowess on adjusting the carburetor and checking the points before he will let her take the General to LA.

Standing in front of the hotel Anne feels ridiculous. She would be the first person to make fun of the jackass with the cane, especially a woman. At least when she had the walking cast it looked necessary, *now it just looks like I'm some asshole.* Mattie bought it for her, some antique thing. The old brass handle looks worn, the wood shaft beautifully worked with inlaid silver. *I wonder what happened to the last owner?* At last she sees the familiar Toyota coming for her and she steps toward the curb.

A smiling Tyler jumps out, "Need some help Ma'am?"

"No," she answers and desires to crack his smartass head with the cane. Anne straps her seatbelt just in time for Tyler to narrowly miss an oncoming garbage truck. Both Anne's feet are busy trying to find the magic brake pedal once again. The inside of the car is filled with sounds from some new band Anne has never heard of, mixed with the sounds of her own anxiety. Finally they must be close because he pulls into a parking lot. Tyler turns to get out, but Anne grabs his shoulder.

"Can I ask you something?" Her serious note seems to change his normally affable character. He nods.

"I have to go," Anne confesses.

"Right now?"

"No, but in a week." Tyler looks relieved and resigned, but not disturbed at all.

"Well, you live in a hotel; I don't think anybody thought you were staying forever." Anne searches his eyes, trying to see if he's concealing some hidden obsessive emotion, but he looks nonchalant about what he's saying. Anne is not getting what she wanted here, or maybe she's looking for something that doesn't exist. The problem is she wants people to answer her questions without having to ask them.

"I really like your sister," she starts. There's a pause as she waits for him to interrupt her.

"Yeah, I think she likes you. And I'm totally cool with my sister seeing a girl if that's what you mean. Are you okay?" he looks at her like she's strapped to a gurney in a Hannibal Lecter mask. She decides to end the serious questions.

"Sorry, long day. Just think; if you hadn't recognized me at Pikes I never would have met Mattie."

He looks at her oddly, "I didn't recognize you; Mattie did."

She is still trying to wrap her head around what Tyler said when they get to the door of the bar.

Someone's complaining about the five dollar cover to the bouncer.

"Dude, wait until you see how hot the singer is, it's worth it," at which point the bouncer winks to the customer.

Anne wants to punch both of them. Instead she hands him her money briskly and hopes the disappointed look on her face is punishment enough.

Tyler responds by saying "dick" after they're inside and far out of earshot. *At least I didn't have the only impotent response.*

Mattie takes the stage about twenty minutes later and Anne is shocked how different it is to be a face in the crowd. The first time was mesmerizing, the second time she noticed all the subtle greatness in their lyrics and her vocals, but tonight at least one third of her attention is taken looking for men lusting after her. *How could they not love her, want her? Didn't I?* Sadness washes over her as Anne realizes that she can't hoard all of Mattie's sunshine for herself. Anne wants Mattie to sing for her alone, but that wouldn't make a very good career. *What you really can't stand is someone getting the attention.* Mattie's dress is slit almost to her waist on the side and as she sways back and forth, her body gets more and more exposed. Instead of thinking how lucky she is, Anne thinks about what the two guys who came in before her are thinking and saying to one another. Maybe they think that they could get a Chinese finger trap. *Stop it.* In her mind they seem to be laughing at her, their cuckold, their joke. Each time they laugh or say something it's about Anne, how she's not enough for Mattie. Mattie seems to be singing only to them, winking their way, teasing them with her wares. Without saying anything to Tyler, Anne gets up and stumbles awkwardly toward the bar.

She orders another beer and a shot of Crown Royal. The numbing helps quiet her overactive interior monologue. Anne need to focus, she could lose it all tonight. She has to care the least, that's the rule. Who wins? Whoever cares the least; and that must be Anne. *Then why are you so desperate for her to look at you? Why do you notice every guy looking at her, at how much cleavage, or how far the slit in her dress goes up? You lie, and worse you're lying to yourself. Not only do you care; you care so much about this one that it's going to ruin this relationship and probably the next one. You're doomed to a life of being alone, but then again, who deserves that more than you? Now you get to reap what you have sewn.*

Anne wants to leave; she wants to run away from this moment of truth. She has been so scared of caring that now as she stands on the precipice, she is nearly immobilized with fear. Even with her interior meltdown, time passes and so does the show. Suddenly her ears perk up again, something in Mattie's lyrics. This time she is sure that she heard her own words.

THE END OF THE ROAD

Standing outside Anne waits while Mattie talks with the band. Anne is jealous of them too, suspecting each one of them in turn. *I am a goddamn basket case.*

When Mattie comes up, she grabs Anne's shirt and pulls her to her, kissing her hard and long. Some guy walking by gives an obligatory 'Woo Hoo'. Anne feels a twinge of pain in her chest. Mattie's mouth is sweet and cool, like a fresh strawberry with a mint buried deep inside. Anne doesn't just want her, she needs her. Every cell in her body wants to be near her, wants to be possessed by her.

"I need to talk," Anne says with foreboding.

Mattie looks unphased, "Silly rabbit, you take everything too seriously," and smiles seductively. The dismissal though surely an off comment flashes Anne's anger.

"Think you could ask before you steal my words and use them in some sappy love song?" Anne blurts, immediately regretting it. Mattie's face turns scarlet red and Anne flinches away from an expected blow.

"I'm sorry, I didn't mean to say that" Anne tries to apologize.

"But you were thinking it? Because I'm not a good enough writer like you, I had to steal your stuff. That was a nod to how much your words mean to me." Mattie's crying and shouting, which is not totally fair. Now Anne has ruined it. *Wow, that's record time asshole.*

"I'm sorry. It's just that I need to tell you something and I don't know how to without ruining it all. I have to go."

"So go," Mattie says coldly.

"I have to be in LA for the scripting, I was supposed to be there last week, and I have to be there a week from now or I'm in breach of contract. I'm sorry about what I said, my leg's been throbbing."

Here Anne tries to use her magic wish to make Mattie respond; make her beg to go along. Instead she says nothing, and who could blame her. She's thinking, who knows what she's thinking, but she's definitely crunching some numbers of her own.

"Let's talk about it later, come on, I'll take you home."

In the car, relegated to the passenger seat Anne starts to think. Dangerous stuff that thinking. Anne thinks about how Mattie made her close her eyes to increase the dramatic effect before seeing a large installation at the Seattle Art Museum, how she introduced her to the couple that owns a little deli on Pacific Avenue. Anne remembers how she woke Anne up one morning so they could hold each other close as the sun rose. Anne can't lose that. *She's my best friend.* She has to do something. *I'll throw away my contract, I'll make them video conference me in, I'll say I'm sick.*

Luckily the hotel is close, because Mattie didn't say a word the whole trip and the anticipation is agonizing. By all rights Mattie should just drop her off and never look back. Only she parks and follows Anne. She doesn't say a word in the elevator, or at the door. Anne is not sure what to expect, maybe shouting or hitting, but definitely not what follows.

Inside the room, Mattie tears at Anne's clothes, popping buttons and ripping fabric. There is a rushed feeling, almost a sense of desperation in how they devour each other. Anne is trying to make up for what she said, maybe trying to sell Mattie on the idea of Anne Carter again.

Anne kisses her shoulders and neck, unclasping her bra and cupping warm breasts in her cold hands. They lay on the bed, mouths teasing and playing with the other. Mattie's skin feels so warm and soft against Anne's. *This is so different from being with a man, so much more intimate.* Their bodies rub against each other, as if every square millimeter of contact their bodies made brought them that much closer to being one single entity. Anne kisses her neck, working down her naked body, raising small goose bumps as she goes. The sound of Mattie's rasped breathing is like music to her ears, *I want her to love this, I need her to need this.*

THE END OF THE ROAD

Suddenly Mattie grabs Anne's neck and pulls her up to kiss her softly, simultaneously rolling her onto her back and freeing her of her pants. She is enveloped in her warm, soft embrace. Their bodies intertwine each finding purchase against the other and the time continuum shifts, colors become subdued, all Anne can hear is the sound of Mattie's breathing in her ear. She slides back and forth with athletic abandon. Part of Anne wants to ask her to stop, she's actually hurting her a little bit, but somehow the agony in her leg only seems to make the pleasure that much more intense. Anne kisses the body offered her. Mattie increases her tempo and Anne's own passion rises to its crescendo. Mattie's nails dig in to Anne's shoulders as the breath catches in her throat, followed by a small almost imperceptible shriek and they collapse next to each other. Anne rubs her back and kisses her softly on the side of her neck. *I'm not even sure if I finished, what's more I don't know if I care.* Anne just wants to be near her, part of her.

"I think I love you," Anne whispers in her ear.

Mattie pushes herself up on her elbow, letting her hair fall down and tickle Anne's nose. She looks her directly in the eye from so close everything is unfocused.

"You have a funny way of showing it," she says.

"I do love you and I am sorry for being, me. I can promise you that nobody hates me more than I do."

Mattie looks sad for a moment, like she might cry. Anne wants to say something; that it's okay, she has to stay with her family and her job, but she can't. Anne knows what she has to do, but she hates it. Anne knows she could say something incredibly stupid here to help her to stay, make it her decision, her fault. Maybe that would be the compassionate thing to do.

"I'm coming with you," Mattie says.

Anne feels relief washing over her, threatening to open those dark and secret places she thought were locked away. This is more than she could have hoped for, more than she dared hope for. Anne wants to sing, wants to dance. Mattie is smiling too, she looks so happy.

So then why is she crying? Mental Note: Ignore the details.

Chapter 28 Livin' the dream

Taking the ferry out of Ante Cortés was out of their way. Certainly no direct route from Seattle to Los Angeles would include Victoria British Columbia, but Mattie confided that she had never visited the Butchart Gardens and Anne wanted to walk through the green splendor of those gardens holding her hand. Anne feared it might be a letdown, her memory made better by years of hazy recollection and bong resin, but it was every ounce the vision she remembered. Anne does her best to pretend Mattie is the first person she has been here with, anyway Mattie never asks. The cool crisp autumn morning mixes with the fragrant greenery to perfume every step of their way. The soft crunch of the gravel underfoot punctuates their journey and makes hidden their little whispers and small laughs from the prying ears of old ladies. High tea in the cottage restaurant feels surreal, the little sandwiches and very sweet tea contrast strongly to the vision most people would have of a cross-country biker lesbians. *Easy on those titles.* Personally Anne likes the dichotomy of it all; she revels in defying people expectations. Sitting on a bench in the Japanese gardens the air hangs still and there is no sound.

It's the kind of place to propose to the woman you love, but Anne likes Mattie too much for that. They are close friends, best friends even, this time feels somehow more like a dream. It does get her mind thinking of what could be, what might be and unfortunately, what will be. *Will there be a three bedroom in suburbia for us? I don't know if I can tell her that that's not in the cards for me or not. Maybe I have to feed the illusion of our domestic tranquility while constantly fighting to correct our course from the spontaneous chaos that has become my routine. Honestly I can't even stand the idea of us playing house. The ideals my parents tried so adamantly to instill within me died with Bill, any attempt to recreate that would only serve to dishonor his memory. Instead I am creating my own Utopia; the issue is whether or not I can ever find someone who agrees with that vision. But why do we all have to have the same vision of success? Why isn't there room in the vast world for my unique vision of what a life should be? I have never dictated what someone else's life needed to be, why should their opinions alter mine?*

THE END OF THE ROAD

All that sounds fine, but looking at Mattie, Anne is sure that she will have more to say about the whole thing than "Okay." Anne squeezes her hand and it's time to go. The sun is setting and they still have to find their Hotel. They load up on the General. A parting gift from Tomas was a matching rear seat that doesn't look standard, but it is so intoxicating for Anne to feel Mattie's warm arms around her that she wouldn't care if it was a lazy-boy dragging behind her. It feels like home to have her here, like Anne was lost and just finally found her way back. Anne kicks the beast and he fires right up, Tomas was a wizard. Anne hopes she garnered some sliver of his knowledge from their time. Listening closely to the sound of the engine, Anne listens for the tone of the combustion and the lag on letting off the throttle.

It's still a little lean, so she adjusts the screw on the carburetor just an eighth turn. Mattie gives her an extra squeeze, Anne's not sure why. Visors down and they leave the gardens behind. *I wonder if we'll ever be back. I wonder if I'll be back with her or someone else or alone?*

Anne lets the GPS do the navigation; trying to focus on the road and the sensation of Mattie's arms around her waist. *Mattie loves me for me, not the money she hopes I have, or the influence she hopes I might have over the casting director, but me.* Elizabeth booked their hotel for them and she sounded excited, Anne wonders if anything that sounds like it will help her Author stabilize would be exciting for Liz. It's an old mansion in the residential portion of Victoria. Pulling through the gate it looks like an old English manor, almost invisible from the road with all the evergreens and ferns. It's perfect, and Anne needed it to be perfect.

Lying in their bed, the heat of passion still warming the room Anne traces circles on the skin of Mattie's back, long figure eights that dance across her sweaty skin and raise goose bumps. Anne lays her body on top of her, supporting most of her weight on her elbows. The feeling of their skin touching in so many places makes her feel less an individual and more a single entity, like somehow they have joined themselves into one large single organism. Outside it's started to rain, or more like mist, it looks like they're in the middle of a cloud. Anne opens the balcony door and gives Mattie a robe. Standing in the mist there is a steady cloud of steam rising off their exposed skin. Anne pulls her close and kisses her. Her lips are so soft and yielding right now.

No matter what happens, I am happy now, let me always remember that.

"I love you," Anne whispers softly in her ear.

There is a momentary pause before she responds, "I love you too."

Anne tries to let the pause go. Anne tries desperately to not focus on that microsecond pause. It couldn't have possibly been more than a second, maybe Mattie's mind was elsewhere. Or her hair delayed the sound of her voice. She is absolutely sure that the pause doesn't mean anything. She is so completely positive that there is absolutely nothing to read into that miniscule pause that she promises herself that she won't linger on it for even one little second, that's just how unimportant in the grand scheme of things it really is. *Hmmmm.*

The next morning comes early so they can be on the only ferry to Bremerton. Once the General is stowed safely they find a seat watching the fair city of Victoria fade into the background. The air is brisk on the ocean, there's something primal about its smell. As if it calls out to all whose ancestors once crawled from its depths. The rocking of the ship makes Anne a little nauseous and more than a little tired. Anne falls asleep with her head in Mattie's lap. The sound of her phone wakes her with a start. They are about a half mile from shore and they must have just regained reception. Her phone continues to go insane for almost thirty seconds. She must have twenty voicemails. Anne looks at her phone and sees that she had a single missed call from Jordan. Anne smiles and takes her phone to call him. She was sure e was curious about how the trip was going and the Butchart gardens.

Anne had promised to take him years ago after he saw the pictures from her and Bill's trip. Their call is pleasant and once he has heard her gossip, it's over. Anne is so glad that he doesn't seem to care at all that she is with a woman. Utah is a very conservative state and certainly every example will not be like that one. Mattie is on the other side of the ship, but based on her body language it's not as pleasant a call as Anne's. They are called to return to their vehicles, but she's still on the phone, The Ferry operators waving their arms to usher people toward the vehicles.

Anne waits until the staff is personally coaxing them down the stairs toward the vehicles. Finally Mattie ends the phone call, but it's definitely not over. Helmets on, they pull out into Bremerton downtown, such that it is. The first convenient place Anne pulls over to ask Mattie if she wants some breakfast. She says yes and they find a small place where Anne ends up eating by herself while Mattie continues her heated conversation outside. Mattie finally comes in and eats her lukewarm breakfast. She's mad, so Anne tries to look inconspicuous, lest the anger get pointed at her. *It's probably about me, statistically if someone is angry, it's me.*

"I love you," Anne whispers once Mattie's had some breakfast and a couple of deep breaths.

"I love you," Mattie responds although there is a tiredness that shouldn't be present until at least their fifth anniversary. Again Anne denies the tone any validity.

Rolling along the 101 they make their way around the Olympic Peninsula. The trees are so thick here that in many places Anne has to remove her sunglasses. The anger or resentment of the morning is gone when they stop for a burger. They're laughing again as they stop to hike the dense forest. *See, it was all just our imagination. I told you.* The smell of renewal, lichen grows thick and ferns shoot up from fallen logs. The crowns of the pines far above filter the sunlight to dancing shards of light. They kiss in a meadow while the sun warms them. By the time they get back to the General their pant legs are soaked from the forest's dew. The deep thumping of the General resonates now more than it did. Anne finds herself checking him more often, which is to say ever. Anne skips the small gas stations in favor of Chevron with Techron. *I'm not sure if Techron is good for an old Indian, but it sure sounds good.*

On the furthest North West point of the peninsula they find a wonderful beach. Until here it was all just forest, but now the pines part and the magnificent power of the Pacific crashes on the rocks and sand below. Certainly it's not the kind of beach you lay on to get a tan, but the ocean mist is invigorating. It has a harsh beauty; it reminds her of the Craters of the moon in some ways. Anne finds a stick and writes; I love Mattie, in the sand. Mattie smiles and adds her own decoration. Holding hands they walk along the beach sometimes giggling like young girls, sometimes in silence. Anne starts to wonder where they're going, the tide has stranded more than a few newbies who weren't paying attention.

Out of the sight of the few visitors she kisses Mattie hard and with urgency. Her cold hands fumble with her clothes, tearing at the seams trying to get access. Mattie's hands are deft and skilled at finding just the right way to get to Anne's passion. Like a painter on a canvas or a violinist on a Stradivarius, she is a true artist. Anne bites her lip, hard enough she tastes a little blood. Nuzzling her face into Mattie's neckline she lets go. She allows Mattie to have her. *I would do anything for her.* Anne tries to capture this moment in her mind. Anne wants this and so many others they've shared. Walking back, their hands clasped Anne begins to think that maybe this can work.

Chapter 29 Where the road ends

The 101 keeps them close to the coast and so also close to great food. They find oyster bars tucked behind barns and Candy shops in front of random commercial buildings. There are occasional Wineries and Cideries providing inebriating beverages along the way. They stop anytime the fancy takes them, which is often. Anne is at times shocked by the poverty of the area, especially the logging areas, but overall it has a rustic feeling that seems genuine. The buildings are distressed by the sea, its constant barrage of saline graying wood and stripping paint. The food is simple for the most part, but the quality of the ingredients more than compensates for any lack of ingenuity. Personally she is tired of everything having to be plussed all the time. *Like David Sedaris I remember a time when food could be simple and judged on the quality of the ingredients and talent of the chef, not on the unique combination of its ingredients. Today's secret ingredients are Chutney and wood shavings. Fucking Iron chef ruined this country.*

They make it to Seaside, Oregon to stay the night. Their rooms' patio opens to the beach and they leave it open all night. The crashing waves give Anne strange dreams. She is trying to escape from something but it keeps following her wherever she tries to hide. The strange thing is, Anne somehow knows this devil and she's not very good at hiding. It's like she's running in slow motion with heavy, nonresponsive legs. The faster she runs the faster it pursues. The world is silent but for the sound of someone quietly sobbing. Anne wakes up in a sweat, her heart pounding. It's not sunrise yet, so she tries to be quiet. Staring out at the dark horizon and darker waves Anne knows exactly what it was. Anne doesn't want to know, but she does. *Mattie's leaving.* Anne wonders when Mattie will tell her. Staring into the abyss of the Pacific Anne wonders what she will do. Will she cry and throw herself on the ground? Will she offer to find Mattie a new band in Los Angeles? Will she bribe her with whatever life she could dream of? Or will she instead be honest about the life she has chosen to live and try to find a way to help Mattie find the same? *Will I allow her the freedom I demanded for myself so many years ago?* No panic or sadness this morning, Anne must have worked something out in her dreams.

When Mattie wakes up Anne has made tea from the corner shop. Anne had a new batch of the Highlander Grog shipped to her, so all she did was buy hot water and sugar. Mattie smiles, Anne throws her clothes at her to get dressed so they can get breakfast. From the moment Mattie sees the tea she knows something is up, but it's only fair to make her wait as Anne has waited.

They find a little over decorated breakfast spot. The dubious interior makes her question how good their meal will be, but the girl at the Hotel recommended it. Anne order Eggs Benedict with crab in place of the Canadian bacon, while Mattie gets the fruit plate. When they're alone Mattie is looking at her and Anne's looking back. They both know something without knowing everything.

"So when do you need to leave?" Anne asks.

Relief washes over Mattie's face along with a healthy dose of sadness and a few errant tears, which makes Anne feel better.

"How did you know?"

"I didn't, but you've been acting funny." *I wonder if Bill thought the same thing of me.*

Mattie fidgets in her chair for a second, which in body language translates to the fact that she thought she was acting perfectly normal.

"Lonnie called and I just can't leave the group right now. We were supposed to go on tour next month; Tim quit his job for it. As soon as the tour's over they can find a new singer and I'll come with you."

Anne listens intently, this sounds like the same kind of argument she gave Bill before leaving for LA. What Mattie doesn't know, what she won't know until she's sitting on the other side of this particular conversation, is how much better it is to be the one leaving. The luxury of motion, progress and following your dreams makes it all seem fine. There is no pain, no sadness once the boil is lanced. She might look sad and even cry before it's over, but once she hits that plane she'll be off to new adventures. Bill had to live this, now it's Anne's turn, to live in the vacuum that's left, the hollow place that replaces what you had. But what can Anne say now, when she took the opportunity to pursue her dreams with all the gusto she could manage. Anne got everything she ever asked for, the least she can do for Mattie is to allow her the same thing. The other thing she knows is that they could never survive the resentment she would feel if she didn't go. It would sit between them on the General, stare at them across the dinner table, and poison them slowly and painfully from the inside.

What Anne is left with now is the sliver of hope that Mattie is a better human being than she was. Anne gets to lay awake at night and wonder if Mattie has found someone else. Someone younger than she is, someone better looking or maybe just more exciting. *Who isn't better than you?* Anne gets to stare into oblivion each night and wonder if she's enough to keep Mattie interested and committed. Anne gets exactly what she has always deserved, that's why she can sit here smiling. *You're smiling because you don't know what else to do. That's why I won't guilt her into staying.*

"I was wondering what you were going to do about the tour," Anne tells her. "You have to go, I'll be jealous, but the truth is I followed my dreams, you should get to follow yours."

Mattie smiles but remains conspicuously silent.

"When do you have to leave?" Anne asks.

"Two days after we get to LA."

Anne smiles again because that's the role she has to play here. Just like all the roles she has played in her life. The doting wife and loving mother were some early roles which won her many acclaims until she tried on the Famous Writer mask for size. She has worn the masks of the dutiful daughter, housekeeper, Nanny, self possessed author, caring friend, petulant patient, considerate girlfriend and alluring stranger. Sometimes with all the roles she has played she has to wonder who the base character is anymore. Or maybe she's afraid of knowing who the base character is, quite possibly her inner skinny fourteen year old with acne and a flat chest. Why else would she have reacted so insanely to the smallest attention out in Hollywood?

THE END OF THE ROAD

Because you're weak, you've always been weak.

The Eggs Benedict are incredible and she stuffs the appropriately sized portions into her mouth, chewing and swallowing, smile, and repeat. Anne smiles as often as she thinks about it. They go to a little gift shop buying themselves some small things. *This is the part where I play the world's greatest girlfriend, the real Anne would still be at the restaurant begging and groveling.*

Riding the highway is the only place Mattie's impending departure isn't the first thing on her mind. The road rolls under them and for an instant Anne thinks that maybe they're staying still with the world moving underneath them. Maybe like the days before Galileo they are the center of the universe, everything revolving around them.

The rugged coastline is beautiful; they stop for Clam chowder. They make their way through to Tillamook and have some cheese.

They drive through Sonoma and the wine country, sipping California Chardonnays and Merlots, Paul Giamatti be damned. Anne has the best prime rib of her life; Mattie gets sick on the chicken. Anne holds her hair as she throws up and when she falls asleep, wraps her arms tightly around her. Anne runs to the drug store for anything she thinks may help, plus ginger snaps and 7-UP. *That's what my mother gave me when I was sick.*

Mattie's better the next day and they press on. Anne wonders where this road ends. In California she has to check the points on the General as she promised Tomas she would. Anne thinks he would be proud to see her with her little tool set laid out. Anne pulls the plugs just for shits and giggles and decides to swap them. Anne swears there is a difference and Mattie tells her what a wonderful Mechanic she has become. Anne kisses her like she really means it. *And I do.*

They venture into Southern California, but Mattie's sickness cost them the time to go to Disneyland. Anne would have really liked to take Mattie there, but it gives them something to look forward to. They pull into the hotel Monaco in Los Angeles; this has been Anne's home base in Los Angeles every time she has come out here.

Maybe this is where the road ends. There is something horribly final about pulling into the parking garage. An era has ended, the honeymoon is now spent.

Anne checks in and the desk gives her two room keys, the clerk only slightly raises one eyebrow. Anne gives the second one to Mattie, although she has to leave tomorrow, Anne doesn't know that she won't need it. Anne gets the same room she had last year, *I wonder how they worked that out?*

Her work computer and materials are already set up when we walks in. She is a little surprised not to see Elizabeth sitting in the chair urging her on. But she's not here, in person anyway. Anne can smell her influence. Anne laughs because there is an ankle range of motion machine in the corner. *She really is a surrogate mother.*

Mattie comes up behind her; slipping her hands over Anne's eyes. Her breath is hot and sweet on Anne's neck.

"Close your eyes," she says seductively.

Her hands move and she pulls back. Anne can hear rustling, exchanging of items from bags, all sorts of sounds. Anne wonders what life would be like without the gift of sight. Maybe she would have been a better person. Mattie's voice is so soft and sweet it's like honey drawn over hot bread. Then Anne hears music, light at first. Then Mattie's singing, a melody she hasn't heard, but words taken directly from her book. Anne hears her name and opens her eyes. Mattie is standing starkly naked singing in front of her, as if somehow reading her mind. Anne tries hard to swallow the growing lump in her throat and the stinging in her eyes.

How did I become this babbling baby woman-child?

Anne removes her clothes slowly, methodically undoing each button, peeling away her armor. Then she is standing naked before Mattie, her voice so soft the song is almost a whisper. There are no candles, no rose petals, but they caress and make love to each other until they feel the world move beneath them. Anne knows it took a lot of trust for Mattie to sing like that for her, exposing herself body and soul. Anne rolls her on her side; she wants to kiss her mouth. *I want to bite her lip.* When it's over they're both staring at strangers, it was that different an experience for both of them. It takes a tremendous amount of trust to be that soft and vulnerable with each other. In a world hardened by distrust and cynicism, a real moment between lovers seems an increasingly rare thing. Anne tries to capture the moment, the way Mattie smells, the feel of her skin; Mattie's hair tickling her nose, Anne wants to remember all of it. She has to remember all of it, because there is a ball of anxiety in her stomach that tells her she didn't deserve this, and there is no way she will ever have it again.

Please let me save this and push out just one of the bad memories.

They make love twice more that night, not as soft, but intimate and almost frantic, like a drowning victim clinging to her rescuer. In the morning Anne takes Mattie to the airport, saying their tearful goodbyes and promises of the future she knows better than to believe. Then Anne watches her walk away, she turns around twice and the second time Anne thinks for a moment that she might run back, but in the end she fades from view and is gone.

Anne rubs the tank of the General, "It's just us now buddy." He doesn't respond until she turns the throttle and they pull from the curb. The rhythmic pulse of the engine reminds her of a child patting a baby's bottom, trying to sooth them. They take the long way back to the Hotel, which in Los Angeles can be extra long. Anne parks him in his spot, the spot they have been good enough to save for her. Walking away she stops to look back, and then walks back to the parking spot. Running her hands over the seat and handlebars she tells her old friend, "Thanks for always being there."

In her room Anne can still sense the lingering scent of sex. Anne lays down face first where Mattie slept, trying to soak up her smell somehow.

She looks at the desk and knows she should work. Anne needs to get herself in the Pandora's Lust mindset. She immediately wants to write her experience with Mattie into the next book, but it's too soon, too raw. Anne looks at the words on the page, her ideas screwed up by network writers. Anne needs to keep the different writers from making this so much their own that they create logical fallacies. Problem is; it's all one huge logical fallacy. It is garbage and everyone knows it, unfortunately it is popular garbage.

Anne orders a steak and a beer from room service and sits at the desk to do her homework. *I was meant for more than this.*

Chapter 30 And the road goes on...

Anne hands back her key to the front desk. *I'm going to miss this place, but I know I'll be back next season, as long as there is a next season.* Juan at the front desk says he'll make sure Anne gets her same room next year. Anne actually stayed for an extra month and the reward is under her arm. Anne wrote another book, not a cliché novel, but something real. Anne wrote a story about someone, a real character that changes and grows and suffers and wins and loses. Anne just started typing one night and couldn't stop. Before she knew it there were five chapters on the computer and more just waiting to pour out onto the page. Juan, the clerk, has to have a hug; Anne grants him his wish this one time. Walking outside the General is ready and waiting for her. Anne throws the bags into the sidecar, plenty of room there and puts her helmet on. Anne looks at the laptop bag and wonders if she should have saved a copy of the new book somewhere else also, before heading out on that dangerous road. Too late for that now, maybe she'll do it at her next hotel. She really wants to show up in New York to hand the finished manuscript to Elizabeth in person. *No longer a Slut Poet, or even a Harlequin Rhymester; now I am a real writer.*

They detailed the General for her this morning and he looks fabulous. The dark Army green and the white stars belie the treasure that he is, because the General is more than a bike. He's more than a status symbol; he's even more than a friend. He is Anne's redemption, her escape, her plan b and her constant companion. He takes her places and saves her from herself. He's never too busy thinking about himself to be there for her, he lives for her alone. Anne gooses the throttle and he roars down the Los Angeles side street. People look at them, because they are beautiful. The carburetor is tuned perfectly for this elevation, but if it changes they have the tools and talent between them to face whatever challenges come their way.

Anne looks at the laptop and thinks; *really, it's the General's book.* He inspired it and he earned it. He helped her lose herself and find herself. *Like the Phoenix we rose from the ashes to be reborn, harder and faster than ever.* They roll passed the Pollo Loco, where some of the more intricate plot points were resolved in the wee hours of the evening. Anne thinks of the dedications she made for this book, to Jordan for reminding her of what she had forgotten, to Mattie for teaching her what she should have known, but mostly for the General for always getting her where she needed to go. It made her smile to imagine the questioning looks on people faces as they read the last one.

Anne is on fire; she is unquestionably sure that this is the one. People are going to read it and love it, they have to. They owe her, after all. The freeway ramp ahead is clogged so she decides to take the highway out of town. Negotiating the roads in Los Angeles is a full time study. The weather is perfect for riding, the cool March weather is just about to fade into April loveliness. Anne ponders the myriad of choices ahead of her. It's too early for mountain riding, but the deserts would be awesome. If they took a slow southern route they could be back in Utah for Jordan's graduation. That would save her from having to take an airplane.

She smiles thinking about Jordan's acceptance to Duke, who would have thought her son capable of so much? *Well, I would have.* Now if she can just keep that dipshit girlfriend of his from getting herself knocked up; something about Utah (I blame the Mormons) makes kids want to get married at nineteen. Before they've seen the world, or experienced life on their own. Anne wants Jordan to go out there and live, she needs him to go out there and live his life. Anne really can't wait to show him the graduation gift she got for him. It's a jet black Harley Davidson Fat Boy. Anne had thought to go with something more original, a refinished classic like the General, but anti lock brakes and the additional safety features convinced her otherwise. In a nod to the General it has matching stars on the tank; *I just hope nobody lets on and spoils the surprise.*

While she's there it is also finally time to deal with the storage shed. Jordan agreed to help her sort through what to keep and what to let go. Anne is not looking forward to it, but at least she doesn't have to do it alone. She is also changing Kaden's grave marker. Anne wanted something simple when it all happened, or that's what they told her she wanted. In truth she wanted something to match his life and show the world what they would have had to contend with from a spirit like his. *He deserved so much more, this is the least I can do.* Quite a busy summer in good old Utah, it seems. Anne also has to make time to swing by New York for a meeting with the Publisher about the new book. Anne wants to pitch it herself; she has higher hopes than last time. Anne needs to buy Elizabeth something nice, maybe a puppy. She hasn't been requiring quite as much clean up lately and thinks Liz must be feeling unneeded. They head east, up into the canyons; the steady incline tests her carburetor adjustments, which seem spot on.

Anne passes a bus load of elementary students who are waving and making so much noise she can hear them through the windows, over the wind and the General. For a second she swears she can see Kaden waving to her from the bus.

I miss him so much. I don't think that wound will ever fully close, at least I hope not. I think I would have to forget him to have that pain totally gone and that is just too high a cost.

Anne passes the bus and the road continues, pressing ever forward, toward something.

Anne needs to decide where to go, what path to take. Anne knows what paths she wanted to take, what paths she should have taken, but really she needs to focus on what to do at this moment, at this very junction. *Which way's it gonna be?* Mattie is playing in Santa Fe next week. Anne has not seen her since she left LA and they have only spoken a few times. She's not sure how things stand, but as she feared things did not go how either of them said they would. There is an art show in Sonoma Anne would like to catch at the same time. Anne still has Steven's phone number, the man from Kansas City; they had spoken a couple of times and he said she was welcome any time. Mexico is always on the radar, but that may be a trip for another year, something to look forward to. Anne could just go straight to Utah, visiting friends from St. George to Logan. Anne doesn't want to admit how afraid she is of going to Santa Fe. Anne wants to be better than she has been, older, wiser, but fears she is still just the same old scared little girl. Anne can't decide and has to pull over at a rest stop to decide. Walking around, she kicks the gravel into a more distinguished pattern until the decision comes to her.

THE END OF THE ROAD

Is this the end of the road? Yes it is; and no it is not. That's the thing about roads, they start and they end, but if you look hard enough and are open to it, there is always another road. You always have another path to choose, a chance to fix your course. Standing on the side of the road in California she is sure that the road is still ahead of her; she doesn't know if it's left or right, North or South, but in the end all that matters is that she keeps moving forward. The only failure for her would be to stop, to settle, to allow all those roads she hasn't traveled to remain so. The rolling blackness beckons and she is unafraid. In fact, as always, she is excited. She knows what roads she hopes to take, which ones to avoid. Anne hopes she's smarter in picking a path through this life. Anne pulls a quarter out of her pocket, wondering if chance should dictate her fate. The face of Washington stares at her as the edge presses into her palm. *Time to decide.*

She is going to ride. There is no end to this road, so the destination is unimportant. There is time for a stop anywhere and everywhere. The General is with her just like he's always been there for her. He'll get her out if they need to flee, bring her stuff if they need to stay, waiting patiently, and content to sit on his kickstand.

She is free to be the woman she can be, not the woman she is afraid of not being. Anne doesn't have to be the Hero or Villain in her story. Her life is this road right now, shifting below her as she stays still above, willing its revolving path to lie out before her. Anne tries to push aside the masks of wounded lover, wise mother or jilted artist. Anne knows what she wants and owes it to herself and the General to go get it. Anne knows the course ahead and has adjusted the carburetor accordingly. Anne questions the finer points, but thinks they'll be okay. She visually inspects the tires for wear. Putting the unused coin back into her pocket, she kicks under the kickstand lever and sits down hard on the kick-starter. The low thump brings the General back to life. Anne rubs the tank for luck and they pull out onto the highway, the morning sun bright on her eyes. The long black ribbon stretches into the distance; she hits the throttle hard and settles in for a long ride.

The End of the Road